Brother
Odd

ALSO BY DEAN KOONTZ

The Husband · *Forever Odd* · *Velocity* · *Life Expectancy*
· *The Taking* · *Odd Thomas* · *The Face* · *By the Light of the Moon* ·
One Door Away From Heaven · *From the Corner of His Eye*
· *False Memory* · *Seize the Night* · *Fear Nothing* · *Mr. Murder* ·
Dragon Tears · *Hideaway* · *Cold Fire* · *The Bad Place*
· *Midnight* · *Lightning* · *Watchers* · *Strangers* · *Twilight Eyes* ·
Darkfall · *Phantoms* · *Whispers* · *The Mask*
· *The Vision* · *The Face of Fear* · *Night Chills* · *Shattered* ·
The Voice of the Night · *The Servants of Twilight*
· *The House of Thunder* · *The Key to Midnight* ·
The Eyes of Darkness · *Shadowfires* · *Winter Moon*
· *The Door to December* · *Dark Rivers of the Heart* · *Icebound* ·
Strange Highways · *Intensity* · *Sole Survivor*
· *Ticktock* · *The Funhouse* · *Demon Seed* ·

DEAN KOONTZ'S FRANKENSTEIN
Book One: Prodigal Son · with Kevin J. Anderson
Book Two: City of Night · with Ed Gorman

DEAN KOONTZ

Brother Odd

Bantam Books

BROTHER ODD
A Bantam Book / December 2006

Published by Bantam Dell
A Division of Random House, Inc.
New York, New York

Book design by Virginia Norey

A signed, limited edition has been privately printed by Charnel House.
Charnelhouse.com

Bantam Books is a registered trademark of Random House, Inc.,
and the colophon is a trademark of Random House, Inc.

ISBN: 978-0-553-80480-5

Printed in the United States of America

To some folks I've known a long time and admire
because they do good work and are good people:
Peter Styles, Richard Boukes, Bill Anderson (Hello, Danielle),
Dave Gaulke, and Tom Fenner (Hello, Gabriella, Katia, and Troy).
We'll have a fine party on the Other Side,
but let's not be in a hurry.

Teach us . . .
To give and not to count the cost;
To fight and not to heed the wounds;
To toil and not to seek for rest . . .

—St. Ignatius Loyola

Brother
Odd

CHAPTER 1

E MBRACED BY STONE, STEEPED IN SILENCE, I SAT
at the high window as the third day of the week surrendered
to the fourth. The river of night rolled on, indifferent to the
calendar.

I hoped to witness that magical moment when the snow began
to fall in earnest. Earlier the sky had shed a few flakes, then nothing more. The pending storm would not be rushed.

The room was illuminated only by a fat candle in an amber
glass on the corner desk. Each time a draft found the flame,
melting light buttered the limestone walls and waves of fluid
shadows oiled the corners.

Most nights, I find lamplight too bright. And when I'm writing, the only glow is the computer screen, dialed down to gray
text on a navy-blue field.

Without a silvering of light, the window did not reflect my
face. I had a clear view of the night beyond the panes.

Living in a monastery, even as a guest rather than as a monk,
you have more opportunities than you might have elsewhere to

see the world as it is, instead of through the shadow that you cast upon it.

St. Bartholomew's Abbey was surrounded by the vastness of the Sierra Nevada, on the California side of the border. The primeval forests that clothed the rising slopes were themselves cloaked in darkness.

From this third-floor window, I could see only part of the deep front yard and the blacktop lane that cleaved it. Four low lamp-posts with bell-shaped caps focused light in round pale pools.

The guesthouse is in the northwest wing of the abbey. The ground floor features parlors. Private rooms occupy the higher and the highest floors.

As I watched in anticipation of the storm, a whiteness that was not snow drifted across the yard, out of darkness, into lamplight.

The abbey has one dog, a 110-pound German-shepherd mix, perhaps part Labrador retriever. He is entirely white and moves with the grace of fog. His name is Boo.

My name is Odd Thomas. My dysfunctional parents claim a mistake was made on the birth certificate, that Todd was the wanted name. Yet they have never called me Todd.

In twenty-one years, I have not considered changing to Todd. The bizarre course of my life suggests that Odd is more suited to me, whether it was conferred by my parents with intention or by fate.

Below, Boo stopped in the middle of the pavement and gazed along the lane as it dwindled and descended into darkness.

Mountains are not entirely slopes. Sometimes the rising land takes a rest. The abbey stands on a high meadow, facing north.

Judging by his pricked ears and lifted head, Boo perceived a visitor approaching. He held his tail low.

I could not discern the state of his hackles, but his tense posture suggested that they were raised.

From dusk the driveway lamps burn until dawn ascends. The monks of St. Bart's believe that night visitors, no matter how seldom they come, must be welcomed with light.

The dog stood motionless for a while, then shifted his attention toward the lawn to the right of the blacktop. His head lowered. His ears flattened against his skull.

For a moment, I could not see the cause of Boo's alarm. Then . . . into view came a shape as elusive as a night shadow floating across black water. The figure passed near enough to one of the lampposts to be briefly revealed.

Even in daylight, this was a visitor of whom only the dog and I could have been aware.

I see dead people, spirits of the departed who, each for his own reason, will not move on from this world. Some are drawn to me for justice, if they were murdered, or for comfort, or for companionship; others seek me out for motives that I cannot always understand.

This complicates my life.

I am not asking for your sympathy. We all have our problems, and yours seem as important to you as mine seem to me.

Perhaps you have a ninety-minute commute every morning, on freeways clogged with traffic, your progress hampered by impatient and incompetent motorists, some of them angry specimens with middle fingers muscular from frequent use. Imagine, however, how much more stressful your morning might be if in the passenger seat was a young man with a ghastly ax wound in his head and if in the backseat an elderly woman, strangled by her husband, sat pop-eyed and purple-faced.

The dead don't talk. I don't know why. And an ax-chopped spirit will not bleed on your upholstery.

Nevertheless, an entourage of the recently dead is disconcerting and generally not conducive to an upbeat mood.

The visitor on the lawn was not an ordinary ghost, maybe not a ghost at all. In addition to the lingering spirits of the dead, I see one other kind of supernatural entity. I call them *bodachs*.

They are ink-black, fluid in shape, with no more substance than shadows. Soundless, as big as an average man, they frequently slink like cats, low to the ground.

The one on the abbey lawn moved upright: black and featureless, yet suggestive of something half man, half wolf. Sleek, sinuous, and sinister.

The grass was not disturbed by its passage. Had it been crossing water, it would not have left a single ripple in its wake.

In the folklore of the British Isles, a bodach is a vile beast that slithers down chimneys at night and carries off children who misbehave. Rather like Inland Revenue agents.

What I see are neither bodachs nor tax collectors. They carry away neither misbehaving children nor adult miscreants. But I have seen them enter houses by chimneys—by keyholes, chinks in window frames, as protean as smoke—and I have no better name for them.

Their infrequent appearance is always reason for alarm. These creatures seem to be spiritual vampires with knowledge of the future. They are drawn to places where violence or fiery catastrophe is destined to erupt, as if they feed on human suffering.

Although he was a brave dog, with good reason to be brave, Boo shrank from the passing apparition. His black lips peeled back from his white fangs.

The phantom paused as if to taunt the dog. Bodachs seem to know that some animals can see them.

I don't think they know that I can see them, too. If they did know, I believe that they would show me less mercy than mad mullahs show their victims when in a mood to behead and dismember.

At the sight of this one, my first impulse was to shrink from the window and seek communion with the dust bunnies under my bed. My second impulse was to pee.

Resisting both cowardice and the call of the bladder, I raced from my quarters into the hallway. The third floor of the guesthouse offers two small suites. The other currently had no occupant.

On the second floor, the glowering Russian was no doubt scowling in his sleep. The solid construction of the abbey would not translate my footfalls into his dreams.

The guesthouse has an enclosed spiral staircase, stone walls encircling granite steps. The treads alternate between black and white, making me think of harlequins and piano keys, and of a treacly old song by Paul McCartney and Stevie Wonder.

Although stone stairs are unforgiving and the black-and-white pattern can be disorienting, I plunged toward the ground floor, risking damage to the granite if I fell and struck it with my head.

Sixteen months ago, I lost what was most precious to me and found my world in ruins; nevertheless, I am not usually reckless. I have less to live for than I once did, but my life still has purpose, and I struggle to find meaning in the days.

Leaving the stairs in the condition that I found them, I hurried across the main parlor, where only a night lamp with a beaded shade relieved the gloom. I pushed through a heavy oak door with a stained-glass window, and saw my breath plume before me in the winter night.

The guesthouse cloister surrounds a courtyard with a reflecting pool and a white marble statue of St. Bartholomew. He is arguably the least known of the twelve apostles.

Here depicted, a solemn St. Bartholomew stands with his right hand over his heart, left arm extended. In his upturned palm is what appears to be a pumpkin but might be a related variety of squash.

The symbolic meaning of the squash eludes me.

At this time of year, the pool was drained, and no scent of wet limestone rose from it, as in warmer days. I detected, instead, the faintest smell of ozone, as after lightning in a spring rain, and wondered about it, but kept moving.

I followed the colonnade to the door of the guesthouse receiving room, went inside, crossed that shadowy chamber, and returned to the December night through the front door of the abbey.

Our white shepherd mix, Boo, standing on the driveway, as I had last seen him from my third-floor window, turned his head to look at me as I descended the broad front steps. His stare was clear and blue, with none of the eerie eyeshine common to animals at night.

Without benefit of stars or moon, most of the expansive yard receded into murk. If a bodach lurked out there, I could not see it.

"Boo, where's it gone?" I whispered.

He didn't answer. My life is strange but not so strange that it includes talking canines.

With wary purpose, however, the dog moved off the driveway,

onto the yard. He headed east, past the formidable abbey, which appears almost to have been carved from a single great mass of rock, so tight are the mortar joints between its stones.

No wind ruffled the night, and darkness hung with folded wings.

Seared brown by winter, the trampled grass crunched underfoot. Boo moved with far greater stealth than I could manage.

Feeling watched, I looked up at the windows, but I didn't see anyone, no light other than the faint flicker of the candle in my quarters, no pale face peering through a dark pane.

I had rushed out of the guest wing wearing blue jeans and a T-shirt. December stropped its teeth on my bare arms.

We proceeded eastward alongside the church, which is part of the abbey, not a separate building.

A sanctuary lamp glows perpetually, but it isn't sufficient to fire the colorful stained glass. Through window after window, that dim light seemed to watch us as though it were the single sullen eye of something in a bloody mood.

Having led me to the northeast corner of the building, Boo turned south, past the back of the church. We continued to the wing of the abbey that, on the first floor, contains the novitiate.

Not yet having taken their vows, the novices slept here. Of the five who were currently taking instruction, I liked and trusted four.

Suddenly Boo abandoned his cautious pace. He ran due east, away from the abbey, and I pursued him.

As the yard relented to the untamed meadow, grass lashed my knees. Soon the first heavy snow would compact these tall dry blades.

For a few hundred feet, the land sloped gently before leveling off, whereupon the knee-high grass became a mown lawn again. Before us in the gloom rose St. Bartholomew's School.

In part the word *school* is a euphemism. These students are unwanted elsewhere, and the school is also their home, perhaps the only one that some of them will ever have.

This is the original abbey, internally remodeled but still an impressive pile of stone. The structure also houses the convent in which reside the nuns who teach the students and care for them.

Behind the former abbey, the forest bristled against the storm-ready sky, black boughs sheltering blind pathways that led far into the lonely dark.

Evidently tracking the bodach, the dog went up the broad steps to the front door of the school, and through.

Few doors in the abbey are ever locked. But for the protection of the students, the school is routinely secured.

Only the abbot, the mother superior, and I possess a universal key that allows admittance everywhere. No guest before me has been entrusted with such access.

I take no pride in their trust. It is a burden. In my pocket, the simple key sometimes feels like an iron fate drawn to a lodestone deep in the earth.

The key allows me quickly to seek Brother Constantine, the dead monk, when he manifests with a ringing of bells in one of the towers or with some other kind of cacophony elsewhere.

In Pico Mundo, the desert town in which I had lived for most of my time on earth, the spirits of many men and women linger. But here we have just Brother Constantine, who is no less disturbing than all of Pico Mundo's dead combined, one ghost but one too many.

With a bodach on the prowl, Brother Constantine was the least of my worries.

Shivering, I used my key, and hinges squeaked, and I followed the dog into the school.

Two night-lights staved off total gloom in the reception lounge. Multiple arrangements of sofas and armchairs suggested a hotel lobby.

I hurried past the unmanned information desk and went through a swinging door into a corridor lighted by an emergency lamp and red EXIT signs.

On this ground floor were the classrooms, the rehabilitation clinic, the infirmary, the kitchen, and the communal dining room. Those sisters with a culinary gift were not yet preparing break-fast. Silence ruled these spaces, as it would for hours yet.

I climbed the south stairs and found Boo waiting for me on the second-floor landing. He remained in a solemn mood. His tail did not wag, and he did not grin in greeting.

Two long and two short hallways formed a rectangle, serving the student quarters. The residents roomed in pairs.

At the southeast and northwest junctions of the corridors were nurses' stations, both of which I could see when I came out of the stairs in the southwest corner of the building.

At the northwest station, a nun sat at the counter, reading. From this distance, I could not identify her.

Besides, her face was half concealed by a wimple. These are not modern nuns who dress like meter maids. These sisters wear old-style habits that can make them seem as formidable as war-riors in armor.

The southeast station was deserted. The nun on duty must have been making her rounds or tending to one of her charges.

When Boo padded away to the right, heading southeast, I followed without calling to the reading nun. By the time that I had taken three steps, she was out of my line of sight.

Many of the sisters have nursing degrees, but they strive to make the second floor feel more like a cozy dormitory than like a hospital. With Christmas twenty days away, the halls were hung with garlands of fake evergreen boughs and festooned with genuine tinsel.

In respect of the sleeping students, the lights had been dimmed. The tinsel glimmered only here and there, and mostly darkled into tremulous shadows.

The doors of some student rooms were closed, others ajar. They featured not just numbers but also names.

Halfway between the stairwell and the nurses' station, Boo paused at Room 32, where the door was not fully closed. On block-lettered plaques were the names ANNAMARIE and JUSTINE.

This time I was close enough to Boo to see that indeed his hackles were raised.

The dog passed inside, but propriety made me hesitate. I ought to have asked a nun to accompany me into these students' quarters.

But I wanted to avoid having to explain bodachs to her. More important, I didn't want to risk being overheard by one of those malevolent spirits as I was talking about them.

Officially, only one person at the abbey and one at the convent know about my gift—if in fact it is a gift rather than a curse. Sister Angela, the mother superior, shares my secret, as does Father Bernard, the abbot.

Courtesy had required that they fully understand the troubled young man whom they would be welcoming as a long-term guest.

To assure Sister Angela and Abbot Bernard that I was neither a fraud nor a fool, Wyatt Porter, the chief of police in Pico Mundo, my hometown, shared with them the details of some murder cases with which I had assisted him.

Likewise, Father Sean Llewellyn vouched for me. He is the Catholic priest in Pico Mundo.

Father Llewellyn is also the uncle of Stormy Llewellyn, whom I had loved and lost. Whom I will forever cherish.

During the seven months I had lived in this mountain retreat, I'd shared the truth of my life with one other, Brother Knuckles, a monk. His real name is Salvatore, but we call him Knuckles more often than not.

Brother Knuckles would not have hesitated on the threshold of Room 32. He is a monk of action. In an instant he would have decided that the threat posed by the bodach trumped propriety. He would have rushed through the door as boldly as did the dog, although with less grace and with a lot more noise.

I pushed the door open wider, and went inside.

In the two hospital beds lay Annamarie, closest to the door, and Justine. Both were asleep.

On the wall behind each girl hung a lamp controlled by a switch at the end of a cord looped around the bed rail. It could provide various intensities of light.

Annamarie, who was ten years old but small for her age, had set her lamp low, as a night-light. She feared the dark.

Her wheelchair stood beside the bed. From one of the hand grips at the back of the chair hung a quilted, insulated jacket. From the other hand grip hung a woolen cap. On winter nights, she insisted that these garments be close at hand.

The girl slept with the top sheet clenched in her frail hands, as if ready to throw off the bedclothes. Her face was taut with an expression of concerned anticipation, less than anxiety, more than mere disquiet.

Although she slept soundly, she appeared to be prepared to flee at the slightest provocation.

One day each week, of her own accord, with eyes closed tight, Annamarie practiced piloting her battery-powered wheelchair to each of two elevators. One lay in the east wing, the other in the west.

In spite of her limitations and her suffering, she was a happy child. These preparations for flight were out of character.

Although she would not talk about it, she seemed to sense that a night of terror was coming, a hostile darkness through which she would need to find her way. She might be prescient.

The bodach, first glimpsed from my high window, had come here, but not alone. Three of them, silent wolflike shadows, were gathered around the second bed, in which Justine slept.

A single bodach signals impending violence that may be either near and probable or remote and less certain. If they appear in twos and threes, the danger is more immediate.

In my experience, when they appear in packs, the pending danger has become imminent peril, and the deaths of many people are days or hours away. Although the sight of three of them chilled me, I was grateful that they didn't number thirty.

Trembling with evident excitement, the bodachs bent over Justine while she slept, as if studying her intently. As if feeding on her.

CHAPTER 2

THE LAMP ABOVE THE SECOND BED HAD BEEN turned low, but Justine had not adjusted it herself. A nun had selected the dimmest setting, hoping that it might please the girl.

Justine did little for herself and asked for nothing. She was partially paralyzed and could not speak.

When Justine had been four years old, her father had strangled her mother to death. They say that after she had died, he put a rose between her teeth—but with the long thorny stem down her throat.

He drowned little Justine in the bathtub, or thought he did. He left her for dead, but she survived with brain damage from prolonged lack of oxygen.

For weeks, she lingered in a coma, though that was years ago. These days she slept and woke, but when awake, her capacity for engagement with her caregivers fluctuated.

Photographs of Justine at four reveal a child of exceptional beauty. In those snapshots, she looks impish and full of delight.

Eight years after the tub, at twelve, she was more beautiful than ever. Brain damage had not resulted in facial paralysis or distorted expressions. Curiously, a life spent largely indoors had not left her pale and drawn. Her face had color, and not a blemish.

Her beauty was chaste, like that of a Botticelli madonna, and ethereal. For everyone who knew Justine, her beauty stirred neither envy nor desire, but inspired a surprising reverence and, inexplicably, something like hope.

I suspect that the three menacing figures, hunched over her with keen interest, were not drawn by her beauty. Her enduring innocence attracted them, as did their expectation—their certain knowledge?—that she would soon be dead by violence and, at last, ugly.

These purposeful shadows, as black as scraps of starless night sky, have no eyes, yet I could sense them leering; no mouths, though I could almost hear the greedy sounds of them feasting on the promise of this girl's death.

I once saw them gathered at a nursing home in the hours before an earthquake leveled it. At a service station prior to an explosion and tragic fire. Following a teenager named Gary Tolliver in the days before he tortured and murdered his entire family.

A single death does not draw them, or two deaths, or even three. They prefer operatic violence, and for them the performance is not over when the fat lady sings, but only when she is torn to pieces.

They seem incapable of affecting our world, as though they are not fully present in this place and this time, but are in some way *virtual* presences. They are travelers, observers, aficionados of our pain.

Yet I fear them, and not solely because their presence signals oncoming horror. While they seem unable to affect this world in any significant way, I suspect that I am an exception to the rules that limit them, that I am vulnerable to them, as vulnerable as an ant in the shadow of a descending shoe.

Seeming whiter than usual in the company of inky bodachs, Boo did not growl, but watched these spirits with suspicion and disgust.

I pretended to have come here to assure myself that the thermostat had been properly set, to raise the pleated shades and confirm that the window had been firmly closed against all drafts, to dredge some wax from my right ear and to pry a shred of lettuce from between two teeth, though not with the same finger.

The bodachs ignored me—or pretended to ignore me.

Sleeping Justine had their complete attention. Their hands or paws hovered a few inches over the girl, and their fingers or talons described circles in the air above her, as if they were novelty-act musicians playing an instrument composed of drinking glasses, rubbing eerie music from the wet crystal rims.

Perhaps, like an insistent rhythm, her innocence excited them. Perhaps her humble circumstances, her lamblike grace, her complete vulnerability were the movements of a symphony to them.

I can only theorize about bodachs. I know nothing for certain about their nature or about their origins.

This is true not only of bodachs. The file labeled THINGS ABOUT WHICH ODD THOMAS KNOWS NOTHING is no less immense than the universe.

The only thing I know for sure is how much I do not know. Maybe there is wisdom in that recognition. Unfortunately, I have found no comfort in it.

Having been bent over Justine, the three bodachs abruptly

stood upright and, as one, turned their wolfish heads toward the door, as if in response to a summoning trumpet that I could not hear.

Evidently Boo could not hear it, either, for his ears did not prick up. His attention remained on the dark spirits.

Like shadows chased by sudden light, the bodachs whirled from the bed, swooped to the door, and vanished into the hallway.

Inclined to follow them, I hesitated when I discovered Justine staring at me. Her blue eyes were limpid pools: so clear, seemingly without mystery, yet bottomless.

Sometimes you can be sure she sees you. Other times, like this, you sense that, to her, you are as transparent as glass, that she can look *through* everything in this world.

I said to her, "Don't be afraid," which was twice presumptuous. First, I didn't know that she was frightened or that she was even capable of fear. Second, my words implied a guarantee of protection that, in the coming crisis, I might not be able to fulfill.

Too wise and humble to play the hero, Boo had left the room.

As I headed toward the door, Annamarie, in the first bed, murmured, "Odd."

Her eyes remained closed. Knots of bedsheet were still clutched in her hands. She breathed shallowly, rhythmically.

As I paused at the foot of her bed, the girl spoke again, more clearly than before: "Odd."

Annamarie had been born with myelocele spina bifida. Her hips were dislocated, her legs deformed. Her head on the pillow seemed almost as large as the shrunken body under the blanket.

She appeared to be asleep, but I whispered, "What is it, sweetie?"

"Odd one," she said.

Her mental retardation was not severe and did not reveal itself in her voice, which wasn't thick or slurred, but was high and sweet and charming.

"Odd one."

A chill prickled through me equal to the sharpest bite of the winter night outside.

Something like intuition drew my attention to Justine in the second bed. Her head had turned to follow me. For the first time, her eyes fixed on mine.

Justine's mouth moved, but she did not produce even one of the wordless sounds of which, in her deeper retardation, she was capable.

While Justine strove unsuccessfully to speak, Annamarie spoke again: "Odd one."

The pleated shades hung slack over the windows. The plush-toy kittens on the shelves near Justine's bed sat immobile, without one wink of eye or twitch of whisker.

On Annamarie's side of the room, the children's books on her shelves were neatly ordered. A china rabbit with flexible furry ears, dressed in Edwardian clothes, stood sentinel on her night-stand.

All was still, yet I sensed an energy barely contained. I would not have been surprised if every inanimate object in the room had come to life: levitating, spinning, ricocheting wall to wall.

Stillness reigned, however, and Justine tried to speak again, and Annamarie said, "Loop," in her sweet piping voice.

Leaving the sleeping girl, I moved to the foot of Justine's bed.

For fear that my voice would shatter the spell, I did not speak.

Wondering if the brain-damaged girl had made room for a visitor, I wished the bottomless blue eyes would polarize into a particular pair of Egyptian-black eyes with which I was familiar.

Some days I feel as if I have always been twenty-one, but the truth is that I was once young.

In those days, when death was a thing that happened to other people, my girl, Bronwen Llewellyn, who preferred to be called Stormy, would sometimes say, *Loop me in, odd one.* She meant that she wanted me to share the events of my day with her, or my thoughts, or my fears and worries.

During the sixteen months since Stormy had gone to ashes in this world and to service in another, no one had spoken those words to me.

Justine moved her mouth without producing sound, and in the adjacent bed, Annamarie said in her sleep, "Loop me in."

Room 32 seemed airless. Following those three words, I stood in a silence as profound as that in a vacuum. I could not breathe.

Only a moment ago, I had wished these blue eyes would polarize into the black of Stormy's eyes, that the suspicion of a visitation would be confirmed. Now the prospect terrified me.

When we hope, we usually hope for the wrong thing.

We yearn for tomorrow and the progress that it represents. But yesterday was once tomorrow, and where was the progress in it?

Or we yearn for yesterday, for what was or what might have been. But as we are yearning, the present is becoming the past, so the past is nothing but our yearning for second chances.

"Loop me in," Annamarie repeated.

As long as I remain subject to the river of time, which will be as long as I may live, there is no way back to Stormy, to anything.

The only way back is forward, downstream. The way up is the way down, and the way back is the way forward.

"Loop me in, odd one."

My hope here, in Room 32, should not be to speak with Stormy now, but only at the end of my journey, when time had no more power over me, when an eternal present robbed the past of all appeal.

Before I might see in those blue vacancies the Egyptian black for which I hoped, I looked away, stared at my hands, which clutched the footboard of the bed.

Stormy's spirit does not linger in this world, as some do. She moved on, as she should have done.

The intense undying love of the living can be a magnet to the dead. Enticing her back would be an unspeakable disservice to her. And although renewed contact might at first relieve my loneliness, ultimately there is only misery in hoping for the wrong thing.

I stared at my hands.

Annamarie fell silent in her sleep.

The plush-toy kittens and the china rabbit remained inanimate, thus avoiding either a demonic or a Disney moment.

In a while, my heart beat at a normal rate once more.

Justine's eyes were closed. Her lashes glistened, and her cheeks were damp. From the line of her jaw were suspended two tears, which quivered and then fell onto the sheet.

In search of Boo and bodachs, I left the room.

CHAPTER 3

INTO THE OLD ABBEY, WHICH WAS NOW ST. Bartholomew's School, had been transplanted modern mechanical systems that could be monitored from a computer station in the basement.

The spartan computer room had a desk, two chairs, and an unused file cabinet. Actually, the bottom drawer of the cabinet was packed with over a thousand empty Kit Kat wrappers.

Brother Timothy, who was responsible for the mechanical systems of both the abbey and the school, had a Kit Kat jones. Evidently, he felt that his candy craving was uncomfortably close to the sin of gluttony, because he seemed to be hiding the evidence.

Only Brother Timothy and visiting service personnel had reason to be in this room frequently. He felt his secret was safe here.

All the monks knew about it. Many of them, with a wink and a grin, had urged me to look in the bottom drawer of the file cabinet.

No one could have known whether Brother Timothy had

confessed gluttony to the prior, Father Reinhart. But the existence of his collection of wrappers suggested that he wanted to be caught.

His brothers would be happy to discover the evidence, although not until the trove of wrappers grew even larger, and not until the right moment, the moment that would ensure the greatest embarrassment for Timothy.

Although Brother Timothy was loved by everyone, unfortunately for him, he was also known for his bright blush, which made a lantern of his face.

Brother Roland had suggested that God would have given a man such a glorious physiological response to embarrassment only if He wanted it to be displayed often and to be widely enjoyed.

Posted on a wall of this basement room, referred to by the brothers as the Kit Kat Katacombs, hung a framed needlepoint sampler: THE DEVIL IS IN THE DIGITAL DATA.

Using this computer, I could review the historical performance record as well as the current status of the heating-and-cooling system, the lighting system, the fire-control system, and the emergency-power generators.

On the second floor, the three bodachs still roamed from room to room, previewing victims to enhance the pleasure they would get from carnage when it came. I could learn no more from watching them.

Fear of fire had driven me to the basement. On the screen, I studied display after display relating to the fire-control system.

Every room featured at least one sprinkler head embedded in the ceiling. Every hallway had numerous sprinklers, spaced fifteen feet on center.

According to the monitoring program, all the sprinklers were in order and all the water lines were maintaining the required pressure. The smoke detectors and alarm boxes were functional and periodically self-testing.

I backed out of the fire-control system and called up the schema of the heating-and-cooling systems. I was particularly interested in the boilers, of which the school had two.

Because no natural-gas service extended to the remote Sierra, both boilers were fired by propane. A large pressurized storage tank lay buried at a distance from both the school and the abbey.

According to the monitors, the propane tank contained 84 percent of maximum capacity. The flow rate appeared to be normal. All of the valves were functioning. The ratio of BTUs produced to propane consumed indicated no leaks in the system. Both of the independent emergency-shutdown switches were operative.

Throughout the schema, every point of potential mechanical failure was signified by a small green light. Not a single red indicator marred the screen.

Whatever disaster might be coming, fire would probably not be a part of it.

I looked at the needlepoint sampler framed on the wall above the computer: THE DEVIL IS IN THE DIGITAL DATA.

Once, when I was fifteen, some seriously bad guys in porkpie hats handcuffed me, chained my ankles together, locked me in the trunk of an old Buick, picked up the Buick with a crane, dropped the car into a hydraulic compressing machine of the kind that turns any once-proud vehicle into a three-foot cube of bad modern art, and punched the CRUSH ODD THOMAS button.

Relax. It's not my intention to bore you with an old war story.

I raise the issue of the Buick only to illustrate the fact that my supernatural gifts do not include reliable foresight.

Those bad guys had the polished-ice eyes of gleeful socio-paths, facial scars that suggested they were at the very least adventurous, and a way of walking that indicated either painful testicular tumors or multiple concealed weapons. Yet I did not recognize that they were a threat until they knocked me flat to the ground with a ten-pound bratwurst and began to kick the crap out of me.

I had been distracted by two other guys who were wearing black boots, black pants, black shirts, black capes, and peculiar black hats. Later, I learned they were two schoolteachers who had each independently decided to attend a costume party dressed as Zorro.

In retrospect, by the time I was locked in the trunk of the Buick with the two dead rhesus monkeys and the bratwurst, I realized that I should have recognized the real troublemakers the minute I had seen the porkpie hats. How could anyone in his right mind attribute good intentions to three guys in identical porkpie hats?

In my defense, consider that I was just fifteen at the time, not a fraction as experienced as I am these days, and that I have never claimed to be clairvoyant.

Maybe my fear of fire was, in this case, like my suspicion of the Zorro impersonators: misguided.

Although a survey of selected mechanical systems had given me no reason to believe that impending flames had drawn the bodachs to St. Bart's School, I remained concerned that fire was a danger. No other threat seemed to pose such a challenge to a large community of the mentally and physically disabled.

Earthquakes were not as common or as powerful in the mountains of California as in the valleys and the flatlands. Besides, the new abbey had been built to the standards of a fortress, and the old one had been reconstructed with such diligence that it should be able to ride out violent and extended temblors.

This high in the Sierra, bedrock lay close underfoot; in some places, great granite bones breached the surface. Our two buildings were anchored in bedrock.

Here we have no tornadoes, no hurricanes, no active volcanoes, no killer bees.

We *do* have something more dangerous than all those things. We have people.

The monks in the abbey and the nuns in the convent seemed to be unlikely villains. Evil can disguise itself in piety and charity, but I had difficulty picturing any of the brothers or sisters running amok with a chain saw or a machine gun.

Even Brother Timothy, on a dangerous sugar high and crazed by Kit Kat guilt, didn't scare me.

The glowering Russian staying on the second floor of the guesthouse was a more deserving object of suspicion. He did not wear a porkpie hat, but he had a dour demeanor and secretive ways.

My months of peace and contemplation were at an end.

The demands of my gift, the silent but insistent pleas of the lingering dead, the terrible losses that I had not always been able to prevent: These things had driven me to the seclusion of St. Bartholomew's Abbey. I needed to simplify my life.

I had not come to this high redoubt forever. I had only asked God for a time-out, which had been granted, but now the clock was ticking again.

When I backed out of the heating-and-cooling-system schema, the computer monitor went to black with a simple white menu. In that more reflective screen, I saw movement behind me.

For seven months, the abbey had been a still point in the river, where I turned in a lazy gyre, always in sight of the same familiar shore, but now the true rhythm of the river asserted itself. Sullen, untamed, and intractable, it washed away my sense of peace and washed me toward my destiny once more.

Expecting a hard blow or the thrust of something sharp, I spun the office chair around, toward the source of the reflection in the computer screen.

CHAPTER 4

M Y SPINE HAD GONE TO ICE AND MY MOUTH to dust in fear of a nun.

Batman would have sneered at me, and Odysseus would have cut me no slack, but I would have told them that I had never claimed to be a hero. At heart, I am only a fry cook, currently unemployed.

In my defense, I must note that the worthy who had entered the computer room was not just any nun, but Sister Angela, whom the others call Mother Superior. She has the sweet face of a beloved grandmother, yes, but the steely determination of the Terminator.

Of course I mean the *good* Terminator from the second movie in the series.

Although Benedictine sisters usually wear gray habits or black, these nuns wear white because they are a twice-reformed order of a previously reformed order of post-reform Benedictines, although they would not want to be thought of as being aligned with either Trappist or Cistercian principles.

You don't need to know what that means. God Himself is still trying to figure it out.

The essence of all this reformation is that these sisters are more orthodox than those modern nuns who seem to consider themselves social workers who don't date. They pray in Latin, never eat meat on Friday, and with a withering stare would silence the voice and guitar of any folksinger who dared to offer a socially relevant tune during Mass.

Sister Angela says she and her sisters hark back to a time in the first third of the previous century when the Church was confident of its timelessness and when "the bishops weren't crazy." Although she wasn't born until 1945 and never knew the era she admires, she says that she would prefer to live in the '30s than in the age of the Internet and shock jocks broadcasting via satellite.

I have some sympathy for her position. In those days, there were no nuclear weapons, either, no organized terrorists eager to blow up women and children, and you could buy Black Jack chewing gum anywhere, and for no more than a nickel a pack.

This bit of gum trivia comes from a novel. I have learned a great deal from novels. Some of it is even true.

Settling into the second chair, Sister Angela said, "Another restless night, Odd Thomas?"

From previous conversations, she knew that I don't sleep as well these days as I once did. Sleep is a kind of peace, and I have not yet earned peace.

"I couldn't go to bed until the snow began to fall," I told her. "I wanted to see the world turn white."

"The blizzard still hasn't broken. But a basement room is a most peculiar place to stand watch for it."

"Yes, ma'am."

She has a certain lovely smile that she can sustain for a long time in patient expectancy. If she held a sword over your head, it would not be as effective an instrument of interrogation as that forbearing smile.

After a silence that was a test of wills, I said, "Ma'am, you look as though you think I'm hiding something."

"Are you hiding something, Oddie?"

"No, ma'am." I indicated the computer. "I was just checking on the school's mechanical systems."

"I see. Then you're covering for Brother Timothy? Has he been committed to a clinic for Kit Kat addiction?"

"I just like to learn new things around here . . . to make myself useful," I said.

"Your breakfast pancakes every weekend are a greater grace than any guest of the abbey has ever brought to us."

"Nobody's cakes are fluffier than mine."

Her eyes are the same merry blue as the periwinkles on the Royal Doulton china that my mother owned, pieces of which Mom, from time to time, threw at the walls or at me. "You must have had quite a loyal following at the diner where you worked."

"I was a star with a spatula."

She smiled at me. Smiled and waited.

"I'll make hash browns this Sunday. You've never tasted my hash browns."

Smiling, she fingered the beaded chain on her pectoral cross.

I said, "The thing is, I had a bad dream about an exploding boiler."

"An exploding-boiler dream?"

"That's right."

"A real nightmare, was it?"

"It left me very anxious."

"Was it one of *our* boilers exploding?"

"It might have been. In the dream, the place wasn't clear. You know how dreams are."

A twinkle brightened her periwinkle eyes. "In this dream, did you see nuns on fire, screaming through a snowy night?"

"No, ma'am. Good heavens, no. Just the boiler exploding."

"Did you see disabled children flinging themselves from windows full of flame?"

I tried silence and a smile of my own.

She said, "Are your nightmares always so thinly plotted, Oddie?"

"Not always, ma'am."

She said, "Now and then I dream of Frankenstein because of a movie I saw when I was a little girl. In *my* dream, there's an ancient windmill hung with ragged rotting sails creaking 'round in a storm. A ferocity of rain, sky-splitting bolts of lightning, leaping shadows, stairwells of cold stone, hidden doors in bookcases, candlelit secret passageways, bizarre machines with gold-plated gyroscopes, crackling arcs of electricity, a demented hunchback with lantern eyes, always the lumbering monster close behind me, and a scientist in a white lab coat carrying his own severed head."

Finished, she smiled at me.

"Just an exploding boiler," I said.

"God has many reasons to love you, Oddie, but for certain He loves you because you're such an inexperienced and incompetent liar."

"I've told some whoppers in my time," I assured her.

"The claim that you have told whoppers is the biggest whopper you have told."

"At nun school, you must've been president of the debating team."

"Fess up, young man. You didn't dream about an exploding boiler. Something else has you worried."

I shrugged.

"You were checking on the children in their rooms."

She knew that I saw the lingering dead. But I had not told her or Abbot Bernard about bodachs.

Because these bloodthirsty spirits are drawn by events with high body counts, I hadn't expected to encounter them in a place as remote as this. Towns and cities are their natural hunting grounds.

Besides, those who accept my assertion that I see the lingering dead are less likely to believe me if too soon in our acquaintance I begin to talk, as well, about sinuous shadowy demons that delight in scenes of death and destruction.

A man who has one pet monkey might be viewed as charmingly eccentric. But a man who has made his home into a monkey house, with scores of chattering chimpanzees capering through the rooms, will have lost credibility with the mental-health authorities.

I decided to unburden myself, however, because Sister Angela is a good listener and has a reliable ear for insincerity. Two reliable ears. Perhaps the wimple around her face serves as a sound-focusing device that brings to her greater nuances in other people's speech than those of us without wimples are able to hear.

I'm not saying that nuns have the technical expertise of Q, the genius inventor who supplies James Bond with way-cool gadgets in the movies. It's a theory I won't dismiss out of hand, but I can't prove anything.

Trusting in her goodwill and in the crap-detecting capability made possible by her wimple, I told her about the bodachs.

She listened intently, her face impassive, giving no indication whether or not she thought I was psychotic.

With the power of her personality, Sister Angela can compel you to meet her eyes. Perhaps a few strong-willed people are able to look away from her stare after she has locked on to their eyes, but I'm not one of them. By the time I told her all about bodachs, I felt pickled in periwinkle.

When I finished, she studied me in silence, her expression unreadable, and just when I thought she had decided to pray for my sanity, she accepted the truth of everything I'd told her by saying simply, "What must be done?"

"I don't know."

"That's a most unsatisfactory answer."

"Most," I agreed. "The thing is, the bodachs showed up only half an hour ago. I haven't observed them long enough to be able to guess what's drawn them here."

Cowled by voluminous sleeves, her hands closed into pink, white-knuckled fists. "Something's going to happen to the children."

"Not necessarily all the children. Maybe some of them. And maybe not just to the children."

"How much time do we have until . . . whatever?"

"Usually they show up a day or two ahead of the event. To savor the sight of those who are . . ." I was reluctant to say more.

Sister Angela finished my sentence: ". . . soon to die."

"If there's a killer involved, a human agent instead of, say, an exploding propane-fired boiler, they're sometimes as fascinated with him as with the potential victims."

"We have no murderers here," said Sister Angela.

"What do we really know about Rodion Romanovich?"

"The Russian gentleman in the abbey guesthouse?"

"He glowers," I said.

"At times, so do I."

"Yes, ma'am, but it's a concerned sort of glower, and you're a nun."

"And he's a spiritual pilgrim."

"We have proof you're a nun, but we only have his word about what he is."

"Have you seen bodachs following him around?"

"Not yet."

Sister Angela frowned, short of a glower, and said, "He's been kind to us here at the school."

"I'm not accusing Mr. Romanovich of anything. I'm just curious about him."

"After Lauds, I'll speak to Abbot Bernard about the need for vigilance in general."

Lauds is morning prayer, the second of seven periods in the daily Divine Office that the monks observe.

At St. Bartholomew's Abbey, Lauds immediately follows Matins—the singing of psalms and readings from the saints—which begins at 5:45 in the morning. It concludes no later than 6:30.

I switched off the computer and got to my feet. "I'm going to look around some more."

In a billow of white habit, Sister Angela rose from her chair. "If tomorrow is to be a day of crisis, I'd better get some sleep. But in an emergency, don't hesitate to call me on my cell number at any hour."

I smiled and shook my head.

"What is it?" she asked.

"The world turns and the world changes. Nuns with cell phones."

"An easy thing to get your mind around," she said. "Easier than factoring into your philosophy a fry cook who sees dead people."

"True. I guess the equivalent of me would actually be like in that old TV show—a flying nun."

"I don't allow flying nuns in my convent," she said. "They tend to be frivolous, and during night flight, they're prone to crashing through windows."

CHAPTER 5

WHEN I RETURNED FROM THE BASEMENT computer room, no bodachs swarmed the corridors of the second floor. Perhaps they were gathered over the beds of other children, but I didn't think so. The place felt clean of them.

They might have been on the third floor, where nuns slept unaware. The sisters, too, might be destined to die in an explosion.

I couldn't go uninvited onto the third floor, except in an emergency. Instead I went out of the school and into the night once more.

The meadow and the surrounding trees and the abbey upslope still waited to be white.

The bellied sky, the storm unborn, could not be seen, for the mountain was nearly as dark as the heavens and reflected nothing on the undersides of the clouds.

Boo had abandoned me. Although he likes my company, I am not his master. He has no master here. He is an independent agent and pursues his own agenda.

Not sure how to proceed or where to seek another clue of what had drawn the bodachs, I crossed the front yard of the school, moving toward the abbey.

The temperature of blood and bone had fallen with the arrival of the bodachs; but malevolent spirits and December air, together, could not explain the cold that curled through me.

The true source of the chill might have been an understanding that our only choice is pyre or pyre, that we live and breathe to be consumed by fire or fire, not just now and at St. Bartholomew's, but always and anywhere. Consumed or purified by fire.

The earth rumbled, and the ground shivered underfoot, and the tall grass trembled though no breeze had yet arisen.

Although this was a subtle sound, a gentle movement, that most likely had not awakened even one monk, instinct said *earthquake*. I suspected, however, that Brother John might be responsible for the shuddering earth.

From the meadow rose the scent of ozone. I had detected the same scent earlier, in the guesthouse cloister, passing the statue of St. Bartholomew offering a pumpkin.

When after half a minute the earth stopped rumbling, I realized that the primary potential for fire and cataclysm might not be the propane tank and the boilers that heated our buildings. Brother John, at work in his subterranean retreat, exploring the very structure of reality, required serious consideration.

I hurried to the abbey, past the quarters of the novitiates, and south past the abbot's office. Abbot Bernard's personal quarters were above the office, on the second floor.

On the third floor, his small chapel provided him with a place for private prayer. Faint lambent light shivered along the beveled edges of those cold windows.

At 12:35 in the morning, the abbot was more likely to be

snoring than praying. The trembling paleness that traced the cut lines in the glass must have issued from a devotional lamp, a single flickering candle.

I rounded the southeast corner of the abbey and headed west, past the last rooms of the novitiate, past the chapter room and the kitchen. Before the refectory, I came to a set of stone stairs.

At the bottom of the stairs, a single bulb revealed a bronze door. A cast bronze panel above this entrance bore the Latin words LIBERA NOS A MALO.

Deliver us from evil.

My universal key unlocked the heavy bolt. Pivoting silently on ball-bearing hinges, the door swung inward, a half-ton weight so perfectly balanced that I could move it with one finger.

Beyond lay a stone corridor bathed in blue light.

The slab of bronze swung shut and locked behind me as I walked to a second door of brushed stainless steel. In this grained surface were embedded polished letters that spelled three Latin words: LUMIN DE LUMINE.

Light from light.

A wide steel architrave surrounded this formidable barrier. Inlaid in the architrave was a twelve-inch plasma screen.

Upon being touched, the screen brightened. I pressed my hand flat against it.

I could not see or feel the scanner reading my fingerprints, but I was nonetheless identified and approved. With a pneumatic hiss, the door slid open.

Brother John says the hiss is not an inevitable consequence of the operation of the door. It could have been made to open silently.

He incorporated the hiss to remind himself that in every

human enterprise, no matter with what virtuous intentions it is undertaken, a serpent lurks.

Beyond the steel door waited an eight-foot-square chamber that appeared to be a seamless, wax-yellow, porcelain vessel. I entered and stood there like a lone seed inside a hollow, polished gourd.

When a second heedful hiss caused me to turn and look back, no trace of the door could be seen.

The buttery light radiated from the walls, and as on previous visits to this realm, I felt as though I had stepped into a dream. Simultaneously, I experienced a detachment from the world *and* a heightened reality.

The light in the walls faded. Darkness closed upon me.

Although the chamber was surely an elevator that carried me down a floor or two, I detected no movement. The machinery made no sound.

In the darkness, a rectangle of red light appeared as another portal hissed open in front of me.

A vestibule offered three brushed-steel doors. The one to my right and the one to my left were plain. Neither door had a visible lock; and I had never been invited through them.

On the third, directly before me, were embedded more polished letters: PER OMNIA SAECULA SAECULORUM.

For ever and ever.

In the red light, the brushed steel glowed softly, like embers. The polished letters blazed.

Without a hiss, *For ever and ever* slid aside, as though inviting me to eternity.

I stepped into a round chamber thirty feet in diameter, barren but for a cozy arrangement of four wingback chairs at the center.

A floor lamp served each chair, though currently only two shed light.

Here sat Brother John in tunic and scapular, but with his hood pushed back, off his head. In the days before he'd become a monk, he had been the famous John Heineman.

Time magazine had called him "the most brilliant physicist of this half-century, but increasingly a tortured soul," and presented, as a sidebar to their main article, an analysis of Heineman's "life decisions" written by a pop psychologist with a hit TV show on which he resolved the problems of such troubled people as klepto-maniac mothers with bulimic biker daughters.

The New York Times had referred to John Heineman as "a riddle wrapped in a mystery inside an enigma." Two days later, in a brief correction, the newspaper noted that it should have attrib-uted that memorable description not to actress Cameron Diaz after she had met Heineman, but to Winston Churchill, who first used those words to describe Russia in 1939.

In an article titled "The Dumbest Celebrities of the Year," *Entertainment Weekly* called him a "born-again moron" and "a hopeless schlub who wouldn't know Eminem from Oprah."

The *National Enquirer* had promised to produce evidence that he and morning-show anchor Katie Couric were an item, while the *Weekly World News* had reported that he was dating Princess Di, who was not—they insisted—as dead as everyone thought.

In the corrupted spirit of much contemporary science, various learned journals, with a bias to defend, questioned his research, his theories, his right to publish his research and theories, his right even to conduct such research and to *have* such theories, his motives, his sanity, and the unseemly size of his fortune.

Had the many patents derived from his research not made him

a billionaire four times over, most of those publications would have had no interest in him. Wealth is power, and power is the only thing about which contemporary culture cares.

If he hadn't quietly given away that entire fortune without issuing a press release and without granting interviews, they wouldn't have been so annoyed with him. Just as pop stars and film critics live for their power, so do reporters.

If he'd given his money to an approved university, they would not have hated him. Most universities are no longer temples of knowledge, but of power, and true moderns worship there.

At some time during the years since all that had happened, if he had been caught with an underage hooker or had checked into a clinic for cocaine addiction so chronic that his nose cartilage had entirely rotted away, all would have been forgiven; the press would have adored him. In our age, self-indulgence and self-destruction, rather than self-sacrifice, are the foundations for new heroic myths.

Instead, John Heineman had passed years in monastic seclusion and in fact had spent months at a time in hermitage, first elsewhere and then here in his deep retreat, speaking not a word to anyone. His meditations were of a different character from those of other monks, though not necessarily less reverent.

I crossed the shadowy strand surrounding the ordered furniture. The floor was stone. Under the chairs lay a wine-colored carpet.

The tinted bulbs and the umber-fabric lampshades produced light the color of caramelized honey.

Brother John was a tall, rangy, broad-shouldered man. His hands—at that moment resting on the arms of the chair—were large, with thick-boned wrists.

Although a long countenance would have been more in harmony with his lanky physique, his face was round. The lamplight directed the crisp and pointed shadow of his strong nose toward his left ear, as if his face were a sundial, his nose the gnomon, and his ear the mark for nine o'clock.

Assuming that the second lighted lamp was meant to direct me, I sat in the chair opposite him.

His eyes were violet and hooded, and his gaze was as steady as the aim of a battle-hardened sharpshooter.

Considering that he might be engaged in meditation and averse to interruption, I said nothing.

The monks of St. Bartholomew's are encouraged to cultivate silence at all times, except during scheduled social periods.

The silence during the day is called the Lesser Silence, which begins after breakfast and lasts until the evening recreation period following dinner. During Lesser Silence, the brothers will speak to one another only as the work of the monastery requires.

The silence after Compline—the night prayer—is called the Greater Silence. At St. Bartholomew's, it lasts through breakfast.

I did not want to encourage Brother John to speak with me. He knew that I would not have visited at this hour without good reason; but it would be his decision to break silence or not.

While I waited, I surveyed the room.

Because the light here was always low and restricted to the center of the chamber, I'd never had a clear look at the continuous wall that wrapped this round space. A dark luster implied a polished surface, and I suspected that it might be glass beyond which pooled a mysterious blackness.

As we were underground, no mountain landscape waited to be

revealed. Contiguous panels of thick curved glass, nine feet high, suggested instead an aquarium.

If we were surrounded by an aquarium, however, whatever lived in it had never revealed itself in my presence. No pale shape ever glided past. No gape-mouthed denizen with a blinkless stare had swum close to the farther side of the aquarium wall to peer at me from its airless world.

An imposing figure in any circumstances, Brother John made me think now of Captain Nemo on the bridge of the *Nautilus*, which was an unfortunate comparison. Nemo was a powerful man and a genius, but he didn't have both oars in the water.

Brother John is as sane as I am. Make of that what you wish.

After another minute of silence, he apparently came to the end of the line of thought that he had been reluctant to interrupt. His violet eyes refocused from some far landscape to me, and in a deep rough voice, he said, "Have a cookie."

CHAPTER 6

I N THE ROUND ROOM, IN THE CARAMEL LIGHT, beside each armchair stood a small table. On the table beside my chair, a red plate held three chocolate-chip cookies.

Brother John bakes them himself. They're wonderful.

I picked up a cookie. It was warm.

From the time I had unlocked the bronze door with my universal key until I entered this room, not even two minutes had passed.

I doubted that Brother John had fetched the cookies himself. He had been genuinely lost in thought.

We were alone in the room. I hadn't heard retreating footsteps when I entered.

"Delicious," I said, after swallowing a bite of the cookie.

"As a boy, I wanted to be a baker," he said.

"The world needs good bakers, sir."

"I couldn't stop thinking long enough to become a baker."

"Stop thinking about what?"

"The universe. The fabric of reality. Structure."

"I see," I said, though I didn't.

"I understood subatomic structure when I was six."

"At six, I made a pretty cool fort out of Lego blocks. Towers and turrets and battlements and everything."

His face brightened. "When I was a kid, I used forty-seven sets of Legos to build a crude model of quantum foam."

"Sorry, sir. I have no idea what quantum foam is."

"To grasp it, you have to be able to envision a very small land-scape, one ten-billionth of a millionth of a meter—and only as it exists within a speck of time that is one-millionth of a billionth of a billionth of a second."

"I'd need to get a better wristwatch."

"This landscape I'm talking about is twenty powers of ten below the level of the proton, where there is no left or right, no up or down, no before or after."

"Forty-seven sets of Legos would've cost a bunch."

"My parents were supportive."

"Mine weren't," I said. "I had to leave home at sixteen and get work as a fry cook to support myself."

"You make exceptional pancakes, Odd Thomas. Unlike quantum foam, everybody knows what pancakes are."

After creating a four-billion-dollar charitable trust to be owned and administered by the Church, John Heineman had disappeared. The media had hunted him assiduously for years, without success. They were told he had gone into seclusion with the intention of becoming a monk, which was true.

Some monks become priests, but others do not. Although they are all brothers, some are called Father. The priests can say Mass and perform sacred rites that the unordained brothers cannot, though otherwise they regard one another as equals. Brother John is a monk but not a priest.

Be patient. The organization of monastic life is harder to understand than pancakes, but it's not a brain buster like quantum foam.

These monks take vows of poverty, chastity, obedience, and stability. Some of them surrender humble assets, while others leave behind prosperous careers. I think it's safe to say that only Brother John has turned his back on four billion dollars.

As John Heineman wished, the Church used a portion of that money to remake the former abbey as a school and a home for those who were both physically and mentally disabled and who had been abandoned by their families. They were children who would otherwise rot in mostly loveless public institutions or would be quietly euthanized by self-appointed "death angels" in the medical system.

On this December night, I was warmed by being in the company of a man like Brother John, whose compassion matched his genius. To be honest, the cookie contributed significantly to my improved mood.

A new abbey had been built, as well. Included were a series of subterranean rooms constructed and equipped to meet Brother John's specifications.

No one called this underground complex a laboratory. As far as I could discern, it wasn't in fact a lab, but something unique of which only his genius could have conceived, its full purpose a mystery.

The brothers, few of whom ever came here, called these quarters John's Mew. *Mew,* in this case, is a medieval word meaning a place of concealment. A hideout.

Also, a mew is a cage in which hunting hawks are kept while they are molting. *Mew* also means "to molt."

I once heard a monk refer to Brother John "down there growing all new feathers in the mew."

Another had called these basement quarters a cocoon and wondered when the revelation of the butterfly would occur.

Such comments suggested that Brother John might become someone other than who he is, someone greater.

Because I was a guest and not a monk, I could not tease more out of the brothers. They were protective of him and of his privacy.

I was aware of Brother John's true identity only because he revealed it to me. He did not swear me to secrecy. He had said instead, "I know you won't sell me out, Odd Thomas. Your discretion and your loyalty are figured in the drift of stars."

Although I had no idea what he meant by that, I didn't press him for an explanation. He said many things I didn't fully understand, and I didn't want our relationship to become a verbal sonata to which a rhythmic *Huh? Huh? Huh?* was my only contribution.

I had not told him my secret. I don't know why. Maybe I would just prefer that certain people I admire do not have any reason to think of me as a freak.

The brothers regarded him with respect bordering on awe. I also sensed in them a trace of fear. I might have been mistaken.

I didn't regard him as fearsome. I sensed no threat in him. Sometimes, however, I saw that he himself was afraid of something.

Abbot Bernard does not call this place John's Mew, as do the other monks. He refers to it as the adytum.

Adytum is another medieval word that means "the most sacred part of a place of worship, forbidden to the public, the innermost shrine of shrines."

The abbot is a good-humored man, but he never speaks the word *adytum* with a smile. The three syllables cross his lips always in a murmur or a whisper, solemnly, and in his eyes are yearning and wonder and perhaps dread.

As to why Brother John traded success and the secular world for poverty and the monastery, he had only said that his studies of the structure of reality, as revealed through that branch of physics known as quantum mechanics, had led him to revelations that humbled him. "Humbled and spooked me," he said.

Now, as I finished the chocolate-chip cookie, he said, "What brings you here at this hour, during the Greater Silence?"

"I know you're awake much of the night."

"I sleep less and less, can't turn my mind off."

A periodic insomniac myself, I said, "Some nights, it seems my brain is someone else's TV, and they won't stop channel surfing."

"And when I *do* nod off," said Brother John, "it's often at inconvenient times. In any day, I'm likely to miss one or two periods of the Divine Office—sometimes Matins and Lauds, sometimes Sext, or Compline. I've even missed the Mass, napping in this chair. The abbot is understanding. The prior is too lenient with me, grants absolution easily and with too little penance."

"They have a lot of respect for you, sir."

"It's like sitting on a beach."

"What is?" I asked, smoothly avoiding *Huh?*

"Here, in the quiet hours after midnight. Like sitting on a beach. The night rolls and breaks and tosses up our losses like bits of wreckage, all that's left of one ship or another."

I said, "I suppose that's true," because in fact I thought I understood his mood if not his full meaning.

"We ceaselessly examine the bits of wreckage in the surf, as though we can put the past together again, but that's just torturing ourselves."

That sentiment had teeth. I, too, had felt its bite. "Brother John, I've got an odd question."

"Of course you do," he said, either commenting on the arcane nature of my curiosity or on my name.

"Sir, this may seem to be an ignorant question, but I have good reason to ask it. Is there a remote possibility that your work here might . . . blow up or something?"

He bowed his head, raised one hand from the arm of his chair, and stroked his chin, apparently pondering my question.

Although I was grateful to him for giving me a well-considered answer, I would have been happier if he had without hesitation said, *Nope, no chance, impossible, absurd.*

Brother John was part of a long tradition of monk and priest scientists. The Church had created the concept of the university and had established the first of them in the twelfth century. Roger Bacon, a Franciscan monk, was arguably the greatest mathematician of the thirteenth century. Bishop Robert Grosseteste was the first man to write down the necessary steps for performing a scientific experiment. Jesuits had built the first reflecting telescopes, microscopes, barometers, were first to calculate the constant of gravity, the first to measure the height of the mountains on the moon, the first to develop an accurate method of calculating a planet's orbit, the first to devise and publish a coherent description of atomic theory.

As far as I knew, over the centuries, not one of those guys had accidentally blown up a monastery.

Of course, I don't know everything. Considering the infinite amount of knowledge that one could acquire in a virtually innumerable array of intellectual disciplines, it's probably more accurate to say that I don't know *anything*.

Maybe monk scientists have occasionally blown a monastery to bits. I am pretty sure, however, they never did it intentionally.

I could not imagine Brother John, philanthropist and cookie-maker, in a weirdly lighted laboratory, cackling a mad-scientist cackle and scheming to destroy the world. Although brilliant, he was human, so I *could* easily see him looking up in alarm from an experiment and saying *Whoops,* just before unintentionally reducing the abbey to a puddle of nano-goo.

"Something," he finally said.

"Sir?"

He raised his head to look at me directly again. "Yes, perhaps something."

"Something, sir?"

"Yes. You asked whether there was a possibility that my work here might blow up or something. I can't see a way it could blow up. I mean, not the work itself."

"Oh. But something else could happen."

"Maybe yes, probably no. Something."

"But maybe yes. Like what?"

"Whatever."

"What whatever?" I asked.

"Whatever can be imagined."

"Sir?"

"Have another cookie."

"Sir, *anything* can be imagined."

"Yes. That's right. Imagination knows no limits."

"So *anything* might go wrong?"

"*Might* isn't *will*. Any terrible, disastrous thing might happen, but probably nothing will."

"Probably?"

"Probability is an important factor, Odd Thomas. A blood vessel *might* burst in your brain, killing you an instant from now."

At once I regretted not having taken a second cookie.

He smiled. He looked at his watch. He looked at me. He shrugged. "See? The probability was low."

"The anything that might happen," I said, "supposing that it *did* happen, could it result in a lot of people dying horribly?"

"Horribly?"

"Yes, sir. Horribly."

"That's a subjective judgment. Horrible to one person might not be the same as horrible to another."

"Shattering bones, bursting hearts, exploding heads, burning flesh, blood, pain, screaming—that kind of horrible."

"Maybe yes, probably no."

"This again."

"More likely, they would just cease to exist."

"That's death."

"No, it's different. Death leaves a corpse."

I had been reaching for a cookie. I pulled my hand back without taking one from the plate.

"Sir, you're scaring me."

A settled blue heron astonishes when it reveals its true height by unfolding its long sticklike legs; likewise, Brother John proved even taller than I remembered when he rose from his chair. "I've been badly scared myself, badly, for quite a few years now. You learn to live with it."

Getting to my feet, I said, "Brother John . . . whatever this work is you do here, are you sure you should be doing it?"

"My intellect is God-given. I've a sacred obligation to use it."

His words resonated with me. When one of the lingering dead has been murdered and comes to me for justice, I always feel obliged to help the poor soul.

The difference is that I rely both on reason and on something that you might call a sixth sense, while in his research Brother John is strictly using his intellect.

A sixth sense is a miraculous thing, which in itself suggests a supernatural order. The human intellect, however, for all its power and triumphs, is largely formed by this world and is therefore corruptible.

This monk's hands, like his intellect, were also God-given, but he could choose to use them to strangle babies.

I did not need to remind him of this. I only said, "I had a terrible dream. I'm worried about the children at the school."

Unlike Sister Angela, he did not instantly recognize that my dream was a lie. He said, "Have your dreams come true in the past?"

"No, sir. But this was very . . . real."

He pulled his hood over his head. "Try to dream of something pleasant, Odd Thomas."

"I can't control my dreams, sir."

In a fatherly way, he put an arm around my shoulders. "Then

perhaps you shouldn't sleep. The imagination has terrifying power."

I was not conscious of crossing the room with him, but now the arrangement of armchairs lay behind us, and before me, a door slid soundlessly open. Beyond the door lay the antechamber awash in red light.

Having crossed the threshold alone, I turned to look back at Brother John.

"Sir, when you traded being just a scientist for being a monk scientist, did you ever consider, instead, being a tire salesman?"

"What's the punch line?"

"It's not a joke, sir. When my life became too complicated and I had to give up being a fry cook, I considered the tire life. But I came here instead."

He said nothing.

"If I could be a tire salesman, help people get rolling on good rubber, at a fair price, that would be useful work. If I could be a tire salesman *and nothing else,* just a good tire salesman with a little apartment and this girl I once knew, that would be enough."

His violet eyes were ruddy with the light of the vestibule. He shook his head, rejecting the tire life. "I want to know."

"Know what?" I asked.

"Everything," he said, and the door slid shut between us.

Polished-steel letters on brushed steel: PER OMNIA SAECULA SAECULORUM.

For ever and ever.

Through hissing doors, through buttery light and blue, I went to the surface, into the night, and locked the bronze door with my universal key.

LIBERA NOS A MALO said the door.

Deliver us from evil.

As I climbed the stone steps to the abbey yard, snow began to fall. Huge flakes turned gracefully in the windless dark, turned as if to a waltz that I could not hear.

The night did not seem as frigid as it had been earlier. Perhaps I had been colder in John's Mew than I realized, and by comparison to that realm, the winter night seemed mild.

In moments, the flakes as big as frosted flowers gave way to smaller formations. The air filled with fine shavings of the unseen clouds.

This was the moment that I had been waiting for at the window of my small guest suite, before Boo and bodach had appeared in the yard below.

Until coming to this monastery, I had spent my life in the town of Pico Mundo, in the California desert. I had never seen snow fall until, earlier in the night, the sky had spit out a few flakes in a false start.

Here in the first minute of the true storm, I stood transfixed by the spectacle, taking on faith what I had heard, that no two snowflakes are alike.

The beauty took my breath, the way the snow fell and yet the night was still, the intricacy of the simplicity. Although the night would have been even more beautiful if she had been here to share it with me, for a moment all was well, all manner of things were well, and then of course someone screamed.

CHAPTER 7

THE SHARP CRY OF ALARM WAS SO BRIEF THAT you might have thought it was imagined or that a night bird, chased by snow to the shelter of the forest, had shrilled just as it flew overhead and away.

In the summer of the previous year, when gunmen stormed the mall in Pico Mundo, I had heard so many screams that I hoped my ears would fail me thereafter. Forty-one innocent people had been shot. Nineteen perished. I would have traded music and the voices of my friends for a silence that would exclude for the rest of my life all human cries of pain and mortal terror.

We so often hope for the wrong things, and my selfish hope was not fulfilled. I am not deaf to pain or blind to blood—or dead, as for a while I might have wished to be.

Instinctively, I hurried around the nearby corner of the abbey. I turned north along the refectory, in which the monks take their meals, and no lights were aglow at one o'clock in the morning.

Squinting through the screening snow, I scanned the night toward the western forest. If someone was out there, the storm hid him.

The refectory formed an inner corner with the library wing. I headed west again, past deep-set windows beyond which lay a darkness of ordered books.

As I turned the southwest corner of the library, I almost fell over a man lying facedown on the ground. He wore the hooded black habit of a monk.

Surprise brought cold air suddenly into my lungs—a brief ache in the chest—and expelled it in a pale rushing plume.

I dropped to my knees at the monk's side, but then hesitated to touch him, for fear that I would find he had not merely fallen, that he had been beaten to the ground.

The world beyond this mountain retreat was largely barbarian, a condition it had been striving toward for perhaps a century and a half. A once-glorious civilization was now only a pretense, a mask allowing barbarians to commit ever greater cruelties in the name of virtues that a truly civilized world would have recognized as evils.

Having fled that barbaric disorder, I was reluctant to admit that no place was safe, no retreat beyond the reach of anarchy. The huddled form on the ground beside me might be proof, more solid than bodachs, that no haven existed to which I could safely withdraw.

Anticipating his smashed face, his slashed face, I touched him as snow ornamented his plain tunic. With a shudder of expectation, I turned him on his back.

The falling snow seemed to bring light to the night, but it was a ghost light that illuminated nothing. Although the hood had slipped back from the victim's face, I could not see him clearly enough to identify him.

Putting a hand to his mouth, I felt no breath, also no beard. Some of the brothers wear beards, but some do not.

I pressed my fingertips to his throat, which was still warm, and felt for the artery. I thought I detected a pulse.

Because my hands were half numb with cold and therefore less sensitive to heat, I might not have felt a faint exhalation, when I had touched his lips.

As I leaned forward to put my ear to his mouth, hoping to hear at least a sigh of breath, I was struck from behind.

No doubt the assailant meant to shatter my skull. He swung just as I bent forward, and the club grazed the back of my head, thumped hard off my left shoulder.

I pitched forward, rolled to the left, rolled again, scrambled to my feet, ran. I had no weapon. He had a club and maybe something worse, a knife.

The hands-on kind of killers, the gunless kind, might stave in with a club or strangle with a scarf, but most of them carry blades, as well, for backup, or for entertainment that might come as foreplay or as aftermath.

The guys in the porkpie hats, mentioned earlier, had blackjacks and guns and even a hydraulic automobile press, and *still* they had carried knives. If your work is deathwork, one weapon is not enough, just as a plumber would not answer an urgent service call with a single wrench.

Although life has made me old for my age, I am still fast in my youth. Hoping my assailant was older and therefore slower, I sprinted away from the abbey, into the open yard, where there were no corners in which to be cornered.

I hurled myself through the snowfall, so it seemed as though a wind had sprung up, pasting flakes to my lashes.

In this second minute of the storm, the ground remained black, unchanged by the blizzard's brush. Within a few bounding steps, the land began to slope gently toward woods that I could not see, open dark descending toward a bristling dark.

Intuition insisted that the forest would be the death of me. Running into it, I would be running to my grave.

The wilds are not my natural habitat. I am a town boy, at home with pavement under my feet, a whiz with a library card, a master at the gas grill and griddle.

If my pursuer was a beast of the new barbarism, he might not be able to make a fire with two sticks and a stone, might not be able to discern true north from the growth of moss on trees, but his lawless nature would make him more at home in the woods than I would ever be.

I needed a weapon, but I had nothing except my universal key, a Kleenex, and insufficient martial-arts knowledge to make a deadly weapon of them.

Cut grass relented to tall grass, and ten yards later, nature put weapons under my feet: loose stones that tested my agility and balance. I skidded to a halt, stooped, scooped up two stones the size of plums, turned, and threw one, threw it hard, and then the other.

The stones vanished into snow and gloom. I had either lost my pursuer or, intuiting my intent, he had circled around me when I stopped and stooped.

I clawed more missiles off the ground, turned 360 degrees, and surveyed the night, ready to pelt him with a couple of half-pound stones.

Nothing moved but the snow, seeming to come down in skeins as straight as the strands of a beaded curtain, yet each flake turning as it fell.

I could see no more than fifteen feet. I had never realized that snow could fall heavily enough to limit visibility this much.

Once, twice, I thought I glimpsed someone moving at the limits of vision, but it must have been an illusion of movement because I couldn't fix on any shape. The patterns of snow on night gradually dizzied me.

Holding my breath, I listened. The snow did not even whisper its way to the earth, but seemed to salt the night with silence.

I waited. I'm good at waiting. I waited sixteen years for my disturbed mother to kill me in my sleep before at last I moved out and left her home alone with her beloved gun.

If, in spite of the periodic peril that comes with my gift, I should live an average life span, I've got another sixty years before I will see Stormy Llewellyn again, in the next world. That will be a long wait, but I am patient.

My left shoulder ached, and the back of my head, grazed by the club, felt less than wonderful. I was cold to the bone.

For some reason, I had not been pursued.

If the storm had been storming long enough to whiten the ground, I could have stretched out on my back and made snow angels. But the conditions were not yet right for play. Maybe later.

The abbey was out of sight. I wasn't sure from which direction I had come, but I wasn't worried that I would lose my way. I have never been lost.

Announcing my return with an uncontrollable chattering of teeth, holding a stone in each hand, I warily retraced my route across the meadow, found the short grass of the yard again. Out of the silent storm, the abbey loomed.

When I reached the corner of the library where I had nearly fallen over the prone monk, I found neither victim nor assailant. Concerned that the man might have regained consciousness and, badly hurt and disoriented, might have crawled away, only to pass out once more, I searched in a widening arc, but found no one.

The library formed an L with the back wall of the guest wing, from which I had set out in pursuit of a bodach little more than an hour ago. At last I dropped the stones around which my hands were clenched and half frozen, unlocked the door to the back stairs, and climbed to the third floor.

In the highest hallway, the door to my small suite stood open, as I'd left it. Waiting for snow, I'd been sitting in candlelight, but now a brighter light spilled from my front room.

CHAPTER 8

AT SHORTLY PAST ONE IN THE MORNING, THE guestmaster, Brother Roland, was not likely to be changing the bed linens or delivering a portion of the "two hogsheads of wine" that St. Benedict, when he wrote the Rule that established monastic order in the sixth century, had specified as a necessary provision for every guesthouse.

St. Bartholomew's does not provide any wine. The small under-the-counter refrigerator in my bathroom contains cans of Coke and bottles of iced tea.

Entering my front room, prepared to shout "Varlet," or "Black-guard," or some other epithet that would sound appropriate to the medieval atmosphere, I found not an enemy, but a friend. Brother Knuckles, known sometimes as Brother Salvatore, stood at the window, peering out at the falling snow.

Brother Knuckles is acutely aware of the world around him, of the slightest sounds and telltale scents, which is why he survived the world he operated in before becoming a monk. Even as I stepped silently across the threshold, he said, "You'll catch your death, traipsin' about on a night like this, dressed like that."

"I wasn't traipsing," I said, closing the door quietly behind me. "I was skulking."

He turned from the window to face me. "I was in the kitchen, scarfin' down some roast beef and provolone, when I seen you come up the stairs from John's Mew."

"There weren't any lights in the kitchen, sir. I would've noticed."

"The fridge light is enough to make a snack, and you can eat good by the glow from the clock on the microwave."

"Committing the sin of gluttony in the dark, were you?"

"The cellarer's gotta be sure things are fresh, don't he?"

As the abbey's cellarer, Brother Knuckles purchased, stocked, and inventoried the food, beverages, and other material goods for the monastery and school.

"Anyway," he said, "a guy, he eats at night in a bright kitchen that's got no window blinds—he's a guy tastin' his last sandwich."

"Even if the guy's a monk in a monastery?"

Brother Knuckles shrugged. "You can never be too careful."

In exercise sweats instead of his habit, at five feet seven and two hundred pounds of bone and muscle, he looked like a die-casting machine that had been covered in a gray-flannel cozy.

The rainwater eyes, the hard angles and blunt edges of brow and jaw, should have given him a cruel or even threatening appearance. In his previous life, people had feared him, and for good reason.

Twelve years in a monastery, years of remorse and contrition, had brought warmth to those once-icy eyes and had inspired in him a kindness that transformed his unfortunate face. Now, at fifty-five, he might be mistaken for a prizefighter who stayed in the sport too long: cauliflower ears, portobello nose, the humility of a basically sweet palooka who has learned the hard way that brute strength does not a champion make.

A small glob of icy slush slid down my forehead and along my right cheek.

"You're wearin' snow like a poofy white hat." Knuckles headed toward the bathroom. "I'll get you a towel."

"There's a bottle of aspirin by the sink. I need aspirin."

He returned with a towel and the aspirin. "You want some water to wash 'em down, maybe a Coke?"

"Give me a hogshead of wine."

"They must've had livers of iron back in Saint Benny's day. A hogshead was like sixty-three gallons."

"Then I'll only need half a hogshead."

By the time I toweled my hair half dry, he had brought me a Coke. "You come up the stairs from John's Mew and stood there lookin' up at the snow the way a turkey stares up at the rain with its mouth open till it drowns."

"Well, sir, I never saw snow before."

"Then, boom, you're off like a shot around the corner of the refectory."

Settling into an armchair and shaking two aspirin out of the bottle, I said, "I heard someone scream."

"I didn't hear no scream."

"You were inside," I reminded him, "and making a lot of chewing noises."

Knuckles sat in the other armchair. "So who screamed?"

I washed down two aspirin with Coke and said, "I found one of the brothers facedown on the ground by the library. Didn't see him at first in his black habit, almost fell over him."

"Who?"

"Don't know. A heavy guy. I rolled him over, couldn't see his face in the dark—then someone tried to brain me from behind."

His brush-cut hair seemed to bristle with indignation. "This don't sound like St. Bart's."

"The club, whatever it was, grazed the back of my head, and my left shoulder took the worst of it."

"We might as well be in Jersey, stuff like this goin' down."

"I've never been to New Jersey."

"You'd like it. Even where it's bad, Jersey is always real."

"They've got one of the world's largest used-tire dumps. You've probably seen it."

"Never did. Ain't that sad? You live in a place most of your life, you take it for granted."

"You didn't even know about the tire dump, sir?"

"People, they live in New York City all their lives, never go to the top of the Empire State Building. You okay, son? Your shoulder?"

"I've been worse."

"Maybe you should go to the infirmary, ring Brother Gregory, have your shoulder examined."

Brother Gregory is the infirmarian. He has a nursing degree.

The size of the monastic community isn't sufficient to justify a full-time infirmarian—especially since the sisters have one of their own for the convent and for the children at the school—so Brother Gregory also does the laundry with Brother Norbert.

"I'll be okay, sir," I assured him.

"So who tried to knock your block off?"

"Never got a look at him."

I explained how I had rolled and run, thinking my assailant was at my heels, and how the monk I'd almost fallen over was gone when I returned.

"So we don't know," said Knuckles, "did he get up on his own and walk away or was he carried."

"We don't know, either, if he was just unconscious or dead."

Frowning, Knuckles said, "I don't like dead. Anyway, it don't make sense. Who would kill a monk?"

"Yes, sir, but who would knock one unconscious?"

Knuckles brooded for a moment. "One time this guy whacked a Lutheran preacher, but he didn't mean to."

"I don't think you should be telling me this, sir."

With a wave of a hand, he dismissed my concern. His strong hands appear to be all knuckles, hence his nickname.

"I don't mean it was me. I told you, I never done the big one. You do believe me on that score, don't you, son?"

"Yes, sir. But you did say this was an accidental whack."

"Never offed no one accidental either."

"All right then."

Brother Knuckles, formerly Salvatore Giancomo, had been well-paid muscle for the mob before God turned his life around.

"Busted faces, broke some legs, but I never chilled no one."

When he was forty, Knuckles had begun to have second thoughts about his career path. He felt "empty, driftin', like a row-boat out on the sea and nobody in it."

During this crisis of confidence, because of death threats to his boss—Tony "the Eggbeater" Martinelli—Knuckles and some other guys like him were sleeping-over at the boss's home. It wasn't a pajamas-and-s'mores kind of sleepover, but the kind of sleepover where everyone brings his two favorite automatic weapons. Anyway, one evening, Knuckles found himself reading a story to the Eggbeater's six-year-old daughter.

The tale was about a toy, a china-rabbit doll, that was proud of his appearance and thoroughly self-satisfied. Then the rabbit endured a series of terrible misfortunes that humbled him, and with humility came empathy for the suffering of others.

The girl fell asleep with half the story still to be read. Knuckles needed in the worst way to know what happened to the rabbit, but he didn't want his fellow face-busters to think that he was really interested in a kid's book.

A few days later, when the threat to the Eggbeater had passed, Knuckles went to a bookstore and bought a copy of the rabbit's tale. He started from the beginning, and by the time he reached the end, when the china rabbit found its way back to the little girl who had loved him, Knuckles broke down and wept.

Never before had he shed tears. That afternoon, in the kitchen of his row house, where he lived alone, he sobbed like a child.

In those days, no one who knew Salvatore "Knuckles" Giancomo, not even his mother, would have said he was an introspective kind of guy, but he nevertheless realized that he was not crying only about the china rabbit's return home. He was crying about the rabbit, all right, but also about something else.

For a while, he could not imagine what that something else might be. He sat at the kitchen table, drinking cup after cup of coffee, eating stacks of his mother's pizzelles, repeatedly recovering his composure, only to break down and weep again.

Eventually he understood that he was crying for himself. He was ashamed of the man whom he had become, mourning the man whom he had expected to be when he'd been a boy.

This realization left him conflicted. He still wanted to be

tough, took pride in being strong and stoic. Yet it seemed that he had become weak and emotional.

Over the next month, he read and reread the rabbit's story. He began to understand that when Edward, the rabbit, discovered humility and learned to sympathize with other people's losses, he did not grow weak but in fact became stronger.

Knuckles bought another book by the same author. This one concerned an outcast big-eared mouse who saved a princess.

The mouse had less impact on him than the bunny did, but, oh, he loved the mouse, too. He loved the mouse for its courage and for its willingness to sacrifice itself for love.

Three months after he first read the story of the china rabbit, Knuckles arranged a meeting with the FBI. He offered to turn state's evidence against his boss and a slew of other mugs.

He ratted them out in part to redeem himself but no less because he wanted to save the little girl to whom he had read part of the rabbit's story. He hoped to spare her from the cold and crippling life of a crime boss's daughter that daily would harden around her, as imprisoning as concrete.

Thereafter, Knuckles had been placed in Vermont, in the Witness Protection Program. His new name was Bob Loudermilk.

Vermont proved to be too much culture shock. Birkenstocks, flannel shirts, and fifty-year-old men with ponytails annoyed him.

He tried to resist the worst temptations of the world with a growing library of kids' books. He discovered that some book writers seemed subtly to approve of the kind of behavior and the values that he had once embraced, and they scared him. He couldn't find enough thoughtful china rabbits and courageous big-eared mice.

Having dinner in a mediocre Italian restaurant, yearning for

Jersey, he suddenly got the calling to the monastic life. It happened shortly after a waiter put before him an order of bad gnocchi, as chewy as caramels, but that's a story for later.

As a novice, following the path of regret to remorse to absolute contrition, Knuckles found the first unalloyed happiness of his life. At St. Bartholomew's Abbey, he thrived.

Now, on this snowy night years later, as I considered taking two more aspirin, he said, "This minister, name's Hoobner, he felt real bad about American Indians, the way they lost their land and all, so he was always losin' money at blackjack in their casinos. Some of it was a high-vigorish loan from Tony Martinelli."

"I'm surprised the Eggbeater would lend to a preacher."

"Tony figured if Hoobner couldn't keep payin' eight percent a week from his own pocket, then he could steal it from the Sunday collection plate. As it shook down, though, Hoobner would gamble and butt-pinch the cocktail waitresses, but he wouldn't steal. So when he stops payin' the vig, Tony sends a guy to discuss Hoobner's moral dilemma with him."

"A guy not you," I said.

"A guy not me, we called him Needles."

"I don't think I want to know why you called him Needles."

"No, you don't," Knuckles agreed. "Anyway, Needles gives Hoobner one last chance to pay up, and instead of receivin' this request with Christian consideration, the preacher says 'Go to hell.' Then he pulls a pistol and tries to punch Needles's ticket for the trip."

"The preacher shoots Needles?"

"He might've been a Methodist, not a Lutheran. He shoots Needles but only wounds him in the shoulder, and Needles pulls his piece and shoots Hoobner dead."

"So the preacher would shoot somebody, but he wouldn't steal."

"I'm not sayin' that's traditional Methodist teachin'."

"Yes, sir. I understand."

"Fact is, now I think on it, the preacher was maybe a Unitarian. Anyway, he was a preacher, and he was shot dead, so bad things can happen to anyone, even a monk."

Although the chill of the winter night had not entirely left me, I pressed the cold can of Coke to my forehead. "This problem we have here involves bodachs."

Because he was one of my few confidants at St. Bartholomew's, I told him about the three demonic shadows hovering at Justine's bed.

"And they was hangin' around the monk you almost stumbled over?"

"No, sir. They're here for something bigger than one monk being knocked unconscious."

"You're right. That ain't the kind of fight card that draws a crowd anywhere."

He got up from his chair and went to the window. He gazed out at the night for a moment.

Then: "I wonder. . . . You think maybe my past life is catchin' up with me?"

"That was fifteen years ago. Isn't the Eggbeater in prison?"

"He died in stir. But some of those other mugs, they got long memories."

"If a hit man tracked you down, sir, wouldn't you be dead by now?"

"For sure. I'd be parked in an unpadded waitin'-room chair, readin' old magazines in Purgatory."

"I don't think this has anything to do with who you used to be."

He turned from the window. "From your lips to God's ear. Worst thing would be anyone here hurt because of me."

"Everyone here's been lifted up because of you," I assured him.

The slabs and lumps of his face shifted into a smile that you would have found scary if you didn't know him. "You're a good kid. If I ever would've had me a kid, it's nice to think he might've been a little like you."

"Being me isn't something I'd wish on anyone, sir."

"Though if I was your dad," Brother Knuckles continued, "you'd probably be shorter and thicker, with your head set closer to your shoulders."

"I don't need a neck anyway," I said. "I never wear ties."

"No, son, you need a neck so you can stick it out. That's what you do. That's who you *are*."

"Lately, I've been thinking I might get myself measured for a habit, become a novice."

He returned to his chair but only sat on the arm of it, studying me. After consideration, he said, "Maybe someday you'll hear the call. But not anytime soon. You're of the world, and need to be."

I shook my head. "I don't think I need to be of the world."

"The world needs you to be out there in it. You got things to do, son."

"That's what I'm afraid of. The things I'll have to do."

"The monastery ain't a hideout. A mug wants to come in here, take the vows, he should come because he wants to open himself to somethin' bigger than the world, not because he wants to close himself up in a little ball like a pill bug."

"Some things you just have to close yourself away from, sir."

"You mean the summer before last, the shootings at the mall. You don't need no one's forgiveness, son."

"I knew it was coming, they were coming, the gunmen. I should've been able to stop it. Nineteen people died."

"Everyone says, without you, hundreds would've died."

"I'm no hero. If people knew about my gift and knew *still* I couldn't stop it, they wouldn't call me a hero."

"You ain't God, neither. You did all you could, anyone could."

As I put down the Coke, picked up the bottle of aspirin, and shook two more tablets onto my palm, I changed the subject. "Are you going to wake the abbot and tell him that I fell over an unconscious monk?"

He stared at me, trying to decide whether to *allow* me to change the subject. Then: "Maybe in a while. First, I'm gonna try to take an unofficial bed count, see if maybe I can find someone holdin' ice to a lump on his head."

"The monk I fell over."

"Exactly. We got two questions. Second, why would some guy club a monk? But *first,* why would a monk be out at this hour where he could get himself clubbed?"

"I guess you don't want to get a brother in trouble."

"If there's sin involved, I ain't gonna help him keep what he done from his confessor. That won't be no favor to his soul. But if it was just some kinda foolishness, the prior maybe don't have to know."

A prior is a monastery's disciplinarian.

St. Bartholomew's prior was Father Reinhart, an older monk with thin lips and a narrow nose, less than half the nose of which Brother Knuckles could boast. His eyes and eyebrows and hair were all the color of an Ash Wednesday forehead spot.

Walking, Father Reinhart appeared to float like a spirit across the ground, and he was uncannily quiet. Many of the brothers called him the Gray Ghost, though with affection.

Father Reinhart was a firm disciplinarian, though not harsh or unfair. Having once been a Catholic-school principal, he warned that he had a paddle, as yet never used, in which he had drilled holes to reduce wind resistance. "Just so you know," he had said with a wink.

Brother Knuckles went to the door, hesitated, looked back at me. "If somethin' bad is comin', how long we got?"

"After the first bodachs show up . . . it's sometimes as little as a day, usually two."

"You sure you ain't got a concussion or nothin'?"

"Nothing that four aspirin won't help," I assured him. I popped the second pair of tablets into my mouth and chewed them.

Knuckles grimaced. "What're you, a tough guy?"

"I read that they're absorbed into your bloodstream faster this way, through the tissue in your mouth."

"What—you get a flu shot, you have the doc inject it in your tongue? Get a few hours' sleep."

"I'll try."

"Find me after Lauds, before Mass, I'll tell you who got himself conked—and maybe why, if he knows why. Christ be with you, son."

"And with you."

He left and closed the door behind him.

The doors of the suites in the guesthouse, like those of the monks' rooms in another wing, have no locks. Everyone here respects the privacy of others.

I carried a straight-backed chair to the door and wedged it under the knob, to prevent anyone from entering.

Maybe chewing aspirin and letting them dissolve in your mouth speeds up absorption of the medication, but they taste like crap.

When I drank some Coke to wash out the bad taste, the crushed tablets reacted with the soft drink, and I found myself foaming at the mouth like a rabid dog.

When it comes to tragic figures, I've got a much greater talent for slapstick than Hamlet did, and whereas King Lear would step over a banana peel in his path, my foot will find it every time.

CHAPTER 9

THE COMFORTABLE BUT SIMPLE GUEST SUITE had a shower so small that I felt as if I were standing in a coffin.

For ten minutes I let the hot water beat on my left shoulder, which had been tenderized by the mysterious assailant's club. The muscles relaxed, but the ache remained.

The pain wasn't severe. It didn't concern me. Physical pain, unlike some other kinds, eventually goes away.

When I turned off the water, big white Boo was staring at me through the steam-clouded glass door.

After I had toweled dry and pulled on a pair of briefs, I knelt on the bathroom floor and rubbed the dog behind the ears, which made him grin with pleasure.

"Where were you hiding?" I asked him. "Where were you when some miscreant tried to make my brain squirt out my ears? Huh?"

He didn't answer. He only grinned. I like old Marx Brothers movies, and Boo is the Harpo Marx of dogs in more ways than one.

My toothbrush seemed to weigh five pounds. Even in exhaustion, I am diligent about brushing my teeth.

A few years previously, I had witnessed an autopsy in which the medical examiner, during a preliminary review of the corpse, remarked for his recorder that the deceased was guilty of poor dental hygiene. I had been embarrassed for the dead man, who had been a friend of mine.

I hope that no attendants at *my* autopsy will have any reason to be embarrassed for me.

You might think this is pride of a particularly foolish kind. You're probably right.

Humanity is a parade of fools, and I am at the front of it, twirling a baton.

I have persuaded myself, however, that brushing my teeth in anticipation of my untimely demise is simply consideration for the feelings of any autopsy witness who might have known me when I was alive. Embarrassment for a friend, arising from his shortcomings, is never as awful as being mortified by the exposure of your own faults, but it is piercing.

Boo was in bed, curled up against the footboard, when I came out of the bathroom.

"No belly rub, no more ear scratching," I told him. "I'm coming down like a plane that's lost all engines."

His yawn was superfluous for a dog like him; he was here for companionship, not for sleep.

Lacking enough energy to put on pajamas, I fell into bed in my briefs. The coroner always strips the body, anyway.

After pulling the covers to my chin, I realized that I had left the light on in the adjacent bathroom.

In spite of John Heineman's four-billion-dollar endowment,

the brothers at the abbey live frugally, in respect of their vows of poverty. They do not waste resources.

The light seemed far away, growing more distant by the second, and the blankets were turning to stone. To hell with it. I wasn't a monk yet, not even a novice.

I wasn't a fry cook anymore, either—except when I made pancakes on Sundays—or a tire salesman, or much of anything. We not-much-of-anything types don't worry about the cost of leaving a light on unnecessarily.

Nevertheless, I worried. In spite of worrying, I slept.

I dreamed, but not about exploding boilers. Not about nuns on fire, screaming through a snowy night, either.

In the dream, I was sleeping but then awoke to see a bodach standing at the foot of my bed. This dream bodach, unlike those in the waking world, had fierce eyes that glistered with reflections of the light from the half-open bathroom door.

As always, I pretended that I did not see the beast. I watched it through half-closed eyes.

When it moved, it morphed, as things do in dreams, and became not a bodach any longer. At the foot of my bed stood the glowering Russian, Rodion Romanovich, the only other visitor currently staying in the guesthouse.

Boo was in the dream, standing on the bed, baring his teeth at the intruder, but silent.

Romanovich went around the bed to the nightstand.

Boo sprang from the bed to the wall, as though he were a cat, and clung there on the vertical, defying gravity, glaring at the Russian.

Interesting.

Romanovich picked up the picture frame that stood beside the nightstand clock.

The frame protects a small card from a carnival fortune-telling machine called Gypsy Mummy. It declares YOU ARE DESTINED TO BE TOGETHER FOREVER.

In my first manuscript, I recounted the curious history of this object, which is sacred to me. Suffice to say that Stormy Llewellyn and I received it in return for the first coin we fed the machine, after a guy and his fiancée, in line before us, got nothing but bad news for their eight quarters.

Because Gypsy Mummy did not accurately forecast events in this world, because Stormy is dead and I am alone, I know the card means that we will be together forever in the *next* world. This promise is more important than food to me, than air.

Although the light from the bathroom did not reach far enough to allow Romanovich to read the words on the framed card, he read them anyway because, being a dream Russian, he could do anything that he wanted, just as dream horses can fly and dream spiders can have the heads of human babies.

In a murmur, in accented speech, he spoke the words aloud: *"You are destined to be together forever."*

His solemn yet mellifluous voice was suitable for a poet, and those seven words sounded like a line of lyrical verse.

I saw Stormy as she'd been that evening at the carnival, and the dream became about her, about us, about a sweet past beyond recovery.

After less than four hours of troubled sleep, I woke before dawn.

The leaded window showed a black sky, and snow fairies

danced down the glass. In the bottom panes, a few ferns of frost twinkled with a strange light, alternately red and blue.

The digital clock on the nightstand was where it had been when I'd fallen into bed, but the framed fortune-teller's card appeared to have been moved. I felt certain it had been standing upright in front of the lamp. Now it lay flat.

I threw aside the bedclothes and got up. I walked out to the living room, turned on a lamp.

The straight-backed chair remained wedged under the knob of the door to the third-floor hallway. I tested it. Secure.

Before communism bled them of so much of their faith, the Russian people had a history of both Christian and Judaic mysticism. They weren't known, however, for walking through locked doors or solid walls.

The living-room window was three stories above the ground and not approachable by a ledge. I checked the latch anyhow, and found it engaged.

Although lacking nuns on fire, lacking spiders with the heads of human babies, the night disturbance had been a dream. Nothing but a dream.

Looking down from the latch, I discovered the source of the pulsing light that throbbed in the filigree of frost along the edges of the glass. A thick blanket of snow had been drawn over the land while I slept, and three Ford Explorers, each with the word SHERIFF on its roof, stood idling on the driveway, clouds of exhaust pluming from their tailpipes, emergency beacons flashing.

Although still windless, the storm had not relented. Through the screening cold confetti, I glimpsed six widely separated flashlights wielded by unseen men moving in coordinated fashion, as if quartering the meadow in search of something.

CHAPTER 10

BY THE TIME I CHANGED INTO THERMAL LONG johns, pulled on jeans and a crewneck sweater, got feet into ski boots, grabbed my Gore-Tex/Thermolite jacket, rushed downstairs, crossed the parlor, and pushed through the oak door into the guesthouse cloister, dawn had come.

Sullen light brushed a gray veneer over the limestone columns encircling the courtyard. Under the cloister ceiling, darkness held fast, as if the night were so unimpressed by the dreary morning that it might not retreat.

In the courtyard, without ski boots, St. Bartholomew stood in fresh powder, offering a winterized pumpkin in his outstretched hand.

On the east side of the cloister, directly across from the point at which I burst into it, was the guesthouse entrance to the abbatial church. Voices raised in prayer and a tolling bell echoed to me not from the church but instead along a passageway ahead and to my right.

Four steps led up to that barrel-vaulted stone corridor, which itself led twenty feet into the grand cloister. Here a courtyard four times larger than the first was framed by an even more impressive colonnade.

The forty-six brothers and five novices were gathered in this open courtyard in full habit, facing Abbot Bernard, who stood on the bell dais, with one hand rhythmically drawing upon the toll rope.

Matins had concluded, and near the end of Lauds, they had come out of the church for the final prayer and the abbot's address.

The prayer was the Angelus, which is beautiful in Latin, when raised with many voices.

A chanted response rose from the brothers as I arrived: *"Fiat mihi secundum verbum tuum."* Then abbot and all said, *"Ave Maria."*

Two sheriff's deputies waited in the shelter of the cloister as the brothers in the courtyard finished the prayer. The cops were big men and more solemn than the monks.

They stared at me. Clearly I was not a cop, and apparently I was not a monk. My indeterminate status made me a person of interest.

Their stares were so intense that I wouldn't have been surprised if, in the bitter air, their eyes had begun to steam as did their every exhalation.

Having had much experience of police, I knew better than to approach them with the suggestion that their suspicions would best be directed at the glowering Russian, wherever he might coil at this moment. As a consequence, their interest in me would only intensify.

Although anxious to know the reason that the sheriff had been called, I resisted the urge to ask them. They would be inclined to view my ignorance as merely a *pretense* of ignorance, and they would regard me with greater suspicion than they did now.

Once a cop has found you of even passing interest, regarding a criminal matter, you can do nothing to remove yourself from his list of potential suspects. Only events beyond your control can clear you. Like being stabbed, shot, or strangled by the *real* villain.

"Ut digni efficiamur promissionibus Christi," said the brothers, and the abbot said, *"Oremus,"* which meant "Let us pray."

Less than half a minute later, the Angelus concluded.

Usually, after the Angelus, the abbot's address consists of a brief commentary on some sacred text and its application to monastic life. Then he does a soft-shoe number while singing "Tea for Two."

All right, I made up the soft-shoe and "Tea for Two." Abbot Bernard *does* resemble Fred Astaire, which is why I've never been able to get this irreverent image out of my head.

Instead of his usual address, the abbot announced a dispensation from attendance at morning Mass to all those who might be needed to assist the sheriff's deputies in a thorough search of the buildings.

The time was 6:28. Mass would begin at seven o'clock.

Those essential to the conduct of Mass were to attend and, after the service, were to make themselves available to the authorities to answer questions and to assist as needed.

Mass would be over at about 7:50. Breakfast, which is taken in silence, always begins at eight o'clock.

The abbot also excused those assisting the police from Terce, the third of seven periods of daily prayer. Terce is at 8:40 and lasts for about fifteen minutes. The fourth period in the Divine Office is Sext, at eleven-thirty, before lunch.

When most laymen learn that a monk's life is so regimented and that the same routine is followed day after day, they grimace. They think this life must be boring, even tedious.

From my months among the monks, I had learned that, quite the contrary, these men are energized by worship and meditation. During the recreation hours, between dinner and Compline, which is the night prayer, they are a lively bunch, intellectually engaging and amusing.

Well, most of them are as I've described, but a handful are shy. And a couple are too pleased by their selfless offering of their lives to make the offering seem entirely selfless.

One of them, Brother Matthias, has such encyclopedic knowledge of—and such strong opinions about—the operettas of Gilbert and Sullivan that he can bore your ass off.

Monks are not necessarily holy by virtue of being monks. And they are always and entirely human.

At the end of the abbot's remarks, many brothers hurried to the deputies waiting in the shelter of the cloister, eager to assist.

I became aware of one novice lingering in the courtyard, in the descending snow. Although his face was shadowed by his hood, I could see that he was staring at me.

This was Brother Leopold, who had finished his postulancy only in October and had worn the habit of a novice less than two months. He had a wholesome Midwestern face, with freckles and a winning smile.

Of the five current novices, I distrusted only him. My reason for not trusting him eluded me. It was a gut feeling, nothing more.

Brother Knuckles approached me, stopped, shook himself rather like a dog might, and cast the clinging snow from his habit. Pushing back his hood, he said softly, "Brother Timothy is missing."

Brother Timothy, master of the mechanical systems that kept the abbey and school habitable, wasn't one to arrive late for Matins, and certainly wasn't a man who would run off for a secular adventure, in violation of his vows. His greatest weakness was Kit Kat bars.

"He must've been the one I nearly fell over last night, at the corner of the library. I have to speak to the police."

"Not yet. Walk with me," said Brother Knuckles. "We need a place don't have a hundred ears."

I glanced toward the courtyard. Brother Leopold had vanished.

With his fresh face and Midwestern directness, Leopold in no way seems calculating or sly, furtive or deceitful.

Yet he has an unsettling way of arriving and departing with a suddenness that sometimes reminds me of a ghost materializing and dematerializing. He is there, then isn't. Isn't, then is.

With Knuckles, I left the grand cloister and followed the stone passage to the guest cloister, from there through the oak door into the main parlor on the ground floor of the guesthouse.

We went to the fireplace at the north end of the room, though no fire was burning, and sat forward on armchairs, facing each other.

"After we talked last night," Knuckles said, "I did a bed check. Don't have no authority. Felt sneaky. But it seemed the right thing."

"You made an executive decision."

"That's just what I done. Even back when I was dumb muscle

and lost to God, I sometimes made executive decisions. Like, the boss sends me to break a guy's legs, but the guy gets the point after I break one, so I don't do the second. Things like that."

"Sir, I'm just curious. . . . When you presented yourself as a postulant to the Brothers of St. Bartholomew, how long did your first confession last?"

"Father Reinhart says two hours ten minutes, but it felt like a month and a half."

"I'll bet it did."

"Anyway, some brothers leave their doors part open, some don't, but no room's ever locked. I used a flashlight from each doorway to quick scope the bed. Nobody was missin'."

"Anybody awake?"

"Brother Jeremiah suffers insomnia. Brother John Anthony had a gut full of acid from yesterday's dinner."

"The chile rellenos."

"I told 'em I thought maybe I smelled somethin' burnin', I was just checkin' around to be sure there weren't no problem."

"You lied, sir," I said, just to tweak him.

"It ain't a lie that's gonna put me in the pit with Al Capone, but it's one step on a slippery slope I been down before."

His hand, so brutal-looking, invested the sign of the cross with a special poignancy, and called to mind the hymn "Amazing Grace."

The brothers arise at five o'clock, wash, dress, and line up at 5:40 in the courtyard of the grand cloister, to proceed together into the church for Matins and Lauds. At two o'clock in the morning, therefore, they're sacked out, not reading or playing a Game Boy.

"Did you go over to the novitiate wing, check on the novices?"

"No. You said the brother facedown in the yard was in black, you almost fell over him."

In some orders, the novices wear habits similar to—or the same as—those worn by the brothers who have professed their final vows, but at St. Bartholomew's, the novices wear gray, not black.

Knuckles said, "I figured the unconscious guy in the yard, he maybe came to, got up, went back to bed—or he was the abbot."

"You checked on the abbot?"

"Son, I ain't gonna try that smelled-somethin'-burnin' routine on the abbot in his private quarters, him as smart as three of me. Besides, the guy in the yard was heavy, right? You said heavy. And Abbot Bernard, you gotta tie him down in a mild wind."

"Fred Astaire."

Knuckles winced. He pinched the lumpy bridge of his mushroom nose. "Wish you never told me that 'Tea for Two' thing. Can't keep my mind on the abbot's mornin' address, just waitin' for his soft-shoe."

"When did they discover Brother Timothy was missing?"

"I seen he ain't in line for Matins. By Lauds, he still don't show, so I duck outta church to check his room. He's just pillows."

"Pillows?"

"The night before, what looked like Brother Timothy under the blanket, by flashlight from his doorway, was just extra pillows."

"Why would he do that? There's no rule about lights out. There's no bed check."

"Maybe Tim, he didn't do it himself, somebody else faked it to buy time, keep us from realizin' Tim was gone."

"Time for what?"

"Don't know. But if I'd seen he was gone last night, I would've known it was him you found in the yard, and I'd have woke the abbot."

"He's a little heavy, all right," I said.

"Kit Kat belly. If a brother was missin' when I did bed check, the cops would've been here hours ago, before the storm got so bad."

"And now the search is harder," I said. "He's . . . dead, isn't he?"

Knuckles looked into the fireplace, where no fire burned. "My professional opinion is, I kinda think so."

I'd had too much of Death. I'd fled from Death to this haven, but of course in running from him, I had only run into his arms.

Life you can evade; death you cannot.

CHAPTER 11

THE LAMB OF DAWN BECAME A MORNING LION
with a sudden roar of wind that raked the parlor windows
with ticking teeth of snow. A mere snowstorm swelled into a
biting blizzard.

"I liked Brother Timothy," I said.

"He was a sweet guy," Knuckles agreed. "That amazing blush."

I remembered the outer light that revealed the inner brightness of the monk's innocence. "Somebody put pillows under
Tim's blankets so he wouldn't be missed till the storm could com-
plicate things. The killer bought time to finish what he came here
to do."

"He who?" Knuckles asked.

"I told you, sir, I'm not psychic."

"Ain't askin' for psychic. Thought you seen some clues."

"I'm not Sherlock Holmes, either. I better talk to the police."

"Maybe you should think on whether that's smart."

"But I should tell them what happened."

"You gonna tell 'em about bodachs?"

In Pico Mundo, the chief of police, Wyatt Porter, was like a father to me. He had known about my gift since I was fifteen.

I didn't relish sitting with the county sheriff and explaining that I saw dead people as well as demons, wolfish and swift.

"Chief Porter can call the sheriff here and vouch for me."

Knuckles looked doubtful. "And how long might that take?"

"Maybe not long, if I can reach Wyatt quick."

"I don't mean how long for Chief Porter to tell the locals you're real. I mean how long for the locals to believe it."

He had a point. Even Wyatt Porter, an intelligent man, who knew my grandmother well and knew me, required convincing when I first took him information that solved a stalled murder investigation.

"Son, nobody but you sees bodachs. If the kids or all of us is gonna get slammed by somebody, by somethin'—you got the best chance of figurin' out what-how-when, the best chance to stop it."

On the mahogany floor lay a Persian-style carpet. In the figured world of wool between my feet, a dragon twisted, glaring.

"I don't want that much responsibility. I can't carry it."

"God seems to think you can."

"Nineteen dead," I reminded him.

"When it might've been two hundred. Listen, son, don't think the law is always like Wyatt Porter."

"I know it's not."

"These days law thinks it's about nothin' but laws. Law don't remember it was once handed down from somewhere, that it once meant not just *no*, but was a way to live and a reason to live that way. Law now thinks nobody but politicians made it or remake it, so maybe it ain't a surprise some people don't care anymore about law, and even some lawmen don't understand the real reason for law. You pour your story out to a wrong kind of lawman, he's never gonna see you're on his side. Never gonna believe you're gifted. A lawman like that, he thinks you're what's wrong with the world the way it used to be, the way he's glad it ain't anymore. He thinks you're a psych case. He can't trust you. He won't. Suppose they take you in for observation, or even for suspicion if they find a body, what do we do then?"

I didn't like the arrogant expression of the dragon in the woven wool, or the way bright threads lent violence to its eyes. I shifted my left foot to cover its face.

"Sir, maybe I don't mention my gift or bodachs. I could just say I found a monk on the ground, then I was clubbed by someone."

"What was you doin' out at that hour? Where was you comin' from, goin' to, what was you *up* to? Why your funny name? You mean you're the kid was a hero at the Green Moon Mall summer before last? How come trouble follows you, or is it maybe you yourself are trouble?"

He was playing the devil's advocate.

I half believed I could feel the carpet dragon squirming under my foot.

"I don't really have much to tell them that would be helpful," I relented. "I guess we could wait until they find the body."

"They won't find it," Brother Knuckles said. "They ain't lookin' for a Brother Tim who's been murdered, the body hidden. What they're lookin' for is a Brother Tim somewhere who slashed his wrists or hung himself from a rafter."

I stared at him, not fully comprehending.

"It's only two years since Brother Constantine committed suicide," he reminded me.

Constantine is the dead monk who lingers in this world, and sometimes manifests as an energetic poltergeist in unexpected ways.

For reasons no one understands, he climbed into the church tower one night, while his brothers slept, tied one end of a rope around the mechanism that turns the three-bell carillon, knotted the other end around his neck, climbed onto the tower parapet, and jumped, ringing awake the entire community of St. Bartholomew's.

Among men of faith, perhaps self-destruction is the most damning of all transgressions. The effect on the brothers had been profound; time had not diminished it.

Knuckles said, "Sheriff thinks we're a rough crew, he can't trust us. He's the kind believes albino-monk assassins live here in secret catacombs, goin' out to murder in the night, all that old Ku Klux Klan anti-Catholic stuff, though maybe he don't know it's from the KKK. Funny how people that don't believe in nothin' are so quick to believe every crazy story about people like us."

"So they expect that Brother Timothy killed himself."

"Sheriff probably thinks we'll all kill ourselves before we're done. Like those Jim Jones Kool-Aid drinkers."

I thought wistfully of Bing Crosby and Barry Fitzgerald. "Saw an old movie the other night—*Going My Way.*"

"That wasn't just another time, son. That was another planet."

The outer door of the parlor opened. A sheriff's deputy and four monks entered. They had come to search the guesthouse, though it was not likely that a suicidal brother would have repaired to this wing to drink a quart of Clorox.

Brother Knuckles recited the last few lines of a prayer and

made the sign of the cross, and I followed his example, as though we had retreated here to pray together for Brother Timothy's safe return.

I don't know if this deception qualified as a half-step down the slippery slope. I had no sensation of sliding. But of course we never notice the descent until we're rocketing along at high velocity.

Knuckles had convinced me that I would find no friends among these authorities, that I must remain a free agent to discover the nature of the looming violence that drew the bodachs. Consequently, I preferred to avoid the deputies without appearing to be dodging them.

Brother Fletcher, the monastery's cantor and music director, one of the four monks with the deputy, asked for permission to search my suite. I gave it without hesitation.

For the benefit of the deputy, whose eyes were compressed to slits by the weight of his suspicion, Knuckles asked me to help search the pantries and storerooms that were his domain, as cellarer.

When we stepped out of the parlor, into the guesthouse cloister, where wind blustered among the columns, Elvis was waiting for me.

In my previous two manuscripts, I have recounted my experiences with the lingering spirit of Elvis Presley in Pico Mundo. When I left that desert town for a mountain monastery, he had come with me.

Instead of haunting a place, especially an appropriate place like Graceland, he haunts *me*. He thinks that, through me, he will in time find the courage to move on to a higher place.

I suppose I should be glad that I'm being haunted by Elvis instead of, say, by a punker like Sid Vicious. The King is an easy spirit with a sense of humor and with concern for me, though once in a while he weeps uncontrollably. Silently, of course, but copiously.

Because the dead don't talk or even carry text-messaging devices, I needed a long time to learn why Elvis hangs around our troubled world. At first I thought he was reluctant to leave here because this world had been so good to him.

The truth is, he's desperate to see his mother, Gladys, in the next world, but he's reluctant to cross over because he's filled with anxiety about the reunion.

Few men have loved their mothers more than Elvis loved Gladys. She died young, and he grieved for her until his death.

He fears, however, that his use of drugs and his other personal failures in the years that followed her passage must have shamed her. He is embarrassed by his ignominious death—overdosed on prescription medications, facedown in vomit—though this seems to be the preferred exit scene for a significant percentage of rock-and-roll royalty.

I have often assured him that there can be no shame, no anger, no disappointment where Gladys waits, only love and understanding. I tell him that she will open her arms to him on the Other Side.

Thus far my assurances have not convinced him. Of course there is no reason why they should. Remember: In Chapter Six, I admitted that I don't know *anything.*

So as we entered the passageway between the guest and the grand cloisters, I said to Brother Knuckles, "Elvis is here."

"Yeah? What movie's he in?"

This was Knuckles's way of asking how the King was dressed.

Other lingering spirits manifest only in the clothes they were wearing when they died. Donny Mosquith, a former mayor of Pico Mundo, had a heart attack during vigorous and kinky intimacy with a young woman. Cross-dressing in spike heels and women's underwear stimulated him. Hairy in lace, wobbling along the streets of a town that named a park after him when he was alive but later renamed it after a game-show host, Mayor Mosquith does not make a pretty ghost.

In death as in life, Elvis exudes cool. He appears in costumes from his movies and stage performances, as he chooses. Now he wore black boots, tight black tuxedo trousers, a tight and open black jacket that came only to the waistline, a red cummerbund, a ruffled white shirt, and an elaborate black foulard.

"It's the flamenco-dancer outfit from *Fun in Acapulco*," I told Knuckles.

"In a Sierra winter?"

"He can't feel the cold."

"Ain't exactly suitable to a monastery, neither."

"He didn't make any monk movies."

Walking at my side, as we neared the end of the passageway, Elvis put an arm around my shoulders, as though to comfort me. It felt no less substantial than the arm of a living person.

I do not know why ghosts feel solid to me, why their touch is warm instead of cold, yet they walk through walls or dematerialize at will. It's a mystery that I most likely will never solve— like the popularity of aerosol cheese in a can or Mr. William Shatner's brief post-*Star Trek* turn as a lounge singer.

In the large courtyard of the grand cloister, wind rushed down the three-story walls, wielding lashes of brittle snow, whipping up clouds of the softer early snow from the cobblestone floor, thrashing between columns as we hurried along the colonnade toward the kitchen door in the south wing.

Like a crumbling ceiling shedding plaster, the sky lowered on St. Bart's, and the day seemed to be collapsing upon us, great white walls more formidable than the stone abbey, alabaster ruins burying all, soft and yet imprisoning.

CHAPTER 12

KNUCKLES AND I DID IN FACT SEARCH THE pantry and associated storerooms, though we found no trace of Brother Timothy.

Elvis admired the jars of peanut butter that filled one shelf, perhaps recalling the fried-banana-and-peanut-butter sandwiches that had been a staple of his diet when he was alive.

For a while, monks and deputies were busy in the hallways, the refectory, the kitchen, and other nearby rooms. Then quiet descended, except for the wind at windows, as the quest moved elsewhere.

After the library had been searched, I retreated there to worry and to keep a low profile until the authorities departed.

Elvis went with me, but Knuckles wanted to spend a few minutes at his desk in a storeroom, reviewing invoices, before going to Mass. As distressing as Brother Tim's disappearance was, work must go on.

It is a fundamental of the brothers' faith that when the Day comes and time ends, being taken while at honest work is as good as being taken while in prayer.

In the library, Elvis wandered the aisles, sometimes phasing *through* the stacks, reading the spines of the books.

He had periodically been a reader. Following his early fame, he ordered twenty hardcovers at a time from a Memphis bookstore.

The abbey offers sixty thousand volumes. A purpose of monks, especially Benedictines, has always been to preserve knowledge.

Many Old World monasteries were built like fortresses, on peaks, with one approach that could be blockaded. The knowledge of nearly two millennia, including the great works of the ancient Greeks and the Romans, had been preserved through the efforts of monks when invasions of barbarians—the Goths, the Huns, the Vandals—repeatedly destroyed Western civilization, and twice when Islamic armies nearly conquered Europe in some of the bloodiest campaigns in history.

Civilization—says my friend Ozzie Boone—exists only because the world has barely enough of two kinds of people: those who are able to build with a trowel in one hand, a sword in the other; and those who believe that in the beginning was the Word, and will risk death to preserve all books for the truths they might contain.

I think a few fry cooks are essential, as well. To build, to fight, to risk death in a good cause requires high morale. Nothing boosts morale like a perfectly prepared plate of eggs sunny-side up and a pile of crispy hash browns.

Restlessly wandering the library aisles, I turned a corner and came face to face with the Russian, Rodion Romanovich, most recently seen in a dream.

I never claimed to possess James Bond's aplomb, so I'm not embarrassed to admit I startled backward and said, "Sonofa-bitch!"

Bearish, glowering so hard that his bushy eyebrows knitted together, he spoke with a faint accent: "What's wrong with you?"

"You frightened me."

"I certainly did not."

"Well, it felt like frightened."

"You frightened yourself."

"I'm sorry, sir."

"What are you sorry for?"

"For my language," I said.

"I speak English."

"You do, yes, and so well. Better than I speak Russian, for sure."

"Do you speak Russian?"

"No, sir. Not a word."

"You are a peculiar young man."

"Yes, sir, I know."

At perhaps fifty, Romanovich did not appear old, but time had battered his face with much experience. Across his broad fore-head lay a stitchery of tiny white scars. His laugh lines did not suggest that he had spent a life smiling; they were deep, severe, like old wounds sustained in a sword fight.

Clarifying, I said, "I meant I was sorry for my *bad* language."

"Why would I frighten you?"

I shrugged. "I didn't realize you were here."

"I did not realize you were here, either," he said, "but you did not frighten me."

"I don't have the equipment."

"What equipment?"

"I mean, I'm not a scary guy. I'm innocuous."

"And I *am* a scary guy?" he asked.

"No, sir. Not really. No. Imposing."

"I am imposing?"

"Yes, sir. Quite imposing."

"Are you one of those people who uses words more for the sound than for the sense of them? Or do you know what *innocuous* means?"

"It means 'harmless,' sir."

"Yes. And you are certainly not innocuous."

"It's just the black ski boots, sir. They tend to make anybody look like he could kick butt."

"You appear clear, direct, even simple."

"Thank you, sir."

"But you are complex, complicated, even intricate, I suspect."

"What you see is what you get," I assured him. "I'm just a fry cook."

"Yes, you make that quite plausible, with your exceptionally fluffy pancakes. And I am a librarian from Indianapolis."

I indicated the book in his hand, which he held in such a way that I could not see the title. "What do you like to read?"

"It is about poisons and the great poisoners in history."

"Not the uplifting stuff you'd expect in an abbey library."

"It is an important aspect of Church history," said Romanovich. "Throughout the centuries, clergymen have been poisoned by royals and politicians. Catherine de' Medicis murdered the Cardinal of Lorraine with poison-saturated money. The toxin penetrated through his skin, and he was dead within five minutes."

"I guess it's good we're moving toward a cashless economy."

"Why," Romanovich asked, "would just-a-fry-cook spend months in a monastery guesthouse?"

"No rent. Griddle exhaustion. Carpal tunnel syndrome from bad spatula technique. A need for spiritual revitalization."

"Is that common to fry cooks—a periodic quest for spiritual revitalization?"

"It might be the defining characteristic of the profession, sir. Poke Barnett has to go out to a shack in the desert twice a year to meditate."

Layering a frown over his glower, Romanovich said, "What is Poke Barnett?"

"He's the other fry cook at the diner where I used to work. He buys like two hundred boxes of ammunition for his pistol, drives out in the Mojave fifty miles from anyone, and spends a few days blasting the living hell out of cactuses."

"He shoots cactuses?"

"Poke has many fine qualities, sir, but he's not much of an environmentalist."

"You said that he went into the desert to meditate."

"While shooting the cactuses, Poke says he thinks about the meaning of life."

The Russian stared at me.

He had the least readable eyes of anyone I had ever met. From his eyes, I could learn nothing more about him than a paramecium on a glass slide, gazing up at the lens of a microscope, would be able to learn about the examining scientist's opinion of it.

After a silence, Rodion Romanovich changed the subject: "What book are you looking for, Mr. Thomas?"

"Anything with a china bunny on a magical journey, or mice who save princesses."

"I doubt you will find that kind of thing in this section."

"You're probably right. Bunnies and mice generally don't go around poisoning people."

That statement earned another brief silence from the Russian. I don't believe that he was pondering his own opinion of the homicidal tendencies of bunnies and mice. I think, instead, he was trying to decide whether my words implied that I might be suspicious of him.

"You are a peculiar young man, Mr. Thomas."

"I don't try to be, sir."

"And droll."

"But not grotesque," I hoped.

"No. Not grotesque. But droll."

He turned and walked away with his book, which might have been about poisons and famous poisoners in history. Or not.

At the far end of the aisle, Elvis appeared, still dressed as a flamenco dancer. He approached as Romanovich receded, slouching his shoulders and imitating the Russian's hulking, troll-like shamble, scowling at the man as he passed him.

When Rodion Romanovich reached the end of these stacks, before turning out of sight, he paused, looked back, and said, "I do not judge you by your name, Odd Thomas. You should not judge me by mine."

He departed, leaving me to wonder what he had meant. He had not, after all, been named for the mass murderer Joseph Stalin.

By the time Elvis reached me, he had contorted his face into a recognizable and comic impression of the Russian.

Watching the King as he mugged for me, I realized how unusual it was that neither I nor Romanovich had mentioned either Brother Timothy being missing or the deputies swarming the grounds in search of him. In the closed world of a monastery, where deviations from routine are rare, the disturbing events of the morning ought to have been the first subject of which we spoke.

Our mutual failure to remark on Brother Timothy's disappearance, even in passing, seemed to suggest some shared perception of events, or at least a shared attitude, that made us in some important way alike. I had no idea what I meant by that, but I intuited the truth of it.

When Elvis couldn't tease a smile from me with his impression of the somber Russian, he stuck one finger up his left nostril all the way to the third knuckle, pretending to be mining deep for boogers.

Death had not relieved him of his compulsion to entertain. As a voiceless spirit, he could no longer sing or tell jokes. Sometimes he danced, remembering a simple routine from one of his movies or from his Las Vegas act, though he was no more Fred Astaire than was Abbot Bernard. Sadly, in his desperation, he sometimes resorted to juvenile humor that was not worthy of him.

He withdrew his finger from his nostril, extracting an imaginary string of snot, then pretending that it was of extraordinary length, soon pulling yard after yard of it out of his nose with both hands.

I went in search of the reference-book collection and stood for a while reading about Indianapolis.

Elvis faced me over the open book, continuing his performance, but I ignored him.

Indianapolis has eight universities and colleges, and a large public library system.

When the King gently rapped me on the head, I sighed and looked up from the book.

He had an index finger stuck in his right nostril, all the way to the third knuckle, as before, but this time the tip of the finger was impossibly protruding from his left ear. He wiggled it.

I couldn't help smiling. He so badly wants to please.

Gratified to have pried a smile from me, he took the finger from his nose and wiped both hands on my jacket, pretending that they were sticky with snot.

"It's hard to believe," I told him, "that you're the same man who sang 'Love Me Tender.'"

He pretended to use the remaining snot to smooth back his hair.

"You're not droll," I told him. "You're grotesque."

This judgment delighted him. Grinning, he performed a series of quarter bows, as though to an audience, silently mouthing the words *Thank you, thank you, thank you very much.*

Sitting at a library table, I read about Indianapolis, which is intersected by more highways than any other city in the U.S. They once had a thriving tire industry, but no more.

Elvis sat at a window, watching the snow fall. With his hands, he tapped out rhythms on the window sill, but he made no sound.

Later, we went to the guesthouse receiving room at the front of the abbey, to see how the sheriff's-department search was proceeding.

The receiving room, furnished like a small shabby-genteel hotel lobby, was currently unoccupied.

As I approached the front door, it opened, and Brother Rafael entered in a carousel of glittering snow, wind chasing around him and howling like a pipe organ tuned in Hell. Meeting with resistance, he forced the door shut, and the whirling snow settled to the floor, but the wind still raised a muffled groan outside.

"What a terrible thing," he said to me, his voice trembling with distress.

A cold many-legged something crawled under the skin of my scalp, down the back of my neck. "Have the police found Brother Timothy?"

"They *haven't* found him, but they've left anyway." His large brown eyes were so wide with disbelief that he might have been named Brother Owl. "They've *left!*"

"What did they say?"

"With the storm, they're shorthanded. Highway accidents, unusual demands on their manpower."

Elvis listened to this, nodding judiciously, apparently in sympathy with the authorities.

In life, he sought and received actual—as opposed to honorary—special-deputy badges from several police agencies, including from the Shelby County, Tennessee, Sheriff's Office. Among other things, the badges permitted him to carry a concealed weapon. He had always been proud of his association with law enforcement.

One night in March 1976, coming upon a two-vehicle collision on Interstate 240, he displayed his badge and helped the victims until the police arrived. Fortunately, he never accidentally shot anyone.

"They searched all the buildings?" I asked.

"Yes," Brother Rafael confirmed. "And the yards. But what if he went for a walk in the woods and something happened to him, a fall or something, and he's lying out there?"

"Some of the brothers like to walk in the woods," I said, "but not at night, and not Brother Timothy."

The monk thought about that, and then nodded. "Brother Tim is awfully sedentary."

In the current situation, applying the word *sedentary* to Brother Timothy might be stretching the definition to include the ultimate sedentary condition, death.

"If he's not out there in the woods, where is he?" Brother Rafael wondered. A look of dismay overcame him. "The police don't understand us at all. They don't understand *anything* about us. They said maybe he went AWOL."

"Absent without leave? That's ridiculous."

"More than ridiculous, worse. It's an insult," Rafael declared, indignant. "One of them said maybe Tim went to Reno for 'some R and R—rum and roulette.'"

If one of Wyatt Porter's men in Pico Mundo had said such a thing, the chief would have put him on probation without pay and, depending on the officer's response to a dressing down, might have fired him.

Brother Knuckles's suggestion that I keep a low profile with these authorities appeared to have been wise advice.

"What're we going to do?" Brother Rafael worried.

I shook my head. I didn't have an answer.

Hurrying out of the room, speaking more to himself now than to me, he repeated, "What're we going to do?"

I consulted my wristwatch and then went to a front window.

Elvis phased through the closed door and stood outside in the sheeting snow, a striking figure in his black flamenco outfit with red cummerbund.

The time was 8:40 A.M.

Only the tire tracks of the recently departed police vehicles marked the path of the driveway. Otherwise, the storm had plastered over the variety and the roughness of the land, smoothing it into a white-on-white geometry of soft planes and gentle undulations.

From the look of things, eight or ten inches had piled up in about seven and a half hours. The snow was falling much faster now than it had fallen earlier.

Outside, Elvis stood with his head tipped back and his tongue out, in a fruitless attempt to catch flakes. Of course he was but a spirit, unable to feel the cold or taste the snow. Something about the effort he made, however, charmed me . . . and saddened me, as well.

How passionately we love everything that cannot last: the dazzling crystallory of winter, the spring in bloom, the fragile flight of butterflies, crimson sunsets, a kiss, and life.

The previous evening, the TV weather report had predicted a minimum two-foot accumulation. Storms in the High Sierra could be prolonged, brutal, and might result in an even deeper accumulation than what had been forecast.

By this afternoon, certainly before the early winter dusk, St. Bartholomew's Abbey would be snowbound. Isolated.

CHAPTER 13

I TRIED TO BE THE SHERLOCK HOLMES THAT Brother Knuckles hoped I could be, but my deductive reasoning led me through a maze of facts and suspicions that brought me back to where I started: clueless.

Because I am not much fun when I'm pretending to be a thinker, Elvis left me alone in the library. He might have gone to the church, hoping that Brother Fletcher intended to practice on the choir organ.

Even in death, he likes to be around music; and in life he had recorded six albums of gospel and inspirational songs, plus three Christmas albums. He might have preferred to dance to something with a backbeat, but you don't get much rock and roll in a monastery.

A poltergeist could have blasted out "All Shook Up" on the organ, could have pounded through "Hound Dog" on the piano in the guesthouse receiving room, the same way that Brother Constantine, deceased, rings church bells when in the mood. But poltergeists are angry; their rage is the source of their power.

Elvis could never be a poltergeist. He is a sweet spirit.

The wintry morning ticked toward whatever disaster might be coming. Recently I had learned that really brainy guys divide the day into units amounting to one-millionth of a billionth of a billionth of a second, which made each *whole* second that I dithered seem to be an unconscionable waste of time.

I wandered out of the receiving room, from cloister to grand cloister, thereafter into other wings of the abbey, trusting that my intuition would lead me toward some clue to the source of the pending violence that had drawn the bodachs.

No offense intended, but my intuition is better than yours. Maybe you took an umbrella to work on a sunny day and needed it by afternoon. Maybe you declined to date an apparently ideal man, for reasons you didn't understand, only to see him on the evening news, months later, arrested for having sexual relations with his pet llama. Maybe you bought a lottery ticket, using the date of your last proctological examination to select your numbers, and won ten million bucks. My intuition is still way better than yours.

The spookiest aspect of my intuition is what I call psychic magnetism. In Pico Mundo, when I had needed to find someone who was not where I expected him to be, I kept his name or face in mind while driving at random from street to street. Usually I found him within minutes.

Psychic magnetism isn't always reliable. Nothing is one hundred percent reliable this side of paradise, except that your cellphone provider will never fulfill the service promises that you were naïve enough to believe.

St. Bartholomew's population is a tiny fraction of that in Pico Mundo. Here, when giving myself to psychic magnetism, I proceed on foot instead of cruising in a car.

Initially, I kept Brother Timothy in mind: his kind eyes, his legendary blush. Now that the deputies were gone, if I found the monk's body, I faced no risk of being taken away to the nearest sheriff's station for questioning.

Seeking murder victims where their killers have hidden them is not as much fun as an Easter-egg hunt, although if you overlook an egg and find it a month later, the smells can be similar. Because the condition of the cadaver might provide a clue to the identity of the killer, might even suggest his ultimate intentions, the search was essential.

Fortunately, I had skipped breakfast.

When intuition brought me three times to three different outside doors, I stopped resisting the compulsion to take the search into the storm. I zippered shut my jacket, pulled up the hood, tightened it under my chin with a Velcro closure, and put on a pair of gloves that were tucked in a jacket pocket.

The snowfall that I had welcomed the previous night, with my face turned to the sky and my mouth open as if I were a turkey, had been a pathetic production compared to the extravaganza of snow that befell the mountain now, a wide-screen storm as directed by Peter Jackson on steroids.

The wind contradicted itself, seeming to slam into me from the west, then from the north, then from both directions at once, as if it surely must spend itself against itself, and be extinguished by its own fury.

Such schizophrenic wind threw-spun-whipped flakes in stinging sheets, in funnels, in icy lashes, a spectacle some poet once called "the frolic architecture of snow," but in this instance, there was a lot less frolic than fusillade, wind booming as loud as mortar fire and the snow like shrapnel.

My special intuition led me first north toward the front of the abbey, then east, then south. . . . After a while I realized that I had trudged more than once in a circle.

Perhaps psychic magnetism didn't work well in such a distracting environment: the white tumult of the storm, the caterwauling wind, the cold that pinched my face, that stung tears from my eyes and froze them on my cheeks.

As a desert-town boy, I was raised in fierce dry heat, which does not distract, but tends either to enervate or to toughen the sinews of the mind and focus thought. I felt displaced in this cold and whirling chaos, and not entirely myself.

I might have been hampered, as well, by a dread of looking into Brother Timothy's dead face. What I needed to find was, in this case, not what I wanted to find.

Repurposing my search, I let Brother Timothy rest and thought instead of bodachs and wondered what terror might be coming, and in general gave myself to worry about the indefinable threat, with the hope that I would be drawn toward some person or some place that in some way as yet unknowable would prove to be connected to the pending violence.

On the spectrum of detective work, this plan was a dismaying distance from the Sherlock end and closer to the tea-leaf-reading end than I cared to acknowledge.

I found myself, nevertheless, breaking out of the meaningless ramble on which I had been engaged. Moving with more purpose, I slogged east through the ten-inch-deep mantle of snow toward the convent and the school.

Halfway across the meadow, I succumbed to a sudden alarm and ducked, turned, flinched, certain that I was about to receive a blow.

I stood alone.

In spite of the evidence of my eyes, I didn't *feel* that I was alone. I felt watched. More than watched. Stalked.

A sound in the storm but not of the storm, a keening different from the shrill lament of the wind, drew near, receded, drew near, and once more receded.

To the west, the abbey stood barely visible through a thousand shifting veils, white drifts obscuring its foundations, wind-pasted snow erasing portions of its mighty stone walls. The bell tower grew less visible as it rose, seeming to dissolve toward the top, and the steeple—and the cross—could not be seen at all.

Downhill and to the east, the school was as obscure as a ghost ship becalmed in fog, less seen than suggested, a paleness in the lesser paleness of the blizzard.

No one at a window in either building would be able to see me at this distance, in these conditions. My scream would not carry in the wind.

The keening rose again, needful and agitated.

I turned in a circle, seeking the source. Much was obscured by the falling snow and by clouds of already-fallen snow whisked off the ground, and the bleak light deceived.

Although I had only turned in place, the school had entirely vanished along with the lower portion of the meadow. Uphill, the abbey shimmered like a mirage, rippled like an image painted on a sheer curtain.

Because I live with the dead, my tolerance for the macabre is so high that I am seldom spooked. The part-shriek-part-squeal-part-buzz, however, was so otherworldly that my imagination failed to conjure a creature that might have made it, and the marrow in my bones seemed to shrink in the way that mercury, in winter, contracts to the bottom of a thermometer.

I took one step toward where the school ought to be, but then halted, retracted that step. I turned uphill but dared not retreat to the abbey. Something unseen in the camouflaging storm, something with an alien voice full of need and fury, seemed to await me no matter in which direction I proceeded.

CHAPTER 14

STRIPPING VELCRO FROM VELCRO, PUSHING BACK
the insulated hood of my jacket, I raised my head, turned
my head, cocked my head, striving to determine from which
point of the compass the cry arose.

Icy wind tossed my hair and frosted it with snow, boxed my
ears and made them burn.

All magic had been snuffed from the storm. The grace of
falling snow was now a graceless wildness, a churning mael-
strom as raw and flaying as human rage.

I had the strange perception, beyond my power to explain, that
reality had shifted, down there twenty powers of ten below the
level of protons, that nothing was as it had been, nothing as it
should be.

Even with my hood off, I could not locate the source of the
eerie keening. The wind might be distorting and displacing the
sound, but perhaps the cry seemed to come from every side
because more than one shrieking entity prowled the snowblind
morning.

Reason asserted that anything stalking me must be of the Sierra, but this didn't sound like wolves or mountain lions. And bears were cavebound now, lost in dreams of fruit and honey.

I am not a guy who likes to pack a gun. My mother's affection for her pistol—and the threats of suicide that she employed to control me when I was a child—left me with a preference for other forms of self-defense.

Over the years, in pinches and crunches, I have survived—often just barely—by the effective use of such weapons as fists, feet, knees, elbows, a baseball bat, a shovel, a knife, a rubber snake, a real snake, three expensive antique porcelain vases, about a hundred gallons of molten tar, a bucket, a lug wrench, an angry cross-eyed ferret, a broom, a frying pan, a toaster, butter, a fire hose, and a large bratwurst.

As reckless as this strategy might be in my case, I prefer to rely on my wits rather than on a personal armory. Unfortunately, at that moment in the meadow, my wits were so dry that I could wring from them no idea except that perhaps I should make snowballs.

Because I doubted that my eerily keening, unknown stalkers were mischievous ten-year-old boys, I rejected the snowball defense. I pulled the hood over my half-frozen head and fixed the Velcro clasp under my chin.

These cries were purposeful, but in spite of how different they were from other chaotic blusterings of the storm, perhaps they were only wind noises, after all.

When my wits fail me, I resort to self-deception.

I started toward the school again and at once detected movement to my left, at the periphery of vision.

Turning to confront the threat, I saw something white and

quick, visible only because it was angular and bristling in contrast to the undulant billow and whirl of falling and upswept snow. Like a goblin in a dream, it was gone even as it appeared, infolding into the downfall, leaving a vague impression of sharp points, hard edges, gloss and translucency.

The keening stopped. The groan and hiss and whistle of the wind sounded almost welcoming without that other craving cry.

Movies offer no wisdom and have little to do with real life, but I remembered old adventure films in which the ceaseless pounding of jungle drums had put the sweaty pith-helmeted explorers on edge. The abrupt cessation of the drumming was never the relief that it ought to have been, however, because often the silence signaled imminent attack.

I suspected Hollywood had gotten that one right.

Sensing that I was soon to receive something worse and stranger than a poison dart in the throat or an arrow through an eye, I cast aside indecision and hurried toward the school.

Something loomed in the storm ahead and to the right, veiled by snow, suggestive of the bare frosted limbs of a tree thrashing in the wind. Not a tree. No trees stood in the meadow between the abbey and the school.

Instead, I had glimpsed a narrow aspect of a mysterious presence that was more aware than wood, that moved not as the wind commanded it but with a fierce purpose of its own.

Having revealed only enough to make of itself a deeper enigma than it had been previously, the thing drew cloaks of snow around itself, vanishing. It had not gone away, still paralleled me out of sight, like a lion pacing a gazelle that had become separated from its herd.

Intuitively perceived but not seen, another predator rose at my back. I became convinced that I would be seized from behind and that my head would be ripped off as if it were the pull-tab on a can of cola.

I do not want a fancy funeral. I would be embarrassed by flowery tributes delivered over my casket. On the other hand, I do not want my death to be observed solely by the belch of some beast that has slaked its thirst with my precious bodily fluids.

As I plunged across the sloping meadow, kicking through drifts, heart knocking, the all-enveloping whiteness of the blizzard bleached my vision. The fluorescence of the snow made my eyes ache, and the driven flakes appeared to strobe.

In this further-reduced visibility, something crossed my path, perhaps ten feet ahead, from right to left, its size and shape and nature obscured, but not simply obscured, also distorted, surely distorted, because the quick scuttling something, judging by the portion briefly glimpsed in glare, appeared to be a construct of bones jacketed in ice. With its impossible biological architecture, it should have moved, if at all, with a shambling instability but instead exhibited a wicked kind of grace, a visual glissando of rippling motion, gliding past, gone.

I had momentum, and the school was near, so I didn't halt or turn, but crossed the tracks of whatever had passed in front of me. I didn't pause to examine the prints it left. The fact that there *were* prints proved that I hadn't been hallucinating.

No keening rose—just the stillness of imminent attack, the sense of something rearing up behind me to strike—and through my mind flew words like *horde, host, legion, swarm.*

Snow had drifted across the front steps of the school. The footprints of the searchers, who had been here seeking poor Brother Timothy, had already been erased by the wind.

I scrambled up the steps, tore open the door, expecting to be snatched off the threshold, one step from safety. I crossed into the reception lounge, shoved the door shut, leaned against it.

The moment that I was out of the wind, out of the eye-searing glare, in a bath of warm air, the pursuit seemed like a dream from which I had awakened, the beasts in the blizzard only figments of a particularly vivid nightmare. Then something scraped against the far side of the door.

CHAPTER 15

HAD THE VISITOR BEEN A MAN, HE WOULD HAVE knocked. If it had been only the wind, it would have huffed and strained against the door until the planks creaked.

This scrape was the sound of bone on wood, or something like bone. I could imagine an animated skeleton clawing with mindless persistence at the other side of the door.

In all my bizarre experiences, I had never actually encountered an animated skeleton. But in a world where McDonald's now sells salads with low-fat dressing, anything is possible.

The reception lounge was deserted. Had it been staffed, only a nun or two would have been there, anyway.

If something like what I had glimpsed in the storm was able to break the door off its hinges, I would have preferred better backup than the average nun could provide. I needed someone even tougher than Sister Angela with her penetrating periwinkle stare.

The doorknob rattled, rattled, turned.

Doubtful that my resistance alone would keep out this unwanted caller, I engaged the dead-bolt lock.

A scene from an old movie played in my memory: a man standing with his back pressed to a stout oak door, believing himself to be safe from preternatural forces on the farther side.

The film had been about the evils of nuclear energy, about how minimal exposure to radiation will overnight cause ordinary creatures to mutate into monsters and to grow gigantic as well. As we know, in the real world, this has had a devastating impact on the real-estate values in the monster-plagued communities near all of our nuclear power plants.

Anyway, the guy is standing with his back to the door, feeling safe, when a giant stinger, curved like a rhino horn, pierces the oak. It bursts through his chest, exploding his heart.

The monsters in this flick were only marginally more convincing than the actors, on a par with sock puppets, but the skewering-stinger scene stuck in my mind.

Now I stepped away from the door. Watched the knob rattling back and forth. Eased farther away.

I had seen movies in which one kind of fool or another, putting his face to a window to scope the territory, gets shotgunned or gets seized by a creature that doesn't need a gun and that smashes through the glass and drags him screaming into the night. Nevertheless, I went to the window beside the door.

If I lived my entire life according to movie wisdom, I would risk winding up as spinning-eyed crazy as do many of our nation's most successful actors.

Besides, this wasn't a night scene. This was a morning scene, and snow was falling, so probably the worst that would happen, if life imitated films, would be someone breaking into "White Christmas" or the equivalent.

A thin crust of ice had crystallized across the exterior of the windowpanes. I detected something moving outside, but it was no more than a white blur, an amorphous shape, a pallid form quivering with potential.

Squinting, I put my nose to the cold glass.

To my left, the knob ceased rattling.

I held my breath for a moment to avoid further clouding the window with every exhalation.

The visitor on the doorstep surged forward and bumped against the glass, as if peering in at me.

I twitched but did not reel back. Curiosity transfixed me.

The opaque glass still masked the visitor even as it pressed forward insistently. In spite of the obscuring ice, if this had been a face before me, I should have seen at least the hollows of eyes and something that might have been a mouth, but I did not.

What I *did* see, I could not understand. Again, the impression was of bones, but not the bones of any animal known to me. Longer and broader than fingers, they were lined up like piano keys, although they were not in straight keyboards, but were serpentine, and curved through other undulant rows of bones. They appeared to be joined by a variety of knuckles and sockets that I observed, in spite of the veil of ice, were of extraordinary design.

This macabre collage, which filled the window from side to side, from sill to header, abruptly flexed. With a soft click-and-rattle like a thousand tumbling dice on a felt-lined craps table, all the elements shifted as if they were fragments in a kaleidoscope, forming a new pattern more amazing than the previous.

I leaned back from the window just far enough to be able to

appreciate the entire elaborate mosaic, which had both a cold beauty and a fearsome quality.

The joints that linked these ranked rows of bones—if bones they were, and not insectile limbs sheathed in chitin—evidently permitted 360-degree rotation along more than one plane of movement.

With the dice-on-felt sound, the kaleidoscope shifted, producing another intricate pattern as eerily beautiful as the one before it, though a degree more menacing.

I got the distinct feeling that the joints between the bones allowed universal rotation on numerous if not infinite planes, which was not just biologically impossible but *mechanically* impossible.

Perhaps to taunt me, the spectacle remade itself once more.

Yes, I have seen the dead, the tragic dead and the foolish dead, the dead who linger in hatred and the dead who are chained to this world by love, and they are different from one another yet all the same, the same in that they cannot accept the truth of their place in the vertical of sacred order, cannot move in any direction from this place, neither to glory nor to an eternal void.

And I have seen bodachs, whatever they may be. I have more than one theory about them but not a single fact to support a theory.

Ghosts and bodachs are the sum of it. I do not see fairyfolk or elves, neither gremlins nor goblins, neither dryads nor nymphs, nor pixies, neither vampires nor werewolves. A long time ago, I stopped keeping an eye out for Santa Claus on Christmas Eve because, when I was five, my mother told me that Santa was a wicked pervert who would cut off my peepee with a pair of scissors and that if I didn't stop chattering about him, he would be certain to put me on his list and look me up.

Christmas was never the same after that, but at least I still have my peepee.

Although my experience with supernatural presences had been limited to the dead and bodachs, the thing pressed to the window seemed more supernatural than real. I had no idea what it might be, but I was reasonably confident that the words *fiend* and *demon* were more applicable than the word *angel*.

Whatever it was, thing of bone or thing of ectoplasm, it had something to do with the threat of violence that hung over the nuns and the children in their charge. I didn't have to be Sherlock Holmes to figure that out.

Apparently each time the bones shifted, they abraded the ice and shaved some off the glass, for this mosaic was clearer than those that had preceded it, the edges of the bones sharper, the details of the joints slightly more defined.

Seeking a better understanding of the apparition, I leaned close to the glass again, studying the disturbing details of this unearthly osteography.

Nothing supernatural has ever harmed me. My wounds and losses have all been at the hands of human beings, some in porkpie hats but most dressed otherwise.

None of the many elements in the bony mosaic trembled, but I had an impression that it was tight with tension.

Although my breath bloomed directly against the window, the surface did not cloud, most likely because my exhalations remained shallow, expelled with little force.

I had the disturbing thought, however, that my breath was

without warmth, too frigid to cloud the glass, and that I inhaled darkness with the air but breathed no darkness out, which was a strange notion even for me.

I stripped off my gloves, shoved them in my jacket pockets, and placed one hand lightly on the cold glass.

Again the bones clicked, fanned, seemed almost to shuffle in the manner of a deck of cards, and rearranged themselves.

Shavings of ice in fact peeled from the outside of the window.

This new pattern of bones must have expressed a primal image of evil that spoke to my unconscious mind, for I saw nothing of beauty anymore, but felt as though something with a thin flicking tail had skittered the length of my spine.

My curiosity had ripened into a less healthy fascination, and fascination had become something darker. I wondered if I might be spellbound, somehow mesmerized, but I figured that I could not be spellbound if I remained capable of considering the possibility, though I was *something,* if not spellbound, because I found myself contemplating a return to the front steps to consider this visitor without the hampering interface of ice and glass.

A splintering sound came from a couple of the wooden muntins that divided the window into panes. I saw a hairline crack open in the white paint that sealed the wood; the fissure traced a crooked path along a vertical muntin, across a horizontal.

Under the hand that I still pressed to the window, the pane cracked.

The single brittle *snap* of failing glass alarmed me, broke the spell. I snatched my hand back and retreated three steps from the window.

No loose glass fell. The fractured pane remained within the framing muntins.

The thing of bone or ectoplasm flexed once more, conjuring yet another but no less menacing pattern, as if seeking a new arrangement of its elements that would apply greater pressure to the stubborn window.

Although it changed from one malignant mosaic to another, the effect was nonetheless elegant, as economical as the movements of an efficient machine.

The word *machine* resonated in my mind, seemed important, seemed revealing, though I knew this could not be a machine. If this world could not produce such a biological structure as the one to which I now stood fearful witness—and it could not— then just as surely, human beings did not possess the knowledge to engineer and build a machine with this phenomenal dexterity.

The storm-born thing flexed again. This newest kaleidoscopic wonder of bones suggested that, just as no two snowflakes in history have been alike, so no two of the thing's manifestations would produce the same pattern.

My expectation was not merely that the glass would shatter, all eight bright panes at once, but also that every muntin would burst into splinters and that the frame would tear out of the wall, taking chunks of plaster with it, and that the thing would clamber into the school behind a cascade of debris.

I wished that I had a hundred gallons of molten tar, an angry cross-eyed ferret, or at least a toaster.

Abruptly, the apparition flexed *away* from the window, ceased to present a malevolent bony pattern. I thought it must be rearing back to throw itself through that barrier, but the attack did not come. This spawn of the storm became again just a pale blur, a trembling potential seen through frosted glass.

A moment later, it seemed to return to the storm. No

movement shadowed the window, and the eight panes were as lifeless as eight TV screens tuned to a dead channel.

One square of glass remained cracked.

I suppose I knew then how the heart in a rabbit's breast feels to the rabbit, how it feels like a leaping thing alive within, when the coyote is eye to eye and peels its lips back from teeth stained by years of blood.

No keening rose in the storm. Only the wind huffed at the window and whistled through the keyhole in the door.

Even to one accustomed to encounters with the supernatural, the aftermath of such an unlikely event sometimes includes equal measures of wonder and doubt. A fear that makes you shrink from the prospect of any further such experience is matched by a compulsion to see more and to *understand*.

I felt compelled to unlock and open the door. I quashed that compulsion, did not lift a foot, did not raise a hand, just stood with my arms wrapped around myself, as if holding myself together, and took long shuddery breaths until Sister Clare Marie arrived and politely insisted that I remove my ski boots.

CHAPTER 16

G AZING AT THE WINDOW, TRYING TO UNDER-
stand what I had seen and silently congratulating myself
on the fact that I still had clean underwear, I didn't realize that
Sister Clare Marie had entered the reception lounge. She circled
around from behind me, coming between me and the window, as
white and silent as an orbiting moon.

In her habit, with her soft pink face, button nose, and slight
overbite, she needed only a pair of long furry ears to call herself a
rabbit and attend a costume party.

"Child," she said, "you look as if you've seen a ghost."

"Yes, Sister."

"Are you all right?"

"No, Sister."

Twitching her nose, as though she detected a scent that
alarmed her, she said, "Child?"

I do not know why she calls me *child*. I have never heard her
address anyone else that way, not even any of the children in the
school.

Because Sister Clare Marie was a sweet gentle person, I did not want to alarm her, especially considering that the threat had passed, at least for the moment, and considering as well that, being a nun, she didn't carry the hand grenades I would need before venturing again into the storm.

"It's just the snow," I said.

"The snow?"

"The wind and cold and snow. I'm a desert boy, ma'am. I'm not used to weather like this. It's mean out there."

"The weather isn't mean," she assured me with a smile. "The weather is glorious. The world is beautiful and glorious. Humanity can be mean, and turn away from what's good. But weather is a gift."

"All right," I said.

Sensing that I hadn't been convinced, she continued: "Blizzards dress the land in a clean habit, lightning and thunder make a music of celebration, wind blows away all that's stale, even floods raise up everything green. For cold there's hot. For dry there's wet. For wind there's calm. For night there's day, which might not seem like weather to you, but it is. Embrace the weather, child, and you'll understand the *balance* of the world."

I am twenty-one, have known the misery of an indifferent father and a hostile mother, have had a part of my heart cut out by a sharp knife of loss, have killed men in self-defense and to spare the lives of innocents, and have left behind all the friends whom I cherished in Pico Mundo. I believe all this must show that I am a page on which the past has written clearly for anyone to read. Yet Sister Clare Marie sees some reason to call me—and only me—*child,* which sometimes I hope means that she possesses some understanding I do not have, but which most often I suspect means that she is as naïve as she is sweet and that she does not know me at all.

"Embrace the weather," she said, "but please don't puddle on the floor."

This seemed to be an admonition that once might have been better directed at Boo than at me. Then I realized that my ski boots were caked with snow, which was melting on the limestone.

"Oh. Sorry, Sister."

When I took off my jacket, she hung it on a coatrack, and when I shucked off my boots, she picked them up to put them on the rubber mat under the rack.

As she moved away with the boots, I pulled the bottom of my sweater over my head, and used it as a towel to blot my soaked hair and damp face.

I heard the door open and the wind shriek.

Panicked, I pulled down my sweater and saw Sister Clare Marie standing on the threshold, looking less like a rabbit than like an array of sails on a vessel on course in Arctic straits, vigorously knocking my boots together so the snow caked on them would be left outside.

Beyond her, the blizzard didn't seem as though it wanted to be embraced, not this storm of storms. It looked instead as though it wanted to blow down the school and the abbey and the forest beyond, blow down everything on the face of the earth that dared to stand upright, and bury everything, and be done with civilization and with humanity once and for all.

By the time I reached her, before I could shout a warning above the wind, Sister Clare Marie retreated from the threshold.

Neither a demon nor an Amway salesperson loomed out of the

frigid tempest before I pushed the door shut and engaged the dead-bolt lock once more.

As she placed the boots on the rubber mat, I said, "Wait, I'll get a mop, don't open the door, I'll get a mop and clean this up."

I sounded shaky, as if I had once been badly traumatized by a mop and needed to summon the courage to use one.

The nun didn't seem to notice the quaver in my voice. With a sunny smile, she said, "You'll do no such thing. You're a guest here. Letting you do my work, I'd be embarrassed in front of the Lord."

Indicating the puddle of melting slush on the floor, I said, "But I'm the one who made the mess."

"That's not a mess, child."

"It looks like a mess to me."

"That's weather! And it's my work. Besides, Mother Superior wants to see you. She called up to the abbey, and they said you'd been seen going outside, maybe you were coming this way, and here you are. She's in her office."

I watched her fetch a mop from a closet near the front door.

When she turned and saw that I hadn't left, she said, "Go on now, shoo, see what Mother Superior wants."

"You won't open the door to wring out the mop on the stoop, will you, Sister?"

"Oh, there's not enough to wring. It's just a small puddle of weather come inside."

"You won't open the door just to glory in the blizzard, will you?" I asked.

"It *is* a fantastic day, isn't it?"

"Fantastic," I said with no enthusiasm.

"If I've got my chores done before None and rosary, then I might take time for the weather."

None was the midafternoon prayer, at twenty minutes past four, more than six and a half hours from now.

"Good. Just before None—that'll be a nice time for watching a storm. Much nicer than now."

She said, "I might make a cup of hot chocolate and sit by a window and glory in the blizzard from a cozy corner of the kitchen."

"Not too close to the window," I said.

Her pink brow furrowed. "Whyever not, child?"

"Drafts. You don't want to sit in a draft."

"Nothing wrong with a good draft!" she assured me heartily. "Some are cold, some are warm, but it's all just air on the move, circulating so it's healthy to breathe."

I left her swabbing up the small puddle of weather.

If something hideous came through the window with the one cracked pane, Sister Clare Marie, wielding the mop like a cudgel, would probably have the moves and the attitude to get the best of the beast.

CHAPTER 17

O N THE WAY TO THE MOTHER SUPERIOR'S office, I passed the large recreation room, where a dozen nuns were supervising the children at play.

Some of the kids have severe physical disabilities combined with mild mental retardation. They like board games, card games, dolls, toy soldiers. They decorate cupcakes themselves and help make fudge, and they enjoy arts and crafts. They like to have stories read to them, and they want to learn to read, and most of them do learn.

The others have either mild or severe physical disabilities but greater mental retardation than the first group. Some of these, like Justine in Room 32, seem not to be much with us, though most of them have an inner life that expresses itself overtly when least expected.

The betweeners—not as detached as Justine, not as involved as those who want to read—like to work with clay, string beads to make their own jewelry, play with stuffed animals, and perform small tasks that help the sisters. They enjoy hearing stories, too; the stories may be simpler, but the magic of stories remains potent for them.

What all of them like, regardless of their limits, is affection. At a touch, a hug, a kiss on the cheek, at any indication that you value them, respect them, believe in them, they shine.

Later in the day, in either of the two rehabilitation rooms, they will take physical therapy to gain strength, improve agility. Those struggling to communicate will get speech therapy. For some, rehab is actually task instruction, during which they learn to dress themselves, to tell time, to make change and manage small allowances.

Special cases will move on from St. Bart's, be paired with assistance dogs or caregivers, graduate to a supported independence when they are eighteen or older. Because many of these kids are so severely disabled, however, the world will never welcome them, and this place is their home for life.

Fewer of the residents are adults than you might think. These children have been dealt terrible blows, most of them while not yet delivered from their mothers' wombs, others by violence before they were three. They are fragile. For them, twenty years is longevity.

You might think that watching them struggle through various kinds of rehab would be heartbreaking, considering that they are often destined to die young. But there is no heartbreak here. Their small triumphs thrill them as much as winning a marathon might thrill you. They know moments of unadulterated joy, they know wonder, and they have hope. Their spirits won't be chained. In my months among them, I have never heard one child complain.

As medical science has advanced, such institutions as St. Bart's have fewer kids damaged by severe cerebral palsy, by toxoplasmosis, by well-understood chromosomal abnormalities. Their beds are taken these days by the offspring of women who preferred not to give up cocaine or ecstasy, or hallucinogens, for nine boring months, who played dice with the devil. Other children here were badly beaten—skulls cracked, brains damaged—by their drunken fathers, by their mothers' meth-rotted boyfriends.

With so many new cells and lightless pits required, Hell must be going through a construction boom these days.

Some will accuse me of being judgmental. Thank you. And proud of it. You wreck a kid's life, I have no pity for you.

There are doctors who advocate killing these children at birth, with lethal injections, or who would let them die later by declining to treat their infections, allowing simple illnesses to become catastrophic.

More cells. More lightless pits.

Maybe my lack of compassion for these abusers of children—and other failures of mine—means I won't see Stormy on the Other Side, that the fire I face will be consuming rather than purifying. But at least if I wind up in that palpable dark where having no cable TV is the least of the inconveniences, I will have the pleasure of seeking you out if you have beaten a child. I will know just what to do with you, and I will have eternity to do it.

In the recreation room on that snowy morning, perhaps with Hell coming to meet us in the hours ahead, the children laughed and talked and gave themselves to make-believe.

At the piano in the corner sat a ten-year-old boy named Walter. He was a crack baby and a meth baby and a Wild Turkey baby and a God-knows-what baby. He could not speak and rarely made eye contact. He couldn't learn to dress himself. After hearing a melody just once, he could play it note-perfect, with passion and nuance. Although he had lost so much else, this gift of talent had survived.

He played softly, beautifully, lost in the music. I think it was Mozart. I'm too ignorant to know for sure.

While Walter made music, while the children played and laughed, bodachs crawled the room. The three last night had become seven.

CHAPTER 18

SISTER ANGELA, THE MOTHER SUPERIOR, MAN-aged the convent and the school from a small office adjacent to the infirmary. The desk, the two visitors' chairs, and the file cabinets were simple but inviting.

On the wall behind her desk hung a crucifix, and on the other walls were three posters: George Washington; Harper Lee, the author of *To Kill a Mockingbird*; and Flannery O'Connor, the author of "A Good Man Is Hard to Find" and many other stories.

She admires these people for many reasons, but especially for one quality they all shared. She will not identify that quality. She wishes you to ponder the riddle and arrive at your own answer.

Standing in her office doorway, I said, "I'm sorry about my feet, ma'am."

She looked up from a file she was reviewing. "If they have a fragrance, it's not so intense that I smelled you coming."

"No, ma'am. I'm sorry for my stocking feet. Sister Clare Marie took my boots."

"I'm sure she'll give them back, Oddie. We've had no problem with Sister Clare Marie stealing footwear. Come in, sit down."

I settled into one of the chairs in front of her desk, indicated the posters, and said, "They're all Southerners."

"Southerners have many fine qualities, charm and civility among them, and a sense of the tragic, but that's not why these particular faces are inspiring to me."

I said, "Fame."

"Now you're being intentionally dense," she said.

"No, ma'am, not intentionally."

"If what I admired in these three was their fame, then I'd just as well have put up posters of Al Capone, Bart Simpson, and Tupac Shakur."

"That sure would be something," I said.

Leaning forward, lowering her voice, she said, "What's happened to dear Brother Timothy?"

"Nothing good. That's all I know for sure. Nothing good."

"One thing we can be certain of—he didn't dash off to Reno for some R and R. His disappearance must be related to the thing we spoke of last evening. The event the bodachs have come to witness."

"Yes, ma'am, whatever it is. I just saw seven of them in the recreation room."

"Seven." Her soft grandmotherly features stiffened with steely resolution. "Is the crisis at hand?"

"Not with seven. When I see thirty, forty, then I'll know we're coming to the edge. There's still time, but the clock is ticking."

"I spoke with Abbot Bernard about the discussion you and I had last night. And now with the disappearance of Brother Timothy, we're wondering if the children should be moved."

"Moved? Moved where?"

"We could take them into town."

"Ten miles in this weather?"

"In the garage we have two beefy four-wheel-drive extended SUVs with wheelchair lifts. They're on oversize tires to give more ground clearance, plus chains on the tires. Each is fitted with a plow. We can make our own path."

Moving the kids was not a good idea, but I sure wanted to see nuns in monster trucks plowing their way through a blizzard.

"We can take eight to ten in each van," she continued. "Moving half the sisters and all the children might require four trips, but if we start now we'll be done in a few hours, before nightfall."

Sister Angela is a doer. She likes to be on the move physically and intellectually, always conceiving and implementing projects, accomplishing things.

Her can-do spirit is endearing. At that moment, she looked like whichever no-nonsense grandmother had passed down to George S. Patton the genes that had made him a great general.

I regretted having to let the air out of her plan after she'd evidently spent some time inflating it.

"Sister, we don't know for sure that the violence, when it happens, will happen here at the school."

She looked puzzled. "But it's already started. Brother Timothy, God rest his soul."

"We *think* it's started with Brother Tim, but we don't have a corpse."

She winced at the word *corpse*.

"We don't have a body," I amended, "so we don't know for sure what's happened. All we know is that the bodachs are drawn to the kids."

"And the children are here."

"But what if you move the kids in town to a hospital, a school, a church, and when we get them settled in, the bodachs show up there because that's where the violence is going to go down, not here at St. Bart's."

She was as good an analyst of strategy and tactics as Patton's grandma might have been. "So we would have been serving the forces of darkness when we thought we'd been thwarting them."

"Yes, ma'am. It's possible."

She studied me so intently that I convinced myself I could feel her periwinkle-blue stare riffling through the contents of my brain as if I had a simple file drawer between my ears.

"I'm so sorry for you, Oddie," she murmured.

I shrugged.

She said, "You know just enough so that, morally, you've got to act . . . but not enough to be certain exactly what to do."

"In the crunch, it clarifies," I said.

"But only at the penultimate moment, only then?"

"Yes, ma'am. Only then."

"So when the moment comes, the crunch—it's always a plunge into chaos."

"Well, ma'am, whatever it is, it's never not memorable."

Her right hand touched her pectoral cross, and her gaze traveled across the posters on her walls.

After a moment, I said, "I'm here to be with the kids, to walk the halls, the rooms, see if I can get a better feel for what might be coming. If that's all right."

"Yes. Of course."

I rose from the chair. "Sister Angela, there's something I want you to do, but I'd rather you didn't ask me why."

"What is it?"

"Be sure all the doors are dead-bolted, all the windows locked. And instruct the sisters not to go outside."

I preferred not to tell her about the creature that I had seen in the storm. For one thing, on that day I stood in her office I did not yet have words to describe the apparition. Also, when nerves are too frayed, clear thinking unravels, so I needed her to be alert to danger without being in a continuous state of alarm.

Most important, I didn't want her to worry that she had allied herself with someone who might be not merely a fry cook, and not merely a fry cook with a sixth sense, but a *totally insane* fry cook with a sixth sense.

"All right," she said. "We'll be sure we're locked, and there's no reason to go out in that storm, anyway."

"Would you call Abbot Bernard and ask him to do the same thing? For the remaining hours of the Divine Office, the brothers shouldn't go outside to enter the church through the grand cloister. Tell them to use the interior door between the abbey and the church."

In these solemn circumstances, Sister Angela had been robbed of her most effective instrument of interrogation: that lovely smile sustained in patient and intimidating silence.

The storm drew her attention. As ominous as ashes, clouds of snow smoked across the window.

She looked up at me again. "Who's out there, Oddie?"

"I don't know yet," I replied, which was true to the extent that I could not name what I had seen. "But they mean to do us harm."

CHAPTER 19

WEARING AN IMAGINARY DOG COLLAR, I LET
intuition have my leash, and was led in a circuitous route
through the ground-floor rooms and hallways of the school, to a
set of stairs, to the second floor, where the Christmas decorations
did not inspire in me a merry mood.

When I stopped at the open door to Room 32, I suspected that
I had deceived myself. I had not given myself to intuition, after
all, but had been guided by an unconscious desire to repeat the
experience of the previous night, when it seemed that Stormy
had spoken to me through sleeping Annamarie by way of mute
Justine.

At the time, as much as I had desired the contact, I had
spurned it. I had been right to do so.

Stormy is my past, and she will be my future only after my life
in this world is over, when time finishes and eternity begins.
What is required of me now is patience and perseverance. The
only way back is the way forward.

I told myself to turn away, to wander farther onto the second floor. Instead I crossed the threshold and stood just inside the room.

Drowned by her father at four, left for dead but still alive eight years later, the radiantly beautiful girl sat in bed, leaning against plump pillows, eyes closed.

Her hands lay in her lap, both palms upturned, as though she waited to receive some gift.

The voices of the wind were muffled but legion: chanting, snarling, hissing at the single window.

The collection of plush-toy kittens watched me from the shelves near her bed.

Annamarie and her wheelchair were gone. I had seen her in the recreation room, where behind the laughter of children, quiet Walter, who could not dress himself without assistance, played classical piano.

The air seemed heavy, like the atmosphere between the first flash of lightning and the first peal of thunder, when the rain has formed miles above but has not yet reached the earth, when fat drops are descending by the millions, compressing the air below them as one last warning of their drenching approach.

I stood in light-headed anticipation.

Beyond the window, frenzies of driven snow chased down the day, and though obviously the wind still flogged the morning, its voices faded, and slowly a cone of silence settled upon the room.

Justine opened her eyes. Although usually she looks through everything in this world, now she met my gaze.

I became aware of a familiar fragrance. Peaches.

When I worked as a short-order cook in Pico Mundo, before the world grew as dark as it is now, I washed my hair in a peach-scented shampoo that Stormy had given me. It effectively replaced the aromas of bacon and hamburgers and fried onions that lingered in my locks after a long shift at the griddle and grill.

At first dubious about peach shampoo, I had suggested that a bacon-hamburgers-fried-onions scent ought to be appealing, ought to make the mouth water, and that most people had quasi-erotic reactions to the aromas of fried food.

Stormy had said, "Listen, griddle boy, you're not as suave as Ronald McDonald, but you're cute enough to eat *without* smelling like a sandwich."

As any red-blooded boy would have done, I thereafter used peach-scented shampoo every day.

The fragrance that now rose in Room 32 was not of peaches but, more precisely, was of that particular peach shampoo, which I had not brought with me to St. Bart's.

This was wrong. I knew that I should leave at once. The scent of peach shampoo immobilized me.

The past cannot be redeemed. What has been and what *might* have been both bring us to what is.

To know grief, we must be in the river of time, because grief thrives in the present and promises to be with us in the future until the end point. Only time conquers time and its burdens. There is no grief before or after time, which is all the consolation we should need.

Nevertheless, I stood there, waiting, full of hope that was the wrong hope.

Stormy is dead and does not belong in this world, and Justine is profoundly brain-damaged from prolonged oxygen deprivation and cannot speak. Yet the girl attempted to communicate, not on her own behalf but for another who had no voice at all this side of the grave.

What came from Justine were not words but thick knots of sound that reflected the wrenched and buckled nature of her brain, eerily bringing to mind a desperate drowner struggling for air underwater, wretched sounds that were sodden and bloated and unbearably sad.

An anguished *no* escaped me, and the girl at once stopped trying to speak.

Justine's usually unexpressive features tightened into a look of frustration. Her gaze slid away from me, tracked left, tracked right, and then to the window.

She suffered from a partial paralysis general in nature, though her left side was more profoundly affected than her right. With some effort, she raised her more useful arm from the bed. Her slender hand reached toward me, as though beseeching me to come closer, but then pointed to the window.

I saw only the bleak shrouded daylight and the falling snow.

Her eyes met mine, more focused than I had ever seen them, as pellucid as always but also with a yearning in those blue depths that I had never glimpsed before, not even when I had been in this room the previous night and had heard sleeping Annamarie say *Loop me in.*

Her intense stare moved from me to the window, returned to me, slid once more to the window, at which she still pointed. Her hand trembled with the effort to control it.

I moved deeper into Room 32.

The single window provided a view of the cloister below, where the brothers had daily gathered when this had been their first abbey. The open courtyard lay deserted. No one lurked between the columns in the portion of the colonnade that I could see.

Across the courtyard, its stone face softened by veils of snow, rose another wing of the abbey. On the second floor, a few windows shone softly with lamplight in the white gloom of the storm, though most of the children were downstairs at this hour.

The window directly opposite from the panes at which I stood glowed brighter than the others. The longer I gazed at it, the more the light seemed to draw me, as though it were a signal lamp set out by someone in distress.

A figure appeared at that window, a backlighted silhouette, as featureless as a bodach, though it was not one of them.

Justine had lowered her arm to the bed.

Her stare remained demanding.

"All right," I whispered, turning away from the window, "all right," but said no more.

I dared not continue, because on my tongue was a name that I longed to speak.

The girl closed her eyes. Her lips parted, and she began to breathe as if, exhausted, she had fallen into sleep.

I went to the open door but did not leave.

Gradually the strange silence lifted, and the wind breathed at the window again, and muttered as if cursing in a brutal language.

If I had properly understood what had happened, I had been given direction in my search for the meaning of the gathering bodachs. The hour of violence approached, perhaps was not imminent, but approached nonetheless, and duty called me elsewhere.

Yet I stood in Room 32 until the fragrance of peach shampoo faded, until I could detect no trace of it, until certain memories would relinquish their grip on me.

CHAPTER 20

ROOM 14 LAY DIRECTLY ACROSS THE COURT-
yard from Room 32, in the north corridor. A single plaque
had been fixed to the door, bearing one name: JACOB.

A floor lamp beside an armchair, a squat nightstand lamp, and
a fluorescent ceiling fixture compensated for daylight so drear
that it could press itself inside no farther than the window sill.

Because Room 14 contained only a single bed, the space could
accommodate a four-foot-square oak table, at which sat Jacob.

I had seen him a couple of times, but I did not know him. "May
I come in?"

He didn't say yes, but he didn't say no, either. Deciding to take
his silence as an invitation, I sat across from him at the table.

Jacob is one of the few adults housed at the school. He is in his
middle twenties.

I didn't know the name of the condition with which he had
been born, but evidently it involved a chromosomal abnormality.

About five feet tall, with a head slightly too small for his body, a sloped forehead, low-set ears, and soft heavy features, he exhibited some of the characteristics of Down's syndrome.

The bridge of his nose was not flat, however, which is an indicator of Down's, and his eyes did not have the inner epicanthic folds that give the eyes of Down's people an Asian cast.

More telling, he did not exhibit the quick smile or the sunny and gentle disposition virtually universal among those with Down's. He did not look at me, and his expression remained dour.

His head was misshapen as no Down's person's head would ever be. A greater weight of bone accumulated in the left side of his skull than in the right. His features were not symmetrical, but were subtly out of balance, one eye set slightly lower than the other, his left jaw more prominent than his right, his left temple convex and his right temple more than usually concave.

Stocky, with heavy shoulders and a thick neck, he hunched over the table, intent on the task before him. His tongue, which appeared to be thicker than a normal tongue but which didn't usually protrude, was at the moment pinched gently between his teeth.

On the table were two large tablets of drawing paper. One lay to the right of him, closed. The second was propped on a slant-board.

Jacob was drawing on the second tablet. Ordered in an open case, an array of pencils offered lead in many thicknesses and in different degrees of softness.

His current project was a portrait of a strikingly lovely woman, nearly finished. Presented in three-quarter profile, she stared past the artist's left shoulder.

Inevitably, I thought of the hunchback of Nôtre Dame: Quasimodo, his tragic hope, his unrequited love.

"You're very talented," I said, which was true.

He did not reply.

Although his hands were short and broad, his stubby fingers wielded the pencil with dexterity and exquisite precision.

"My name is Odd Thomas."

He took his tongue into his mouth, tucked it into one cheek, and pressed his lips together.

"I'm staying in the guesthouse at the abbey."

Looking around at the room, I saw that the dozen framed pencil portraits decorating the walls were of this woman. Here she smiled; there she laughed; most often she appeared contemplative, serene.

In an especially compelling piece, she had been rendered full-face, eyes brimming bright, cheeks jeweled with tears. Her features had not been melodramatically distorted; instead, you could see that her anguish was great but also that she strove with some success to conceal the depth of it.

Such a complex emotional state, rendered so subtly, suggested that my praise of Jacob's talent had been inadequate. The woman's emotion was palpable.

The condition of the artist's heart, while he had labored on this portrait, was also evident, somehow infused into the work. Drawing, he had been in torment.

"Who is she?" I asked.

"Do you float away when the dark comes?" He had only a mild speech impediment. His thick tongue apparently wasn't fissured.

"I'm not sure I know what you mean, Jacob."

Too shy to look at me, he continued drawing, and after a silence said, "I seen the ocean some days, but not that day."

"What day, Jacob?"

"The day they went and the bell rung."

Although already I sensed a rhythm to his conversation and knew that rhythm was a sign of meaning, I couldn't find the beat.

He was willing to count cadence alone. "Jacob's scared he'll float wrong when the dark comes."

From the pencil case, he selected a new instrument.

"Jacob's gotta float where the bell rung."

As he paused in his work and studied the unfinished portrait, his tragic features were beautified by a look of intense affection.

"Never seen where the bell rung, and the ocean it moves, and it moves, so where the bell rung is gone somewhere new."

Sadness captured his face, but the look of affection did not entirely retreat.

For a while, he chewed worriedly on his lower lip.

When he set to work with the new pencil, he said, "And the dark is gonna come with the dark."

"What do you mean, Jacob—the dark is going to come with the dark?"

He glanced at the snow-scrubbed window. "When there's no light again, the dark is gonna come, too. Maybe. Maybe the dark is gonna come, too."

"When there's no light again—that means tonight?"

Jacob nodded. "Maybe tonight."

"And the other dark that's coming with the night . . . do you mean death, Jacob?"

He thrust his tongue between his teeth again. After rolling the pencil in his fingers to find the right grip, he set to work once more on the portrait.

I wondered if I had been too straightforward when I had used the word *death*. Perhaps he expressed himself obliquely not because that was the only way his mind worked, but because speaking about some subjects too directly disturbed him.

After a while, he said, "He wants me dead."

CHAPTER 21

WITH LEAD HE SHADED LOVE INTO THE woman's eyes.

As one who had no talent except for magic at the griddle and grill, I watched with respect as Jacob created her from memory, as he made real on paper what was in his mind and what was evidently lost to him except by the grace of his art.

When I had given him time to proceed but had gotten not another word from him, I said, "Who wants you dead, Jacob?"

"The Neverwas."

"Help me understand."

"The Neverwas came once to see, and Jacob was full of the black, and the Neverwas said, *'Let him die.'*"

"He came here to this room?"

Jacob shook his head. "A long time ago the Neverwas came, before the ocean and the bell and the floating away."

"Why do you call him the Neverwas?"

"That's his name."

"He must have another name."

"No. He's the Neverwas, and we don't care."

"I never heard anyone named the Neverwas before."

Jacob said, "Never heard no one named the Odd Thomas before."

"All right. Fair enough."

Employing an X-Acto knife, Jacob shaved the point on the pencil.

Watching him, I wished that I could whittle my dull brain to a sharper point. If only I could understand something about the scheme of simple metaphors in which he spoke, I might be able to crack the code of his conversation.

I had made some progress, figuring out that when he said "the dark is gonna come with the dark," he meant that death was coming tonight or some night soon.

Although his drawing ability made him a savant, that was the extent of his special talent. Jacob wasn't clairvoyant. His warning of oncoming death was not a presentiment.

He had seen something, heard something, *knew* something that I had not seen, had not heard, did not know. His conviction that death loomed was based on hard evidence, not on supernatural perception.

Now that the pencil wood had been cut away, he put down the X-Acto knife and used a sandpaper block to sharpen the point of the lead.

Brooding about the riddle that was Jacob, I stared at the snow falling thicker and faster than ever past the window, so thick that maybe you could drown out there, trying to breathe but your lungs filling up with snow.

"Jacob's dumb," he said, "but not stupid."

When I shifted my attention from the window, I discovered he was looking at me for the first time.

"That must be another Jacob," I said. "I don't see dumb here."

At once he shifted his eyes to the pencil, and he put aside the sandpaper block. In a different, singsong voice, he said, "Dumb as a duck run down by a truck."

"Dumb doesn't draw like Michelangelo."

"Dumb as a cow knocked flat by a plow."

"You're repeating something you heard, aren't you?"

"Dumb as a mutt with his nose up his butt."

"No more," I said softly. "Okay? No more."

"There's lots more."

"I don't want to hear. It hurts me to hear this."

He seemed surprised. "Hurts why?"

"Because I like you, Jake. I think you're special."

He was silent. His hands trembled, and the pencil ticked against the table. He glanced at me, heartbreaking vulnerability in his eyes. He shyly looked away.

"Who said those things to you?" I asked.

"You know. Kids."

"Kids here at Saint Bart's?"

"No. Kids before the ocean and the bell and the floating away."

In this world where too many are willing to see only the light that is visible, never the Light Invisible, we have a daily darkness that is night, and we encounter another darkness from time to time that is death, the deaths of those we love, but the third and most constant darkness that is with us every day, at all hours of every day, is the darkness of the mind, the pettiness and mean-ness and hatred, which we have invited into ourselves, and which we pay out with generous interest.

"Before the ocean and the bell and the floating away," Jacob repeated.

"Those kids were just jealous. Jake, see, you could do something better than anything they could do."

"Not Jacob."

"Yes, you."

He sounded dubious: "What could I do better?"

"Draw. Of all the things they could do that you couldn't, there wasn't one thing they could do as well as you can draw. So they were jealous and called you names and made fun of you—to make themselves feel better."

He stared at his hands until the tremors stopped, until the pencil was steady, and then he continued working on the portrait.

His resiliency was not the resiliency of the dumb but of a lamb who can remember hurt but cannot sustain the anger or the bitterness that brittles the heart.

"Not stupid," he said. "Jacob knows what he seen."

I waited, then said, "What did you see, Jake?"

"Them."

"Who?"

"Not scared of them."

"Of who?"

"Them and the Neverwas. Not scared of them. Jacob's only scared he'll float wrong when the dark comes. Never seen where the bell rung, wasn't there when the bell rung, and the ocean it moves, it always moves, so where the bell rung is gone somewhere new."

We had come full circle. In fact I felt as if I had been on a merry-go-round too long.

My wristwatch read 10:16.

I was willing to go around and around some more, in the hope that I would be enlightened instead of dizzied.

Sometimes enlightenment descends upon you when you least expect it: like the time that I and a smiling Japanese chiropractor, who was also an herbalist, were hanging side by side, bound with rope, from a rack in a meat locker.

Some difficult guys with no respect for alternative medicine or human life were intending to return to the meat locker and torture us to get information they wanted. They were not seeking the most effective herbal formula to cure athlete's foot or anything like that. They wanted to tear from us information regarding the whereabouts of a large sum of cash.

Our situation was made more dire by the fact that the difficult guys were mistaken; we didn't have the information they wanted. After hours of torturing us, all they would get for their effort would be the fun of hearing us scream, which probably would have been all right with them if they'd also had a case of beer and some chips.

The chiropractor-herbalist spoke maybe forty-seven words of English, and I only spoke two words of Japanese that I could recall under pressure. Although we were highly motivated to escape before our captors returned with an array of pliers, a blowtorch, cattle prods, a CD of the Village People singing Wagner, and other fiendish instruments, I didn't think we could conspire successfully when my two words of Japanese were *sushi* and *sake*.

For half an hour, our relationship was marked by my sputtering frustration and by his unshakable patience. To my surprise, with a series of ingenious facial expressions, eight words that included *spaghetti* and *linguini* and *Houdini* and *tricky,* he managed to make me understand that in addition to being a chiropractor and an herbalist, he was a contortionist who had once had a nightclub act when he had been younger.

He was not as limber as in his youth, but with my cooperation, he managed to use various parts of my body as stepping-stones to eel backward and up to the rack from which we were suspended, where he chewed through a knot and freed himself, then freed me.

We stay in touch. From time to time he sends me pictures from Tokyo, mostly of his kids. And I send him little boxes of dried, chocolate-covered California dates, which he adores.

Now, sitting across the table from Jacob, I figured that if I could be even half as patient as the smiling chiropractor-herbalist-contortionist, and if I kept in mind that to my Japanese friend I must have seemed as impenetrable as Jacob seemed to me, I might in time not only puzzle out the meaning of Jacob's oblique conversation but might also tease from him the thing that he seemed to know, the vital detail, that would help me understand what terror was fast approaching St. Bartholomew's.

Unfortunately, Jacob was no longer talking. When I had first sat down at the table, he'd been mum. Now he was mum to twenty powers of ten. Nothing existed for him except the drawing on which he worked.

I tried more conversational gambits than a lonely logomaniac at a singles' bar. Some people like to hear themselves talk, but I like to hear myself silent. After five minutes, I exhausted my tolerance for the sound of my voice.

Although Jacob sat here in the tick of time that bridges past and future, he had cast his mind back to another day before the ocean and the bell and the floating away, whatever that might mean.

Rather than waste time pecking at him until I wore my beak down to a nub, I got to my feet and said, "I'll come back this afternoon, Jacob."

If he looked forward to the pleasure of my company, he did a superb job of concealing his delight.

I scanned the framed portraits on the walls and said, "She was your mother, wasn't she?"

Not even that question drew a reaction from him. Painstakingly, he restored her to life with the power of the pencil.

CHAPTER 22

A T THE NORTHWEST CORNER OF THE SECOND floor, Sister Miriam was on duty at the nurses' station.

If Sister Miriam grips her lower lip with two fingers and pulls it down to reveal the pink inner surface, you will see a tattoo in blue ink, *Deo gratias,* which is Latin for "Thanks be to God."

This is not a statement of commitment required of nuns. If it were, the world would probably have even fewer nuns than it does now.

Long before she ever considered the life of the convent, Sister Miriam had been a social worker in Los Angeles, an employee of the federal government. She worked with teenage girls from disadvantaged families, striving to rescue them from gang life and other horrors.

Most of this I know from Sister Angela, the mother superior, because Sister Miriam not only doesn't toot her own horn—she does not have a horn to toot.

As a challenge to a girl named Jalissa, an intelligent fourteen-year-old who had great promise but who had been on the gang path and about to acquire a gang tattoo, Miriam had said, *Girl, what do I have to do to make you think how you're trading a full life for a withered one? I talk sense to you, but it doesn't matter. I cry for you, you're amused. Do I have to bleed for you to get your attention?*

She then offered a deal: If Jalissa would promise, for thirty days, to stay away from friends who were in a gang or who hung out with a gang, and if she would not get a gang tattoo the following day as she intended, Miriam would take her at her word and would have her own inner lip tattooed with what she called "a symbol of *my* gang."

An audience of twelve at-risk girls, including Jalissa, gathered to watch, wince, and squirm as the tattooist performed his needlework.

Miriam refused topical anesthetics. She had chosen the tender tissue of the inner lip because the cringe factor would impress the girls. She bled. Tears flowed, but she made not one sound of pain.

That level of commitment and the inventive ways she expressed it made Miriam an effective counselor. These years later, Jalissa has two college degrees and is an executive in the hotel industry.

Miriam rescued many other girls from lives of crime, squalor, and depravity. You might expect that one day she would become the subject of a movie with Halle Berry in the title role.

Instead, a parent complained about the spiritual element that was part of Miriam's counseling strategy. As a government employee, she was sued by an organization of activist attorneys on the grounds of separation of church and state. They wanted her to cut spiritual references from her counseling, and they insisted that *Deo gratias* be either obscured with another tattoo or expunged. They believed that in the privacy of counseling sessions, she would peel down her lip and corrupt untold numbers of young girls.

You might think this case would be laughed out of court, but you would be as wrong as you were about the Halle Berry movie. The court sided with the activists.

Ordinarily, government employees are not easily canned. Their unions will fight ferociously to save the job of an alcoholic clerk who shows up at work only three days a week and then spends a third of his workday in a toilet stall, tippling from a flask or vomiting.

Miriam was an embarrassment to her union and received only token support. Eventually she accepted a modest severance package.

For a few years thereafter, she held less satisfying jobs before she heard the call to the life she now leads.

Standing behind the counter at the nurses' station, reviewing inventory sheets, she looked up as I approached and said, "Well, here comes young Mr. Thomas in his usual clouds of mystery."

Unlike Sister Angela, Abbot Bernard, and Brother Knuckles, she had not been told of my special gift. My universal key and privileges intrigued her, however, and she seemed to intuit something of my true nature.

"I'm afraid you mistake my perpetual state of bafflement for an air of mystery, Sister Miriam."

If they ever did make a movie about her, the producers would hew closer to the truth if they cast Queen Latifah instead of Halle Berry. Sister Miriam has Latifah's size and royal presence, and perhaps even more charisma than the actress.

She regards me always with friendly but gimlet-eyed interest, as though she knows that I'm getting away with something even if it's not something terribly naughty.

"Thomas is an English name," she said, "but there must be Irish blood in your family, considering how you spread blarney as smooth as warm butter on a muffin."

"No Irish blood, I'm afraid. Although if you knew my family, you would agree that I come from *strange* blood."

"You're not looking at a surprised nun, are you, dear?"

"No, Sister. You don't look at all surprised. Could I ask you a few questions about Jacob, in Room Fourteen?"

"The woman he draws is his mother."

From time to time, Sister Miriam seems just a little psychic herself.

"His mother. That's what I figured. When did she die?"

"Twelve years ago, of cancer, when he was thirteen. He was very close to her. She seems to have been a devoted, loving person."

"What about his father?"

Distress puckered her plum-dark face. "I don't believe he was ever in the picture. The mother never married. Before her death, she arranged for Jacob's care at another church facility. When we opened, he was transferred here."

"We were talking for a while, but he's not easy to follow."

Now I *was* looking at a wimple-framed look of surprise. "Jacob talked with you, dear?"

"Is that unusual?" I asked.

"He doesn't talk with most people. He's so shy. I've been able to bring him out of his shell. . . ." She leaned across the counter toward me, searching my eyes, as if she had seen a fishy secret swim through them and hoped to hook it. "I shouldn't be surprised that he'll speak with you. Not at all surprised. You've got something that makes everyone open up, don't you, dear?"

"Maybe it's because I'm a good listener," I said.

"No," she said. "No, that's not it. Not that you aren't a good listener. You're an exceptionally good listener, dear."

"Thank you, Sister."

"Have you ever seen a robin on a lawn, head cocked, listening for worms moving all but silently under the grass? If you were beside the robin, dear, you would get the worm first every time."

"That's quite an image. I'll have to give it a try come spring. Anyway, his conversation is kind of enigmatic. He kept talking about a day when he wasn't allowed to go to the ocean but, quote, 'they went and the bell rung.'"

"'Never seen where the bell rung,'" Sister Miriam quoted, "'and the ocean it moves, so where the bell rung is gone somewhere new.'"

"Do you know what he means?" I asked.

"His mother's ashes were buried at sea. They rang a bell when they scattered them, and Jacob was told about it."

I heard his voice in memory: *Jacob's only scared he'll float wrong when the dark comes.*

"Ah," I said, feeling just a little Sherlocky, after all. "He worries that he doesn't know the spot where her ashes were scattered, and he knows the ocean is always moving, so he's afraid he won't be able to find her when he dies."

"The poor boy. I've told him a thousand times she's in Heaven, and they'll be together again one day, but the mental picture he has of her floating away in the sea is too vivid to dispel."

I wanted to go back to Room 14 and hug him. You can't fix things with a hug, but you can't make them any worse, either.

"What is the Neverwas?" I asked. "He's afraid of the Neverwas."

Sister Miriam frowned. "I haven't heard him use the term. The Neverwas?"

"Jacob says he was full of the black—"

"The black?"

"I don't know what he means. He said he was full of the black, and the Neverwas came and said, 'Let him die.' This was a long time ago, 'before the ocean and the bell and the floating away.'"

"Before his mother died," she interpreted.

"Yes. That's right. But he's still afraid of the Neverwas."

She trained upon me that gimlet-eyed stare again, as if she hoped she might pierce my cloud of mystery and pop it as if it were a balloon. "Why are you so interested in Jacob, dear?"

I couldn't tell her that my lost girl, my Stormy, had made contact with me from the Other Side and had made known, through the instrument of Justine, another sweet lost girl, that Jacob possessed information concerning the source of the violence that would soon befall the school, perhaps before the next dawn.

Well, I could have told her, I guess, but I didn't want to take a chance that she would pull down my lower lip with the expectation that tattooed on the inside of it would be the word *lunatic*.

Consequently, I said, "His art. The portraits on his wall. I thought they might be pictures of his mother. The drawings are so full of love. I wondered what it must be like to love your mother so much."

"What a peculiar thing to say."

"Isn't it?"

"Don't you love your mother, dear?"

"I guess so. A hard, sharp, thorny kind of love that might be pity more than anything else."

I was leaning against the counter, and she took one of my hands in both of hers, squeezed it gently. "I'm a good listener, too, dear. You want to sit down with me for a while and talk?"

I shook my head. "She doesn't love me or anyone, doesn't believe in love. She's afraid of love, of the obligations that come with it. Herself is all she needs, the admirer in the mirror. And that's the story. There's really nothing more to sit down and talk about."

The truth is that my mother is a funhouse full of scares, such a twisted spirit and psychological mare's nest that Sister Miriam and I could have talked about her without stop until the spring equinox.

But with the morning almost gone, with seven bodachs in the recreation room, with living boneyards stalking the storm, with Death opening the door to a luge chute and inviting me to go for a bobsled ride, I didn't have time to put on a victim suit and tell the woeful tale of my sorrowful childhood. Neither the time nor the inclination.

"Well, I'm always here," said Sister Miriam. "Think of me as Oprah with a vow of poverty. Anytime you want to pour out your soul, I'm here, and you don't have to hold the emotion through commercial breaks."

I smiled. "You're a credit to the nun profession."

"And you," she said, "are still standing there in clouds of mystery."

As I turned from the nurses' station, my attention was drawn to movement at the farther end of the hall. A hooded figure stood in the open stairwell door, where he had apparently been watching me as I talked with Sister Miriam. Aware that he'd been seen, he retreated, letting the door fall shut.

The hood concealed the face, or at least that was the story I tried to sell myself. Although I was inclined to believe that the observer had been Brother Leopold, the suspicious novice with the sunny Iowa face, I was pretty sure the tunic had been black rather than gray.

I hurried to the end of the hall, stepped into the stairwell, and held my breath. Not a sound.

Although the convent on the third floor was forbidden to me and to everyone but the sisters, I ascended to the landing and peered up the last flight of stairs. They were deserted.

No imminent threat loomed, yet my heart raced. My mouth had gone dry. The back of my neck was stippled with cold sweat.

I was still trying to sell myself on the idea that the hood had concealed the face, but I wasn't buying.

Plunging two steps at a time, wishing I were not in my stocking feet, which slipped on the stone, I went down to the ground floor. I opened the stairwell door, looked out, and did not see anyone.

I descended to the basement, hesitated, opened the door at the foot of the stairs, and halted on the threshold, listening.

A long hallway led the length of the old abbey. A second hall crossed the first at midpoint, but I couldn't see into it from where I stood. Down here were the Kit Kat Katacombs, the garage, electrical vaults, machinery rooms, and storerooms. I would need a lot of time to investigate all those spaces.

Regardless of how long and thoroughly I searched, I doubted

that I would find a lurking monk. And if I did find the phantom, I would probably wish that I had not gone looking for him.

When he had been standing in the open stairwell door, a ceiling light had shown down directly on him. The hoods on the monks' tunics are not as dramatic as the hood on a medieval cowl. The fabric does not overhang the forehead sufficiently to cast an identity-concealing shadow, especially not in a direct fall of light.

The figure in the stairwell had been faceless. And worse than faceless. The light spilling into the hood had found nothing there to reflect it, only a terrible black emptiness.

CHAPTER 23

MY IMMEDIATE REACTION TO HAVING SEEN Death himself was to get something to eat.

I had skipped breakfast. If Death had taken me before I'd had something tasty for lunch, I would have been really, really angry with myself.

Besides, I couldn't function properly on an empty stomach. My thinking was probably clouded by plunging blood sugar. Had I eaten breakfast, perhaps Jacob would have made more sense to me.

The convent kitchen is large and institutional. Nevertheless, it's a cozy space, most likely because it is always saturated with mouthwatering aromas.

When I entered, the air was redolent of cinnamon, brown sugar, baked pork chops simmering with sliced apples, and a host of other delicious smells that made me weak in the knees.

The eight sisters on the culinary detail, all with shining faces and smiles, a few with flour smudges on their cheeks, some with their tunic sleeves rolled back a turn or two, all wearing blue aprons over their white habits, were busy at many tasks. Two were singing, and their lilting voices made the most of a charming melody.

I felt as if I had wandered into an old movie and that Julie Andrews, as a nun, might sweep into the room, singing to a sweet little church mouse perched on the back of her hand.

When I asked Sister Regina Marie if I could make a sandwich, she insisted on preparing it for me. Wielding a knife with a dexterity and pleasure almost unseemly for a nun, she sliced two slabs of bread from a plump loaf, carved a stack of thin slices of beef from a cold roast, lathered one piece of bread with mustard, the other with mayonnaise. She assembled beef, Swiss cheese, lettuce, tomato, chopped olives, and bread into a teetering marvel, pressed it flatter with one hand, quartered it, plated it, added a pickle, and presented it to me in the time it took me to wash my hands at the pot sink.

The kitchen offers stools here and there at counters, where you can have a cup of coffee or eat without being underfoot. I sought one of these—and came across Rodion Romanovich.

The bearish Russian was working at a long counter on which stood ten sheet cakes in long pans. He was icing them.

Near him on the granite counter lay the volume about poisons and famous poisoners in history. I noticed a bookmark inserted at about page fifty.

When he saw me, he glowered and indicated a stool near him.

Because I'm an amiable fellow and loath to insult anyone, I find it awkward to decline an invitation, even if it comes from a possibly homicidal Russian with too much curiosity about my reasons for being a guest of the abbey.

"How is your spiritual revitalization proceeding?" Romano-vich asked.

"Slow but sure."

"Since we do not have cactuses here in the Sierra, Mr. Thomas, what will you be shooting?"

"Not all fry cooks meditate to gunfire, sir." I took a bite of the sandwich. Fabulous. "Some prefer to bludgeon things."

With his attention devoted to the application of icing to the first of the ten cakes, he said, "I myself find that baking calms the mind and allows for contemplation."

"So you made the cakes, not just the icing?"

"That is correct. This is my best recipe . . . orange-and-almond cake with dark-chocolate frosting."

"Sounds delicious. So to date, how many people have you killed with it?"

"I long ago lost count, Mr. Thomas. But they all died happy."

Sister Regina Marie brought a glass of Coca-Cola for me, and I thanked her, and she said she had added two drops of vanilla to the Coke because she knew I preferred it that way.

When the sister departed, Romanovich said, "You are univer-sally liked."

"No, not really, sir. They're nuns. They have to be nice to everyone."

Romanovich's brow seemed to include a hydraulic mechanism that allowed it to beetle farther over his deep-set eyes when his mood darkened. "I am usually suspicious of people who are universally liked."

"In addition to being an imposing figure," I said, "you're surprisingly solemn for a Hoosier."

"I am a Russian by birth. We are sometimes a solemn people."

"I keep forgetting your Russian background. You've lost so much of your accent, people might think you're Jamaican."

"You may be surprised that I have never been mistaken for one."

He finished frosting the first cake, slid it aside, and pulled another pan in front of him.

I said, "You do know what a Hoosier is, don't you?"

"A Hoosier is a person who is a native of or an inhabitant of the state of Indiana."

"I'll bet the definition reads that way word for word in the dictionary."

He said nothing. He just frosted.

"Since you're a native Russian and not currently an inhabitant of Indiana, you're not at the moment really a Hoosier."

"I am an expatriate Hoosier, Mr. Thomas. When in time I return to Indianapolis, I will once more be a full and complete Hoosier."

"Once a Hoosier, always a Hoosier."

"That is correct."

The pickle had a nice crunch. I wondered if Romanovich had added a few drops of anything lethal to the brine in the pickle jar. Well, too late. I took another bite of the dill.

"Indianapolis," I said, "has a robust public library system."

"Yes, it does."

"As well as eight universities or colleges with libraries of their own."

Without looking up from the cake, he said, "You are in your stocking feet, Mr. Thomas."

"The better to sneak up on people. With all those libraries, there must be a lot of jobs for librarians in Indianapolis."

"The competition for our services is positively cut-throat. If you wear zippered rubber boots and enter by the mud room at the back of the convent, off the kitchen, you make less mess for the sisters."

"I was mortified at the mess I made, sir. I'm afraid I didn't have the foresight to bring a pair of zippered rubber boots."

"How peculiar. You strike me as a young man who is usually prepared for anything."

"Not really, sir. Mostly I make it up as I go along. So at which of those many Indianapolis libraries do you work?"

"The Indiana State Library opposite the Capitol, at one-forty North Senate Avenue. The facility houses over thirty-four thousand volumes about Indiana or by Indiana writers. The library and the genealogy department are open Monday through Friday, eight o'clock until four-thirty, eight-thirty until four on Saturday. Closed Sunday, as well as state and federal holidays. Tours are available by appointment."

"That's exactly right, sir."

"Of course."

"The third Saturday in May," I said, "at the Shelby County Fairgrounds—I think that's the most exciting time of the year in Indianapolis. Don't you agree, sir?"

"No, I do not agree. The third Saturday in May is the Shelby County Blue River Dulcimer Festival. If you think local and national dulcimer players giving concerts and workshops is exciting, instead of merely charming, then you are an even more peculiar young man than I have heretofore thought."

I shut up for a while and finished my sandwich.

As I was licking my fingers, Rodion Romanovich said, "You do know what a dulcimer is, do you not, Mr. Thomas?"

"A dulcimer," I said, "is a trapezoidal zither with metal strings that are struck with light hammers."

He seemed amused, in spite of his dour expression. "I will wager the definition reads that way word for word in the dictionary."

I said nothing, just licked the rest of my fingers.

"Mr. Thomas, did you know that in an experiment with a human observer, subatomic particles behave differently from the way they behave when the experiment is unobserved while in progress and the results are examined, instead, only after the fact?"

"Sure. Everybody knows that."

He raised one bushy eyebrow. "Everybody, you say. Well, then you realize what this signifies."

I said, "At least on a subatomic level, human will can in part shape reality."

Romanovich gave me a look that I would have liked to capture in a snapshot.

I said, "But what does any of this have to do with cake?"

"Quantum theory tells us, Mr. Thomas, that every point in the universe is intimately connected to every other point, regardless of apparent distance. In some mysterious way, any point on a planet in a distant galaxy is as close to me as you are."

"No offense, but I don't really feel that close to you, sir."

"This means that information or objects, or even people, should be able to move instantly between here and New York City, or indeed between here and that planet in another galaxy."

"What about between here and Indianapolis?"

"That, too."

"Wow."

"We just do not yet understand the quantum structure of reality sufficiently to achieve such miracles."

"Most of us can't figure how to program a video recorder, so we probably have a long way to go on this here-to-another-galaxy thing."

He finished frosting the second cake. "Quantum theory gives us reason to believe that on a deep structural level, every point in the universe is in some ineffable way the *same* point. You have a smear of mayonnaise at the corner of your mouth."

I found it with a finger, licked the finger. "Thank you, sir."

"The interconnectedness of every point in the universe is so complete that if an enormous flock of birds bursts into flight from a marsh in Spain, the disturbance of the air caused by their wings will contribute to weather changes in Los Angeles. And, yes, Mr. Thomas, in Indianapolis, as well."

With a sigh, I said, "I still can't figure out what this has to do with cake."

"Nor can I," said Romanovich. "It has to do not with cake but with you and me."

I puzzled over that statement. When I met his utterly unreadable eyes, I felt as if they were taking me apart on a subatomic level.

Concerned that something was smeared at the other corner of my mouth, I wiped with a finger, found neither mayonnaise nor mustard.

"Well," I said, "I'm stumped again."

"Did God bring you here, Mr. Thomas?"

I shrugged. "He didn't stop me from coming."

"I believe God brought me here," Romanovich said. "Whether God brought you here or not is of profound interest to me."

"I'm pretty sure it wasn't Satan who brought me here," I assured him. "The guy who drove me was an old friend, and he doesn't have horns."

I got off the stool, reached past the cake pans, and picked up the book that he had taken from the library.

"This isn't about poisons and famous poisoners," I said.

The true title of the book did not reassure me—*The Blade of the Assassin: The Role of Daggers, Dirks, and Stilettos in the Deaths of Kings and Clergymen.*

"I have a wide-ranging interest in history," said Romanovich.

The color of the binding cloth appeared to be identical to that of the book that he had been holding in the library. I had no doubt this was the same volume.

"Would you like a piece of cake?" he asked.

Putting the book down, I said, "Maybe later."

"There may not be any left later. Everyone loves my orange-and-almond cake."

"I get hives from almonds," I claimed, and reminded myself to report this whopper to Sister Angela, to prove that, in spite of what she believed, I could be as despicable a liar as the next guy.

I carried my empty glass and bare plate to the main sink and began to rinse them.

Sister Regina Marie appeared as if from an Arabian lamp. "I'll wash them, Oddie."

As she attacked the dish with a soapy sponge, I said, "So Mr. Romanovich has baked quite a lot of sheet cakes for the lunch dessert."

"For dinner," she said. "They smell so good that I'm afraid they're decadent."

"He doesn't strike me as the kind of person who would enjoy a culinary pastime."

"Perhaps he doesn't strike you that way," she agreed, "but he loves to bake. And he's very talented."

"You mean you've eaten his desserts before?"

"Many times. You have, too."

"I don't believe so."

"The lemon-syrup cake with coconut icing last week. That was by Mr. Romanovich. And the week before, the polenta cake with almonds and pistachios."

I said, "Oh."

"And surely you remember the banana-and-lime cake with the icing made from lime-juice reduction."

I nodded. "Surely. Yes, I remember. Delicious."

A sudden great tolling of bells shook through the old abbey, as though Rodion Romanovich had arranged for this clangorous performance to mock me for being so gullible.

The bells were rung for a variety of services in the new abbey, but seldom here, and never at this hour.

Frowning, Sister Regina Marie looked up at the ceiling, and then in the direction of the convent church and bell tower. "Oh, dear. Do you think Brother Constantine is back?"

Brother Constantine, the dead monk, the infamous suicide who lingers stubbornly in this world.

"Excuse me, Sister," I said, and I hurried out of the kitchen, digging in a pocket of my jeans for my universal key.

CHAPTER 24

AFTER THE CONSTRUCTION OF THE NEW ABBEY, the church in the former abbey had not been deconsecrated. Twice every day, a priest came downhill to say Mass; half the sisters attended the first service, half the second.

The late Brother Constantine almost exclusively haunted the new abbey and the new church, though he twice made memorable appearances, sans bells, at the school. He had hanged himself in the new bell tower, and when previously his restless spirit had raised a tolling, the clamor had been in that same structure.

Heeding my warning to Sister Angela, I did not go out into the storm, but followed a ground-floor hallway into the former novitiate wing, and entered the sacristy by the back door.

As loud as the bells had seemed before, they were twice that loud when I stepped out of the sacristy into the church. The vaulted ceiling reverberated not with a celebratory tintinnabulation, not with a glory-of-Christmas sound, not with the joyful ringing that follows a wedding. This was an angry tumult of bronze clappers, a pandemoniacal bong-and-clang.

By the murky stormlight that penetrated the stained-glass windows, I stepped down through the choir stalls. I passed through the sanctuary gate and hurried along the center aisle of the nave, sliding a little in my stocking feet.

My haste did not mean that I looked forward with pleasure to another encounter with the spirit of Brother Constantine. He is about as much fun as strep throat.

Because this noisy manifestation was occurring here instead of in the tower where he had killed himself, it might be in some way related to the violence that was bearing down on the children of St. Bart's School. I had learned virtually nothing about that impending event thus far, and I hoped that Brother Constantine would have a clue or two for me.

In the narthex, I flicked a light switch, turned right, and came to the bell-tower door, which was kept locked out of concern that one of the more physically able children might slip out of supervision and wander this far. Were a child to get to the top of the tower, he would be at risk of falling out of the belfry or down the stairs.

As I turned my key in the lock, I warned myself that I was as susceptible to a fatal plunge as was a wandering child. I didn't mind dying—and being reunited with Stormy, whether in Heaven or in the unknown great adventure she calls "service"— but not until the threat to the children had been identified and met.

If I failed this time, if some were spared but others died, as at the mall during the shooting spree, I would have no place to flee that could promise more solitude and peace than a mountain monastery. And you already know what a crock *that* promise turned out to be.

The spiral staircase in the tower was not heated. The rubber-ized treads felt cold under my stocking feet, but they were not slippery.

Here the bedlam of bells caused the walls to resonate like a drum membrane responding to peals of thunder. As I climbed, I slid my hand along the curved wall, and the plaster hummed under my palm.

By the time I reached the top of the stairs, my teeth discretely vibrated like thirty-two tuning forks. The hairs in my nose tick-led, and my ears ached. I could feel the boom of the bells in my bones.

This was an auditory experience for which every thrashed-out heavy-metal rhapsodist had been searching all his life: tuned-bronze walls of sound crashing down in deafening avalanches.

I stepped into the belfry, where the air was freezing.

Before me was not a three-bell carillon like the one at the new abbey. This tower was wider, the belfry more spacious than the one in the building upslope. In earlier decades, the monks clearly had taken more exuberant pleasure in their tolling, for they had constructed a two-level, five-bell carillon, and the bells were enor-mous, as well.

No ropes or crankwheels were required to swing these bronze behemoths. Brother Constantine rode them as if he were a rodeo cowboy leaping from one back to another among a herd of buck-ing bulls.

His restless spirit, energized by frustration and fury, had be-come a raging poltergeist. An immaterial entity, he had no weight or leverage with which to move the heavy bells, but from him throbbed concentric waves of power as invisible to other people as was the dead monk himself, though visible to me.

As these pulses washed through the belfry, the suspended bronze forms swung wildly. The immense clappers hammered out a more violent knelling than their makers had intended or imagined possible.

I could not feel those waves of power as they washed over me. A poltergeist cannot harm a living person either by touch or directly by his emanations.

If one of the bells broke loose of its mountings and fell on me, however, I nonetheless would be squashed.

Brother Constantine had been gentle in life, so he could not have become evil in death. If he unintentionally harmed me, he would be cast into a deeper despair than the one he currently endured.

In spite of his deeply felt remorse, I would remain squashed.

Back and forth along the carillon, up and down and up the two levels, the dead monk capered. Although he didn't appear demonic, I do not feel that I am being unfair to him by using the word *demented*.

Any lingering spirit is irrational, having lost his way in the vertical of sacred order. A poltergeist is irrational *and* pissed.

Warily, I moved along the walkway that encircled the bells. They swung in wider arcs than usual, intruding on the pathway and forcing me to remain near the perimeter of the space.

Columns stood on the waist-high outer wall, supporting the overhanging roof. Between the columns, on a clear day, were views of the new abbey, of the rising and descending slopes of the Sierra, of a pristine vastness of forest.

The blizzard screened from sight the new abbey and the forest. I could see only the slate roofs and the cobblestone courtyards of the old abbey immediately below.

The storm shrieked as before, but it could not be heard above the booming bells. Wind-harried twists of snow chased one another through the belfry, and out again.

As I slowly circled him, Brother Constantine was aware that I had arrived. Like a robed and hooded goblin, he leaped from bell to bell, his attention always on me.

His eyes bulged grotesquely, not as they had in life, but as the strangling noose had caused them to bulge when his neck had snapped and his trachea had collapsed.

I stopped with my back turned to one of the columns and spread my arms wide, both palms turned up, as if to ask, *What's the point of this, Brother? How does this benefit you?*

Although he knew what I meant, he did not want to contemplate the ultimate ineffectiveness of his rage. He looked away from me and flung himself more frenetically through the bells.

I shoved my hands in my pockets and yawned. I assumed a bored expression. When he looked at me again, I yawned exaggeratedly and shook my head as an actor does when playing to the back rows, as though sadly expressing my disappointment in him.

Here was proof that even in its most desperate hours, when the bones are gnawed by a sharp-toothed chill and the nerves fray in fear of what the next circuit of the clock may bring, life retains a comic quality. The clangor had reduced me to a mime.

This swelling of bells proved to be Brother Constantine's final flare of rage. The concentric waves of power stopped radiating from him, and at once the bells swung less violently, their arcs rapidly diminishing.

Although my socks were thick and made for winter sports, an

icy cold pressed through them from the stone floor. My teeth began to chatter as I strove to continue feigning boredom.

Soon the clappers bumped gently against the bronze, producing soft, clear, mellow notes that were the essential theme music for a melancholy mood.

The voice of the wind did not return in a howling rush because my brutalized ears were still thrumming with the memory of the recent cacophony.

Like one of those masters of martial mayhem in *Crouching Tiger, Hidden Dragon,* who could leap gracefully to rooftops and then descend in an aerial ballet, Brother Constantine glided down from the bells and landed near me on the belfry deck.

He no longer chose to be goggle-eyed. His face was as it had been before the cinching noose, though perhaps he had never looked this mournful in life.

As I was about to speak to him, I became aware of movement on the farther side of the belfry, a dark presence glimpsed between the curves of silenced bronze, silhouetted against the stifled light of the snow-choked day.

Brother Constantine followed my gaze and seemed to identify the new arrival from what little could be seen. Although nothing in this world could harm him anymore, the dead monk shrank back as though in dread.

I had moved away from the head of the stairs, and as the figure circled the bells, it came between me and that sole exit from the belfry.

As my temporary deafness faded and as the cry of the wind rose like a chorus of angry voices, the figure emerged from behind the screening bells. Here was the black-habited monk whom I had seen in the open door to the stairwell, as I'd turned away from Sister Miriam at the nurses' station, little more than twenty minutes ago.

I was closer to him now than I had been then, but I could still see only blackness inside his hood, not the merest suggestion of a face. The wind billowed his tunic but revealed no feet, and at the ends of his sleeves, there were no hands to be seen.

Afforded more than a glimpse of him this time, I realized that his tunic was longer than those the brothers wore, that it trailed on the floor. The fabric was not as common as that from which the monks' habits were fashioned; it had the luster of silk.

He wore a necklace of human teeth strung like pearls, with three fingers, just bleached bones, pendant at the center.

Instead of a cloth cincture at the waist, to gather in the tunic and the scapular, he wore a woven cord of what appeared to be clean, shiny human hair.

He drifted toward me. Although I intended to stand my ground, I stepped back from him as he approached, as reluctant to make contact as was my dead companion, Brother Constantine.

CHAPTER 25

HAD NOT THE SOLES OF MY FEET BEEN STUNG by cold as sharp as needles, had not a burning kind of numbness begun to cramp my toes, I might have thought that I had never awakened to find the red light and the blue light of sheriff's-department vehicles twinkling in the frosted windows of my guesthouse bedroom, that I was still asleep and dreaming.

The great pendular lobes of bronze, to which fevered Freud would have attributed the sleaziest symbolic meaning, and the groin-vaulted ceiling of the belfry, which was also fraught with meaning not solely because of its name but also because of its curves and shadows, made the perfect landscape for a dream, surrounded by the virginal white of the frigid storm.

This minimalist figure of Death, robed and hooded, neither ripe with rot nor squirming with maggots as he would be in comic books and in cheesy slice-and-dice movies, but as clean as a dark polar wind, was as real as the Reaper in Bergman's *The Seventh Seal*. At the same time, he had the qualities of a threatening phantom in a nightmare, amorphous and unknowable, most sharply seen from the corner of the eye.

Death raised his right arm, and from the sleeve appeared a long pale hand, not skeletal but fully fleshed. Although a void remained within the hood, the hand reached toward me, and the finger pointed.

Now I was reminded of *A Christmas Carol* by Charles Dickens. Here was the last of the three spirits to visit the miserly master of the counting house, the ominous silent spirit that Scrooge named the Ghost of Christmas Yet to Come. The ghost had been what Scrooge called it but also something worse, because wherever else the future leads, it leads ultimately to death, the end that is present in my beginning and in yours.

From Death's left sleeve, another pale hand appeared, and this one held a rope, the end of which had been fashioned into a noose. The spirit—or whatever it might be—traded the noose from his left hand to his right, and raveled out an unlikely length of rope from within his tunic.

When he withdrew the loose end of the rope from his sleeve, he tossed it over the rocking bar that, when turned by a crankwheel at the bottom of the tower, would set the five-bell carillon to ringing. He fashioned a gallows knot with such ease that it seemed not like the skill of a seasoned executioner but like a good magician's sleight of hand.

All this had the feel of kabuki, that Japanese form of highly stylized theater. The surreal sets, the elaborate costumes, the bold masks, the wigs, the extravagant emotions, and the broad melo-dramatic gestures of the actors should make Japanese theater as laughable as America's brand of professional wrestling. Yet by some mysterious effect, to the knowledgeable audience, kabuki becomes as real as a razor drawn across a thumb.

In the silence of the bells, with the storm seeming to roar its approval of his performance, Death pointed at me, and I knew that he intended the noose for my neck.

Spirits cannot harm the living. This is our world, not theirs.

Death is not actually a figure that stalks the world in costume, collecting souls.

Both of those things were true, which meant that this menacing Reaper could not do me any harm.

Because my imagination is as rich as my bank account is empty, I could nevertheless imagine the coarse fibers of the rope against my throat, my Adam's apple cinched to sauce.

Taking courage from the fact that he was already dead, Brother Constantine stepped forward, as if to draw Death's attention and give me a chance to make a break for the stairs.

The monk leaped to the bells again, but he no longer could summon the rage required to produce psychokinetic phenomena. He appeared instead to be overcome by fear for me. He wrung his hands, and his mouth wrenched wide in a silent scream.

My confidence that no spirit could harm me was shaken by Brother Constantine's conviction that I was toast.

Although the Reaper was a simpler figure than the kaleidoscope of bones that had stalked me through the storm, I sensed that they were alike in that they were theatrical, mannered, self-conscious in a way that the lingering dead never are. Even a poltergeist at the summit of his wrath does not *design* his rampage for maximum effect on the living, has no intention of spooking anyone, but wants only to work off his frustration, his self-loathing, his rage at being stuck in a kind of purgatory between two worlds.

The dazzling transformations of the bone beast at the window had smacked of vanity: *Behold the wonder of me, stand in awe, and tremble.* Likewise, the Reaper moved as might a conceited dancer on a stage, ostentatious, in expectation of applause.

Vanity is strictly a human weakness. No animal is capable of vanity. People sometimes say cats are vain, but cats are haughty. They are confident of their superiority and do not crave admiration, as do vain men and women.

The lingering dead, though they might have been vain in life, have been stripped of vanity by the discovery of their mortality.

Now this Reaper made a mocking come-to-me gesture, as if I should be so intimidated by his fearsome appearance and his grandeur that I would put the noose around my neck and spare him the struggle to snare me.

The recognition that those two apparitions shared an all-too-human vanity, a conceit unseen in all that is truly otherworldly, was significant. But I didn't know *why.*

In response to his come-to-me gesture, I stepped back from him, and he flew at me with sudden ferocity.

Before I could raise an arm to block him, he got his right hand around my throat and, exhibiting inhuman strength, lifted me off the floor with one hand.

The Reaper's arm was so unnaturally long that I couldn't strike at him or claw at the perfect blackness that pooled within his hood. I was reduced to tearing at the hand that gripped me, trying to pry back his fingers.

Although his hand looked like flesh, flexed like flesh, I could not claw blood from it. My fingernails scraping across his pale skin produced the sound they would have raised from a slate chalkboard.

He slammed me against a column, and the back of my head rapped the stone. For a moment, the blizzard seemed to find its way inside my skull, and a whirl of white behind my eyes almost spun me away into an eternal winter.

When I kicked and kicked, my feet landed without effect in soft billows of black tunic, and his body, if one existed under those silken folds, seemed to have no more solidity than quicksand or than the sucking tar into which Jurassic behemoths had blundered to their destruction.

I gasped for breath and found it. He was holding me, not choking me, perhaps to ensure that, when I was discovered and hauled back into the belfry, the only marks on my throat and under my chin would be those left by the lethal snap of the rope.

As he pulled me away from the column, his left hand rose and tossed the noose, which floated toward me like a ring of dark smoke. I twisted my head away. The rope fell across my face, and back into his hand.

The moment he had succeeded in slipping the noose around my neck and had drawn it tight, he would pitch me out of the belfry, and I would ring the bells to announce my death.

I stopped ripping at his hand, which had me firmly yoked, and grabbed the loop of rope as he tried once more to fit me with that crude necktie.

Struggling to foil the noose, staring down into the emptiness of his hood, I heard myself croak, "I know you, don't I?"

That question, born of intuition, seemed to work magic, as if it were an incantation. Something began to form in the void where a face should have been.

He faltered in the struggle for the noose.

Encouraged, I said more certainly, "I know you."

Within the hood, the basic contours of a face began to take shape, like molten black plastic conforming to a die.

The countenance lacked sufficient detail to spark recognition, glistened darkly as the dim reflection of a face might glimmer and ripple in a night pond where no moonlight brightens the black water.

"Mother of God, I know you," I said, though intuition had still not given me a name.

My third insistence conjured greater dimension in the glossy black face before me, almost as though my words had spawned in him a guilt and an irresistible compulsion to confess his identity.

The Reaper turned his head from me. He threw me aside, and then tossed away the hangman's rope, which raveled down upon me as I collapsed onto the belfry deck.

In a silken black swirl, he sprang onto the parapet between two columns, hesitated there, and then flung himself into the snowstorm.

I thrust up from the floor even as he jumped, and I leaned over the parapet.

His tunic spread like wings, and he sailed down from the tower, landed with balletic grace upon the church roof, and at once flung himself toward the lower roof of the abbey.

Although he seemed to me to have been something other than a spirit, less supernatural than *un*natural, he dematerialized as fully as any ghost might, though in a manner that I had never seen before.

In flight, he seemed to come apart like a clay disk blasted by a skeet-shooter's shotgun. A million flakes of snow and a million fragments of the Reaper laced out into a black-and-white symmetrical pattern, a kaleidoscopic image in midair, which the wind respected only for an instant and then dissolved.

CHAPTER 26

I N THE GROUND-FLOOR RECEPTION LOUNGE, I SAT on the edge of a sofa to pull on my ski boots, which had dried.

My feet were still stiff with cold. I would have liked to slouch deep in an armchair, put my feet on a stool, warm myself with a lap robe, read a good novel, nibble cookies, and be served cup after cup of hot cocoa by my fairy godmother.

If I had a fairy godmother, she would resemble Angela Lansbury, the actress in *Murder, She Wrote*. She would love me unconditionally, would bring me anything my heart desired, and would tuck me into bed each night and put me to sleep with a kiss on the forehead, because she would have been through a training program at Disneyland and would have sworn the godmother's oath while in the presence of Walt Disney's cryogenically preserved corpse.

I stood up in my boots and flexed my half-numb toes.

Beast of bones or no beast of bones, I would have to go outside again into the blizzard, not immediately, but soon.

Whatever forces were at work at St. Bartholomew's, I had never encountered anything like them, had never seen such apparitions, and didn't have much confidence that I would understand their intentions in time to prevent disaster. If I should fail to identify the threat before it was upon us, I needed brave hearts and strong hands to help me protect the children, and I knew where to find them.

Graceful, stately, her footsteps hushed by her flowing white habit, Sister Angela arrived as if she were the avatar of a snow goddess who had stepped down from a celestial palace to assess the effectiveness of the storm spell that she had cast upon the Sierra.

"Sister Clare Marie says you need to speak with me, Oddie."

Brother Constantine had accompanied me from the bell tower and now joined us. The mother superior, of course, could not see him.

"George Washington was famous for his bad false teeth," I said, "but I don't know anything about the dental situations of Flannery O'Connor and Harper Lee."

"Nor do I," she said. "And before you ask, it has nothing to do with their hairstyles, either."

"Brother Constantine did not commit suicide," I told her. "He was murdered."

Her eyes widened. "I've never heard such glorious news followed by such terrible news in the same sentence."

"He lingers not because he fears his judgment in the next world but because he despairs for his brothers at the abbey."

Surveying the reception lounge, she said, "Is he here with us now?"

"Right beside me." I indicated his position.

"Dear Brother Constantine." Her voice broke with sentiment. "We've prayed every day for you, and have missed you every day."

Tears shone in the spirit's eyes.

I said, "He was reluctant to move on from this world while his brothers believed that he'd killed himself."

"Of course. He's been worried that his suicide might cause them to doubt their own commitment to a life in faith."

"Yes. But also I think he worried because they were unaware that a murderer had come among them."

Sister Angela is a quick study, with a steel-trap mind, but her decades of gentle service in the peaceful environment of one convent or another have not stropped her street smarts to a sharp edge.

"But surely you mean some outsider wandered here one night, like those the news is full of, and Brother Constantine had the misfortune to cross his path."

"If that's the case, then the guy came back for Brother Timothy, and just now in the tower here, he tried to murder me."

Alarmed, she put one hand on my arm. "Oddie, you're all right?"

"I'm not dead yet," I said, "but there's still the cake after dinner."

"Cake?"

"Sorry. I'm just being me."

"Who tried to kill you?"

I said only, "I didn't see his face. He . . . wore a mask. And I'm convinced he's someone I know, not an outsider."

She looked at where she knew the dead monk to be. "Can't Brother Constantine identify him?"

"I don't think he saw his killer's face, either. Anyway, you'd be surprised how little help I get from the lingering dead. They want me to get justice for them, they want it very bad, but I think they must abide by some proscription against affecting the course of this world, where they no longer belong."

"And you've no theory?" she asked.

"Zip. I've been told that Brother Constantine occasionally had insomnia, and when he couldn't sleep, he sometimes climbed into the bell tower at the new abbey, to study the stars."

"Yes. That's what Abbot Bernard told me at the time."

"I suspect when he was out and about at night, he saw something he was never meant to see, something to which no witness could be tolerated."

She grimaced. "That makes the abbey sound like a sordid place."

"I don't mean to suggest anything of the kind. I've lived here seven months, and I know how decent and devout the brothers are. I don't think Brother Constantine saw anything despicable. He saw something . . . extraordinary."

"And recently Brother Timothy also saw something extraordinary to which no witness could be tolerated?"

"I'm afraid so."

For a moment, she mulled this information and pressed from it the most logical conclusion. "Then you yourself have been witness to something extraordinary."

"Yes."

"Which would be—what?"

"I'd rather not say until I have time to *understand* what I saw."

"Whatever you saw—that's why we've made sure the doors and all the windows are locked."

"Yes, ma'am. And it's one of the reasons we're now going to take additional measures to protect the children."

"We'll do whatever must be done. What do you have in mind?"

"Fortify," I said. "Fortify and defend."

CHAPTER 27

GEORGE WASHINGTON, HARPER LEE, AND Flannery O'Connor smiled down on me, as if mocking my inability to solve the riddle of their shared quality.

Sister Angela sat at her desk, watching me over the frames of a pair of half-lens reading glasses that had slid down her nose. She held a pen poised above a lined yellow tablet.

Brother Constantine had not accompanied us from the reception lounge. Maybe he had at last moved on from this world, maybe not.

Pacing, I said, "I think most of the brothers are pacifists only as far as reason allows. Most would fight to save an innocent life."

"God requires resistance to evil," she said.

"Yes, ma'am. But willingness to fight isn't enough. I want those who know *how* to fight. Put Brother Knuckles at the head of the list."

"Brother Salvatore," she corrected.

"Yes, ma'am. Brother Knuckles will know what to do when the shit—" My voice failed and my face flushed.

"You could have completed the thought, Oddie. The words *hits the fan* wouldn't have offended me."

"Sorry, Sister."

"I'm a nun, not a naïf."

"Yes, ma'am."

"Who in addition to Brother Salvatore?"

"Brother Victor spent twenty-six years in the Marine Corps."

"I think he's seventy years old."

"Yes, ma'am, but he *was* a marine."

"'No better friend, no worse enemy,'" she quoted.

"*Semper Fi* sure does seem to be what we need."

She said, "Brother Gregory was an army corpsman."

The infirmarian had never spoken of military service.

"Are you sure?" I asked. "I thought he had a nursing degree."

"He does. But he was a corpsman for many years, and in the thick of action."

Medics on the battlefield are often as courageous as those who carry the guns.

"For sure, we want Brother Gregory," I said.

"What about Brother Quentin?"

"Wasn't he a cop, ma'am?"

"I believe so, yes."

"Put him on the list."

"How many do you think we need?" she asked.

"Fourteen, sixteen."

"We've got four."

I paced in silence. I stopped pacing and stood at the window. I started pacing again.

"Brother Fletcher," I suggested.

This choice baffled her. "The music director?"

"Yes, ma'am."

"In his secular life, he was a musician."

"That's a tough business, ma'am."

She considered. Then: "He does sometimes have an attitude."

"Saxophone players tend to have attitude," I said. "I know a saxophonist who tore a guitar out of another musician's hands and shot the instrument five times. It was a nice Fender."

"Why would he do a thing like that?" she asked.

"He was upset about inappropriate chord changes."

Disapproval furrowed her brow. "When this is over, perhaps your saxophonist friend could stay at the abbey for a while. I'm trained to counsel people in techniques of conflict resolution."

"Well, ma'am, shooting the guitar *was* conflict resolution."

She looked up at Flannery O'Connor and, after a moment, nodded as if in agreement with something the writer had said. "Okay, Oddie. You think Brother Fletcher could kick butt?"

"Yes, ma'am, for the kids, I think he could."

"Then we've got five."

I sat in one of the two visitors' chairs.

"Five," she repeated.

"Yes, ma'am."

I looked at my wristwatch. We stared at each other.

After a silence, she changed the subject: "If it comes to a fight, what will they fight *with*?"

"For one thing, baseball bats."

The brothers formed three teams every year. Summer evenings, during recreation hours, the teams played one another in rotation.

"They do have a lot of baseball bats," she said.

"Too bad that monks tend not to go in for shooting deer."

"Too bad," she agreed.

"The brothers split all the cordwood for the fireplaces. They have axes."

She winced at the thought of such violence. "Perhaps we should concentrate more on fortification."

"They'll be first-rate at fortification," I agreed.

Most monastic communities believe that contemplative labor is an important part of worship. Some monks make excellent wine to pay the expenses of their abbey. Some make cheese or chocolates, or crumpets and scones. Some breed and sell beautiful dogs.

The brothers of St. Bart's produce fine handcrafted furniture. Because a fraction of the interest from the Heineman endowment will always pay their operating expenses, they do not sell their chairs and tables and sideboards. They give everything to an organization that furnishes homes for the poor.

With their power tools, supplies of lumber, and skills, they would be able to further secure doors and windows.

Tapping her pen against the list of names on the tablet, Sister Angela reminded me: "Five."

"Ma'am, maybe what we should do is—you call the abbot, talk to him about this, then talk to Brother Knuckles."

"Brother Salvatore."

"Yes, ma'am. Tell Brother Knuckles what we need here, defense and fortification, and let him consult with the other four we've picked. They'll know their brothers better than we do. They'll know the best candidates."

"Yes, that's good. I wish I could tell them who they'll be defending against."

"I wish I could, too, Sister."

All the vehicles that served the brothers and sisters were garaged in the basement of the school.

I said, "Tell Knuckles—"

"Salvatore."

"—that I'll drive one of the school's monster SUVs up there to bring them here, and tell him—"

"You said hostile people are out there somewhere."

I had not said *people*. I had said *them* and *they*.

"Hostile. Yes, ma'am."

"Won't it be dangerous, to and from the abbey?"

"More dangerous for the kids if we don't get some muscle here for whatever's coming."

"I understand. My point is you'd have to make two trips to bring so many brothers, their baseball bats, and their tools. I'll drive an SUV, you drive the other, and we'll get it all done at one time."

"Ma'am, there's nothing I'd like better than having a snowplow race with you—tires chocked, engines revved, starter pistol—but I want Rodion Romanovich to drive the second SUV."

"He's here?"

"He's in the kitchen, up to his elbows in icing."

"I thought you were suspicious of him."

"If he's a Hoosier, I'm a radical dulcimer enthusiast. When we're defending the school, if it comes to that, I don't think it's a good idea for Mr. Romanovich to be inside the defenses. I'll ask him to drive one of the SUVs to the new abbey. When you talk to Brother Knuck . . . alvatore—"

"Knuckalvatore? I'm not familiar with Brother Knuckalvatore."

Until meeting Sister Angela, I wouldn't have thought that nuns and sarcasm could be such an effervescent mix.

"When you talk to Brother Salvatore, ma'am, tell him that Mr. Romanovich will be staying at the new abbey, and Salvatore will be driving that SUV back here."

"I assume Mr. Romanovich will not know that he's taking a one-way trip."

"No, ma'am. I will lie to him. You leave that to me. Regardless of what you think, I am a masterful and prodigious liar."

"If you played a saxophone, you'd be a double threat."

CHAPTER 28

As LUNCHTIME APPROACHED, THE KITCHEN staffers were not only busier than they had been previously but also more exuberant. Now four of the nuns were singing as they worked, not just two, and in English instead of Spanish.

All ten cakes had been frosted with chocolate icing. They looked treacherously delicious.

Having recently finished mixing a large bowl of bright orange buttercream, Rodion Romanovich was using a funnel sack to squeeze an elaborate decorative filigree on top of the first of his orange-almond cakes.

When I appeared at his side, he didn't look up, but said, "There you are, Mr. Thomas. You have put on your ski boots."

"I was so quiet in stocking feet, I was scaring the sisters."

"Have you been off practicing your dulcimer?"

"That was just a phase. These days I'm more interested in the saxophone. Sir, have you ever visited the grave of John Dillinger?"

"As you evidently know, he is buried in Crown Hill Cemetery, in my beloved Indianapolis. I have seen the outlaw's grave, but my primary reason for visiting the cemetery was to pay my respects at the final resting place of the novelist Booth Tarkington."

"Booth Tarkington won the Nobel Prize," I said.

"No, Mr. Thomas. Booth Tarkington won the Pulitzer Prize."

"I guess you would know, being a librarian at the Indiana State Library at one-forty North Senate Avenue, with thirty-four thousand volumes about Indiana or by Indiana writers."

"*Over* thirty-four thousand volumes," Romanovich corrected. "We are very proud of the number and do not like to hear it minimized. We may by this time next year have thirty-*five* thousand volumes about Indiana or by Indiana writers."

"Wow. That'll be a reason for a big celebration."

"I will most likely bake many cakes for the event."

The steadiness of his decorative-icing application and the consistency of details in his filigree design were impressive.

If he'd not had about him an air of deceit equal to that of a chameleon sitting on a tree branch, disguised as bark, waiting for innocent butterflies to approach, I might have begun to doubt his potential for villainy.

"Being a Hoosier, sir, you must have a lot of experience driving in snow."

"Yes. I have had considerable experience of snow both in my adopted Indiana and in my native Russia."

"We have two SUVs, fitted with plows, in the garage. We've got to drive up to the abbey and bring back some of the brothers."

"Are you asking me to drive one of these vehicles, Mr. Thomas?"

"Yes, sir. If you would, I'd be most grateful. It'll save me making two trips."

"For what purpose are the brothers coming to the school?"

"For the purpose," I said, "of assisting the sisters with the children if there should be a power failure related to the blizzard."

He drew a perfect miniature rose to finish off one corner of the cake. "Does not the school have an emergency backup generator?"

"Yes, sir, you bet it does. But it doesn't crank out the same level of power. Lighting will have to be reduced. They'll have to turn heating off in some areas, use the fireplaces. And Sister Angela wants to be prepared in case the generator falters, too."

"Have the main power and the backup generator ever both failed on the same occasion?"

"I don't know, sir. I don't think so. But in my experience, nuns are obsessed with detailed planning."

"Oh, I have no doubt, Mr. Thomas, that if nuns had designed and operated the nuclear plant at Chernobyl, we would not have suffered a radiation disaster."

This was an interesting turn. "Are you from Chernobyl, sir?"

"Do I have a third eye and a second nose?"

"Not that I can see, sir, but then you're largely clothed."

"If we should ever find ourselves sunning on the same beach, you are free to investigate further, Mr. Thomas. May I finish decorating these cakes, or must we rush pell-mell to the abbey?"

Knuckles and the others would need at least forty-five minutes to gather the items they'd be bringing and to assemble for pickup.

I said, "Finish the cakes, sir. They look terrific. How about if you meet me down in the garage at twelve forty-five?"

"You can depend on my assistance. I will have finished the cakes by then."

"Thank you, sir." I started to leave, then turned to him again. "Did you know Cole Porter was a Hoosier?"

"Yes. And so are James Dean, David Letterman, Kurt Vonnegut, and Wendell Willkie."

"Cole Porter, he was perhaps the greatest American songwriter of the century, sir."

"Yes, I agree."

"'Night and Day,' 'Anything Goes,' 'In the Still of the Night,' 'I Get a Kick Out of You,' 'You're the Top.' He wrote the Indiana state song, too."

Romanovich said, "The state song is 'On the Banks of the Wabash, Far Away,' and if Cole Porter heard you crediting it to him, he would no doubt claw his way out of the grave, track you down, and exact a terrible vengeance."

"Oh. Then I guess I was misinformed."

He raised his attention from the cake long enough to give me an ironic look heavy enough to weight down a feather in a high wind. "I doubt that you are ever misinformed, Mr. Thomas."

"No, sir, you're wrong. I'm the first to admit I don't know anything about anything—except that I'm something of a nut about all things Indiana."

"Approximately what time this morning did this Hoosiermania overcome you?"

Man, he was good at this.

"Not this morning, sir," I lied. "All my life, as long as I can remember."

"Maybe you were a Hoosier in a previous life."

"Maybe I was James Dean."

"I am certain you were not James Dean."

"Why do you say that, sir?"

"Such an intense craving for adoration and such a capacity for rudeness as Mr. Dean exhibited could not possibly have been expunged so entirely from just one incarnation to the next."

I thought about that statement from a few different angles. "Sir, I have nothing against the late Mr. Dean, but I don't see any way to interpret that except as a compliment."

Glowering, Rodion Romanovich said, "You complimented my cake decorations, did you not? Well, now we are even."

CHAPTER 29

CARRYING MY JACKET, WHICH I HAD RETRIEVED from the rack in the reception lounge, I went down to the basement, grateful that there were no real catacombs full of moldering corpses. With my luck, one of them would have been Cole Porter.

Those brothers who had wished to be interred on the grounds of the abbey are buried in a shady plot on the perimeter of the forest. It is a peaceful little cemetery. The spirits of those at rest there have all moved on from this world.

I have spent pleasant hours among those headstones, with only Boo for company. He likes to watch the squirrels and rabbits while I stroke his neck and scratch his ears. Sometimes he gambols after them, but they are not frightened by him; even in the days when he was sharp of tooth, he was never a killer.

As if my thoughts had summoned him, I found Boo waiting for me when I turned out of the east-west hallway into the north-south.

"Hey, boy, what're you doing down here?"

Tail wagging, he approached, settled on the floor, and rolled onto his back, all four paws in the air.

Receiving such an invitation, only the hard-hearted and the uselessly busy can refuse. All that is wanted is affection, while all that is offered is everything, symbolized in the defenseless posture of the exposed tummy.

Dogs invite us not only to share their joy but also to live in the moment, where we are neither proceeding from nor moving toward, where the enchantment of the past and future cannot distract us, where a freedom from practical desire and a cessation of our usual ceaseless action allows us to recognize the truth of our existence, the reality of our world and purpose—if we dare.

I gave Boo only a two-minute belly rub and then continued with the usual ceaseless action, not because urgent tasks awaited me, but because, as a wise man once wrote, "Humankind cannot bear very much reality," and I am too human.

The large garage had the feel of a bunker, concrete above and below and on all sides. The fluorescent ceiling fixtures shed a hard light, but they were too widely spaced to dispel every shadow.

Seven vehicles were housed here: four compact sedans, a beefy pickup, two extended SUVs jacked up on big tires with snow chains.

A ramp ascended to a large roll-up door, beyond which the wind howled.

Mounted on a wall was a key box. Inside, fourteen sets of keys, two for each vehicle, hung from seven pegs. Above each peg, a label provided the license number of the vehicle, and a tag on each set of keys carried the same number.

No danger of Chernobyls here.

I pulled on my jacket, got behind the wheel of one of the SUVs, started the engine, and let it idle just long enough to figure how to raise and lower the plow with the simple controls.

When I stepped out of the truck, Boo was there. He looked up, cocked his head, pricked his ears, and seemed to say, *What's wrong with your nose, buddy? Don't you smell the same trouble I smell?*

He trotted away, glanced back, saw that I was following, and led me out of the garage, into the northwest hall once more.

This wasn't Lassie, and I didn't expect to find anything as easy to deal with as Timmy down a well or Timmy trapped in a burning barn.

Boo stopped in front of a closed door, at the same point in the corridor at which he had offered me the opportunity to rub his tummy.

Perhaps he had originally encouraged me to pause at that point to give my fabled intuition a chance to operate. I had been caught in the wheels of compulsion, however, bent on getting to the garage, my mind occupied with thoughts of the trip ahead, able to pause briefly but unable to see and feel.

I felt something now, all right. A subtle but persistent pull, as if I were a fisherman, my line cast out into the deep, some catch hooked on the farther end.

Boo went into the suspect room. After a hesitation, I followed, leaving the door open behind me because in situations like this, when psychic magnetism draws me, I cannot be certain I'm the fisherman and not the fish with the hook in its mouth.

We were in a boiler room, full of the hiss of flame rings and the rumble of pumps. Four large, high-efficiency boilers produced the hot water that traveled ceaselessly through pipes in the walls of the building, to the scores of fan-coil units that heated the many rooms.

Here, too, were chillers that produced supercooled water, which also circulated through the school and convent, providing cool air when a room grew too warm.

On three walls were sophisticated air monitors, which would trigger alarms in every farther corner of the big building *and* shut off the incoming gas line that fired the boilers if they detected the merest trace of free propane in the room. This was supposed to be an absolute guarantee against an explosion.

Absolute guarantee. Foolproof. The unsinkable *Titanic.* The uncrashable *Hindenburg.* Peace in our time.

Human beings not only can't bear too much reality, we *flee* from reality when someone doesn't force us close enough to the fire to feel the heat on our faces.

None of the three air monitors indicated the presence of rogue molecules of propane.

I had to depend upon the monitors because propane is color-less and odorless. If I relied on my senses to detect a leak, I would not know a problem existed until I found myself passing out for lack of oxygen or until everything went boom.

Each monitor box was locked and featured a pressed-metal seal bearing the date of the most recent inspection by the service company responsible for their reliable function. I examined every lock and every seal and discovered no indications of tampering.

Boo had gone to the corner of the room farthest from the door. I found myself drawn there, too.

In its circulation through the building, the supercooled water absorbs heat. It then travels to a large underground vault near the eastern woods, where a cooling tower converts the unwanted heat to steam and blows it into the air to dissipate; thereafter, the water returns to the chillers in this room to be cooled again.

Four eight-inch-diameter PVC pipes disappeared through the wall, near the ceiling, close to the corner where Boo and I had been drawn.

Boo sniffed at a four-foot-square stainless-steel panel set six inches off the floor, and I dropped to my knees before it.

Beside the panel was a light switch. I clicked it, but nothing happened—unless I'd turned lights on in some space beyond the wall.

The access panel was fixed to the concrete wall with four bolts. On a nearby hook hung a tool with which the bolts could be extracted.

After removing the bolts, I set aside the panel and peered into the hole where Boo had already gone. Past the butt-end and tucked tail of the big white dog, I saw a lighted tunnel.

Unafraid of dog farts, but fearful about what else might lie ahead, I crawled through the opening.

Once I had cleared the two-foot width of the poured-in-place concrete wall, I was able to stand. Before me lay a rectangular passageway seven feet high and five feet wide.

The four pipes were suspended side by side from the ceiling and were grouped on the left half of the tunnel. Small center-set lights revealed the pipes dwindling as if to eternity.

Along the floor, on the left, were runs of separated copper pipes, steel pipes, and flexible conduits. They probably carried water, propane, and electrical wires.

Here and there, white patterns of calcification stained the

walls, but the place wasn't damp. It had a clean smell of concrete and lime.

Except for the faint rushing noise of water flowing through the pipes overhead, the passageway lay silent.

I consulted my wristwatch. In thirty-four minutes, I would need to be in the garage to meet the Hoosier's Hoosier.

With purpose, Boo trotted forward, and I followed with no clear purpose at all.

I proceeded as silently as possible in ski boots, and when my shiny quilted thermal jacket whistled as I moved my arms, I took it off and left it behind. Boo made no sound whatsoever.

A boy and his dog are the best of all companions, celebrated in songs and books and movies. When the boy is in the grip of a psychic compulsion, however, and when the dog is fearless, the chance that all will turn out well is about as likely as a Scorsese gangster movie ending in sweetness, light, and the happy singing of cherubic children.

CHAPTER 30

I DISLIKE SUBTERRANEAN PASSAGEWAYS. I ONCE died in such a place. At least I'm pretty sure I died, and was dead for a while, and even haunted a few of my friends, though they didn't know I was with them in a spook state.

If I didn't die, something stranger than death happened to me. I wrote about the experience in my second manuscript, but writing about it didn't help me to understand it.

At intervals of forty or fifty feet, air monitors were mounted on the right-hand wall. I found no signs of tampering.

If the passageway led to the cooling-tower vault, as I was sure that it must, then it would be about four hundred feet long.

Twice I thought I heard something behind me. When I looked over my shoulder, nothing loomed.

The third time, I refused to succumb to the urge to glance back. Irrational fear feeds on itself and grows. You must deny it.

The trick is to be able to differentiate irrational fear from justifiable fear. If you squelch justifiable fear and soldier on, dauntless and determined, that's when Santa Claus will squeeze down the chimney, after all, and add your peepee to his collection.

Boo and I had gone two hundred feet when another passageway opened on the right. This one sloped uphill and curved out of sight.

Four additional PVC pipes were suspended from the ceiling of the intersecting corridor. They turned the corner into our passageway and paralleled the first set of pipes, heading toward the cooling tower.

The second serviceway must have originated in the new abbey.

Instead of bringing the brothers back to the school in the two SUVs, risking attack by whatever might be waiting in the blizzard, we could lead them along this easier route.

I needed to explore the new passageway, though not immediately.

Boo had proceeded toward the cooling tower. Although the dog would not be of help when I was attacked by the creeping thing behind me, I felt better when we kept together, and I hurried after him.

In my mind's eye, the creature at my back had three necks but only two heads. The body was human, but the heads were those of coyotes. It wanted to plant my head on its center neck.

You might wonder where such a baroque irrational fear could have come from. After all, as you know, I'm droll, but I'm not grotesque.

A casual friend of mine in Pico Mundo, a fiftyish Panamint Indian who calls himself Tommy Cloudwalker, told me of an encounter he had with such a three-headed creature.

Tommy had gone hiking and camping in the Mojave, when

winter's tarnished-silver sun, the Ancient Squaw, had relented to spring's golden sun, the Young Bride, but before summer's fierce platinum sun, the Ugly Wife, could with her sharp tongue sear the desert so cruelly that a sweat of scorpions and beetles would be wrung from the sand in a desperate search for better shade and a drop of water.

Maybe Tommy's names for the seasonal suns arise from the legends of his tribe. Maybe he just makes them up. I'm not sure if Tommy is partly genuine or entirely a master of hokum.

In the center of his forehead is a stylized image of a hawk two inches wide and one inch high. Tommy says the hawk is a birthmark.

Truck Boheen, a one-legged former biker and tattooist who lives in a rusting trailer on the edge of Pico Mundo, says he applied the hawk to Tommy's forehead twenty-five years ago, for fifty bucks.

Reason tips the scale toward Truck's version. The problem is, Truck also claims that the most recent five presidents of the United States have come secretly to his trailer in the dead of night to receive his tattoos. I might believe one or two, but not five.

Anyway, Tommy was sitting in the Mojave on a spring night, the sky winking with the Wise Eyes of Ancestors—or stars, if scientists are correct—when the creature with three heads appeared on the farther side of the campfire.

The human head never said a word, but the flanking coyote heads spoke English. They debated each other about whether Tommy's head was more desirable than the head already occupying the neck between them.

Coyote One liked Tommy's head, especially the proud nose.

Coyote Two was insulting; he said Tommy was "more Italian than Indian."

Being something of a shaman, Tommy recognized that this creature was an unusual manifestation of the Trickster, a spirit common to the folklore of many Indian nations. As an offering, he produced three cigarettes of whatever he was smoking, and these were accepted.

With solemn satisfaction, the three heads smoked in silence. After tossing the butts in the campfire, the creature departed, allowing Tommy to keep his head.

Two words might explain Tommy's story: *peyote buttons.*

The following day, however, after resuming his hike, Tommy came across the headless corpse of another hiker. The driver's license in the guy's wallet identified him as Curtis Hobart.

Nearby was a severed head, but it was the one that had been on the center neck between the coyotes. It looked nothing like Curtis Hobart in the driver's-license photo.

Using his satellite phone, Tommy Cloudwalker called the sheriff. Shimmering like mirages in the spring heat, the authorities arrived both overland and by helicopter.

Later, the coroner declared that the head and the body did not belong together. They never located Curtis Hobart's head, and no body was ever found to go with the discarded head that had been dropped on the sand near Hobart's corpse.

As I hurried after Boo, along the passageway toward the cooling tower, I did not know why Tommy's unlikely story should rise out of my memory swamp at this time. It didn't seem germane to my current situation.

Later, all would clarify. Even on those occasions when I am as dumb as a duck run down by a truck, my busy *sub*conscious is laboring overtime to save my butt.

Boo went to the cooling tower, and after unlocking the fire door with my universal key, I followed him inside, where the fluorescent lights were on.

We were at the bottom of the structure. It looked like a movie set through which James Bond would pursue a villain who had steel teeth and wore a double-barreled 12-gauge hat.

A pair of thirty-foot-high sheet-metal towers rose above us. They were linked by horizontal ducts, accessed at different levels by a series of red catwalks.

Inside the towers and perhaps in some of the smaller ducts, things were turning with loud thrumming and whisking noises, perhaps huge fan blades. Driven air hissed like peevish cats and whistled like catcalls.

The walls were lined with at least forty large gray metal boxes, similar to junction boxes, except that each featured a large ON/OFF lever and two signal lights, one red and one green. Only green lights glowed at the moment.

All green. A-OK. Good to go. Hunky-dory.

The machinery offered numerous places where someone could hide; and the noise would make even the most lumbering assailant difficult to hear until he was on top of me; but I chose to take the green lights as a good omen.

Had I been aboard the *Titanic,* I would have been standing on the listing deck, leaning against a railing, gazing at a falling star and wishing for a puppy for Christmas even as the band played "Nearer My God to Thee."

Although much that was precious has been taken from me in this life, I have reason to remain an optimist. After the numerous tight scrapes I've been through, by now I should have lost one leg, three fingers, one buttock, most of my teeth, an ear, my spleen, and my sense of fun. But here I am.

Both Boo and psychic magnetism had drawn me here, and when I proceeded warily into the big room, I discovered the attractant.

Between two more banks of gray metal boxes, on a clear section of wall, hung Brother Timothy.

CHAPTER 31

BROTHER TIM'S SHOD FEET DANGLED EIGHTEEN inches off the floor. Six feet above him at its apex, a 180-degree arc of thirteen peculiar white pegs had been driven into the concrete wall. From these pegs stretched white fibrous bands, like inch-wide lengths of cloth, by which he was suspended.

One of the thirteen lines ended in his mussed hair. Two others terminated in the rolled-down hood bunched at the back of his neck, and the remaining ten disappeared into small rents in the shoulders, sleeves, and flanks of his tunic.

The manner in which those lines had been fixed to him remained at every point concealed.

With his head hung forward, with his arms spread out and angled up from his body, the intention to mock the crucifixion could not have been clearer.

Although lacking visible wounds, he appeared to be dead. Famous for his blush, he was now whiter than pale, gray under the eyes. His slack facial muscles responded to no emotion, only to gravity.

Nevertheless, all of the indicator lights on the surrounding breaker boxes—or whatever they were—remained green, so in a spirit of optimism bordering on lunacy, I said, "Brother Timothy," dismayed to hear my voice so whispery and thin.

The whoosh-whirr-thrum-throb of machinery covered the breathing of the three-headed cigarette fiend behind me, but I refused to turn and confront it. Irrational fear. Nothing loomed at my back. Not a coyote-human Indian demigod, not my mother with her gun.

Raising my voice, I repeated, "Brother Tim?"

Although smooth, his skin appeared to be as juiceless as dust, grainy like paper, as if life had not merely been taken from him but had been sucked out to the last drop.

An open spiral staircase led to the catwalks above and to the high door in the portion of the cooling tower that rose above ground. The police would have entered by that door to search the vault below.

Either they had overlooked this place or the dead monk had not been here when they had swept through.

He had been a good man, and kind to me. He should not be left to hang there, his cadaver employed to mock the God to whom he had devoted his life.

Maybe I could cut him down.

I lightly pinched one of the fibrous white bands, slid my thumb and forefinger up and down that taut ribbon. Not ribbon, though, nor cotton cloth, nor anything that I had felt before.

Glass-smooth, as dry as talcum, yet flexible. And remarkably cold for such a thin filament, so icy that my fingers began to grow numb from even a brief inspection.

The thirteen white pins were wedges, somehow driven into

the concrete as a rock climber drives pitons into cracks with a hammer. Yet the concrete presented not one crack.

The nearest of the thirteen bristled from the wall perhaps eighteen inches above my head. It resembled bleached bone.

I couldn't see how the point of the piton had been embedded in the wall. It seemed to grow from—or to be fused with—the concrete.

Likewise, I wasn't able to discern how the fibrous band had been fixed to the piton. Each suspending line and its anchor appeared to be part of a single unit.

Because he was a thief of heads, the Trickster behind me would have a formidable knife of some kind, perhaps a machete, with which I could cut down Brother Timothy. He wouldn't harm me if I explained that Tommy Cloudwalker and I were friends. I didn't have cigarettes to offer him, but I did have gum, a few sticks of Black Jack.

When I plucked one of the lines from which the dead monk hung, to determine its toughness, it proved more taut than I expected, as tight with tension as a violin string.

The fibrous material produced an ugly note. I had plucked only one, but after a beat, the other twelve lines vibrated, too, and from them arose eerie music reminiscent of a theremin.

My scalp crawled, I felt a hot breath on the nape of my neck, I detected a foul smell, I knew this was irrational fear, a reaction to the creepy condition of Brother Timothy and to the disturbing strains of theremin-like sound, but I turned anyway, I turned, chagrined that I was so easily suckered by my imagination, I turned boldly to the looming Trickster.

He wasn't behind me. Nothing waited behind me except Boo,

who regarded me with a baffled expression that hardened my embarrassment into a diamond-bright luster.

As the cold sound from the thirteen tethers faded, I returned my attention to Brother Timothy, and looked up into his face just as his eyes opened.

CHAPTER 32

MORE ACCURATELY: BROTHER TIMOTHY'S EYE-lids lifted, but he could not open his eyes because he didn't possess eyes any longer. In his sockets were matching kaleido-scopic patterns of tiny bonelike forms. The pattern in the left socket irised into new shapes; the pattern in the right did like-wise; then both changed in perfect synchronization.

I felt well advised to take a step back from him.

Tongueless and toothless, his mouth sagged open. In the wide-ness of his silent scream, a layered construct of bony forms, jointed in ways that defied analysis and description, flexed and rotated and thrust forward only to fold inward, as if he were trying to swallow a colony of hard-shelled arachnids that were alive and reluctant to be consumed.

The skin split from the corners of his mouth to his ears. With not one bead of blood, his upper lip peeled toward his scalp, the way the lid of a sardine can rolls back with the twist of a key, and the lower part of his face peeled down over his chin.

While the intention had been to mock the crucifixion of Christ,

Brother Timothy's body had also been a chrysalis from which something less charming than a butterfly strove to emerge.

Beneath the veneer of a face lay the fullness of what I had only glimpsed in the eye sockets, in the yawning mouth: a phantasmagoria of bony forms linked by hinge joints, by pivot joints, by ellipsoidal joints, by ball-and-socket joints, and by joints for which no names existed, and which were not natural to this world.

The apparition appeared to be a solid mass of bones combined so intimately that they must be fused, compacted so completely that they could have no room to rotate or flex. Yet they *did* rotate and flex and pivot and more, seemed to move not merely in three dimensions but in four, in an unceasing exhibition of dexterity that astonished and amazed.

Imagine that all the universe and all of time are together kept in right motion and in perfect balance by an infinite gearbox, and in your mind look down into that intricate mechanism, and you will have a sense of my incomprehension, awe, and terror as I stood before the uberskeleton that churned and ticked and flexed and clicked, peeling the gossamer remnants of Brother Tim away from itself.

Something moved vigorously under the dead monk's tunic.

If popcorn, Pepsi, and a comfortable chair had been available, I might have stayed. But the cooling tower was an inhospitable place, dusty and drafty, offering no refreshments.

Besides, I had an appointment with the Hoosier librarian cakebaker in the school garage. I am loath to be late for an engagement. Tardiness is rude.

A piton popped out of the wall. The fibrous tether reeled that wedge into the kaleidoscopic boneworks, incorporating it in a wink. Another piton came loose, raveled back to Papa.

This rough beast, its hour come 'round at last, didn't need to slouch to Bethlehem to be born. Sharp white blades slashed through the tunic from within, shredding it. No need for Rosemary; no need to waste years as a baby.

The time had come either to light the black candles and start chanting in admiration—or blow this dump.

Boo had already scrammed. I vamoosed.

I pulled the door shut between the cooling tower and the service passage and fumbled with my key for a moment before I realized that the lock only kept people out; I couldn't lock anyone inside.

The four hundred feet to the school appeared to be immeasurable miles, the ceiling lights receding to Pittsburgh and beyond.

Boo was already out of sight. Maybe he had taken a shortcut through another dimension to the school boiler room.

I wished I'd been hanging on to his tail.

CHAPTER 33

WHEN I HAD SPRINTED ABOUT A HUNDRED feet, I heard the cooling-tower door slam open. The crash boomed like a shotgun blast through the service passageway.

Tommy Cloudwalker's Mojave pal, the three-headed poster boy for the evils of smoking, seemed more likely to exist than did the skeletonized boogeyman that now coveted my bones. But fear of this thing was a *rational* fear.

Brother Timothy had been sweet, kind, and devout; yet look what happened to *him*. A shiftless, unemployed, smart-ass specimen like me, who had never exercised his precious American right to vote, who had accepted a compliment at the expense of the late James Dean, ought to expect a fate even more gruesome than Tim's, though I couldn't imagine one.

I glanced over my shoulder.

As it advanced through alternating pools of shadow and light, my pursuer's method of locomotion could not clearly be discerned, though these were not steps that it had learned at a dance studio. It seemed to be marshaling some of its numerous bones into stubby legs, but not all were legs of the same design, and they moved independently of one another, foiling one another and causing the eager creature to lurch.

I was still moving, repeatedly glancing back, not standing in thoughtful contemplation and making notes of my impressions of the beast, but in retrospect I think that I was most alarmed to see it progressing not on the floor but along the junction of the ceiling and the right-hand wall. It was a climber, which meant the children's quarters on the second floor would be more difficult to defend than I had hoped.

Furthermore, as it came, the entire structure of it appeared to turn ceaselessly, as if it were drilling forward like an auger boring through wood. The word *machine* came to mind, as it had when I watched another of these things flexing itself into one elaborate new pattern after another, against the reception-lounge window.

Tripping again, my pursuer lost its perch and clattered down the wall to the floor. Scissoring jacks of bone cranked it erect, and it came forward, eager but uncertain.

Perhaps it was learning its capabilities, as does any newborn. Maybe this was a Kodak moment, baby's first steps.

By the time I reached the intersection with the passageway that evidently led to the new abbey, I felt confident that I would be able to outrun the thing—unless its learning curve was very steep.

Glancing back again, I saw that it was not just clumsy but also had become translucent. The light from the overhead fixtures did not play across its contours any longer, but seemed to pass through it, as if it were made of milky glass.

For a moment, as it faltered to a halt, I thought it was going to dematerialize, not at all like a machine but like a spirit. Then the translucency passed from it, and it became solid again, and it surged forward.

A familiar keening drew my attention toward the intersecting passage. Far uphill, in the voice that I had heard earlier in the storm, another of these things expressed its sincere desire to have a tête-à-tête with me.

From this distance, I couldn't be certain of its size, but I suspected that it was considerably larger than the lovely that had come out of the chrysalis. It moved with confidence, too, with grace, glissading without benefit of snow, legs churning in a faultless rhythm, with centipede swiftness.

So I did one of the things that I do best: I ran like a sonof-abitch.

I only had two legs instead of a hundred, and I was wearing ski boots when I should have been in athletic shoes with air-cushioned insoles, but I had the benefit of wild desperation and the energy provided by Sister Regina Marie's superb beef sandwich. I almost made it to the boiler room safely ahead of Satan and Satan Junior, or whatever they were.

Then something tangled around my feet. I cried out, fell, and scrambled up at once, flailing at my assailant until I realized that it was the quilted thermal jacket I had shucked off earlier because of the whistling noise it made.

As if a chorus line of frenzied skeletons were tapping out the final bars of the show's big number, the clickety-clack of my pursuer rose to a crescendo.

I turned, and it was *right there.*

As one, the regimented legs, different from but as hideous as those of a Jerusalem cricket, clattered to a halt. Although knuckled, knobbed, ribbed, and bristling, the forward half of the twelve-foot apparition rose off the floor with serpentine elegance.

We were face to face, or would have been if I hadn't been the only one of us with a face.

Across the whole of it, patterns of elaborately integrated bones blossomed, withered, were replaced by new forms and patterns, but in a tickless, clickless quicksilver hush.

This silent exhibition was intended to display its absolute and otherworldly control of its physiology, and to leave me terrified and abashed at my comparative weakness. As when I had watched it at the window, I sensed an overweening vanity in its display of itself, an arrogance that was eerily human, a pompousness and boastfulness that exceeded mere vanity and that might be called vainglory.

I backed up a step, another. "Kiss my ass, you ugly bastard."

In a rending fury, it fell upon me, ice-cold and merciless. Uncountable maxillas and mandibles chewed, spurred heelbones ripped, stiletto-sharp phalanges gouged, a whiplike spine with hooked and razored vertebrae slashed me open from abdomen to throat, and my heart was found and torn apart, and thereafter what I could do for the children of St. Bartholomew's School was limited to what power I might have as one of the lingering dead.

Yes, it could have gone as badly as that, but in fact I just lied to you. The truth is stranger than the lie, though considerably less traumatic.

Everything in my account is true through the point at which I told the bag of bones to kiss my posterior. After issuing that heartfelt vulgarity, I did take one step backward, and then one more.

Because I believed that I had nothing to lose, that my life was already forfeited, I turned boldly from the apparition. I dropped to my hands and knees, and crawled through the four-foot-square aperture between the service passageway and the boiler room.

I expected the thing to snare my feet and to haul me back into its realm. When I reached the boiler room unharmed, I rolled onto my back and scooted away from the open service access, anticipating the intrusion of a questing, pincered, bony appendage.

No keening arose from beyond the wall, but no clitterclatter of retreat, either, though the rumble of the boiler-room pumps might have masked all but the loudest of those noises.

I listened to my thundering heart, delighted to still have it. And all my fingers, and all my teeth, my precious little spleen, and both buttocks.

Considering the walking boneyard's ability to manifest in infinite iterations, I saw no reason why it wouldn't follow me into the boiler room. Even in its current configuration, it would have no trouble passing through the four-foot-square opening.

If the creature entered, I had no weapon with which to drive it back. But if I failed to make a stand, I'd be conceding it access to the school, where at this moment most of the children were at lunch in the ground-floor refectory, others in their rooms on the second floor.

Feeling foolish and inadequate, I erupted to my feet, snatched a fire extinguisher from its wall rack, and held it ready, as though I might be able to kill those bundled bones of contention with a fog of ammonium phosphate, as in bad early sci-fi movies where the heroes are apt to discover, in the penultimate scene, that the rampaging and apparently indestructible monster can be dissolved by something as mundane as salt or laundry bleach, or lavender-scented hairspray.

I could not even be sure that this thing was alive in the sense that people and animals and insects are alive, or even in the sense that plants are alive. I could not explain how a three-dimensional collage of bones, regardless of how astoundingly intricate it might appear, could be alive when it lacked flesh, blood, and visible sense organs. And if it wasn't alive, it couldn't be killed.

A supernatural explanation eluded me, too. Nothing in the theology of any major religion proposed the existence of an entity like this, nor anything in any body of folklore with which I was familiar.

Boo appeared from among the boilers. He studied me and my ammonium-phosphate-fog weapon. He sat, cocked his head, and grinned. He seemed to find me amusing.

Armed with the fire extinguisher and, if that failed, with only Black Jack chewing gum, I stood my ground for a minute, two minutes, three.

Nothing came from beyond the wall. Nothing waited at the threshold, tapping its fleshless toes impatiently.

I set aside the fire extinguisher.

Staying ten feet back from the low opening, I got on my hands and knees to peer into the passageway. I saw the lighted concrete corridor dwindling toward the cooling tower, but nothing that would make me want to call Ghostbusters.

Boo went closer to the service aperture than I dared, peered in, then glanced at me, perplexed.

"I don't know," I said. "I don't get it."

I replaced the stainless-steel panel. As I inserted the first bolt and tightened it with the special tool, I expected something to slam against the farther side, rip the panel away, and drag me out of the boiler room. Didn't happen.

Whatever had prevented the beast of bones from doing to me what it had done to Brother Timothy, I do not know, though I am certain it had wanted me and had intended to take me. I'm pretty sure that my insult—*Kiss my ass, you ugly bastard*—did not cause it to sulk away with hurt feelings.

CHAPTER 34

RODION ROMANOVICH ARRIVED IN THE GARAGE wearing a handsome bearskin hat, a white silk neck scarf, a black three-quarter-length lined leather coat with fur collar and fur cuffs, and—no surprise—zippered rubber boots that rose to his knees. He looked as if he had dressed for a horse-drawn sleigh-ride with the czar.

After my experience with the galloping boneyard, I was lying on my back on the floor, staring at the ceiling, trying to calm myself, waiting for my legs to stop trembling and regain some strength.

Standing over me, peering down, he said, "You are a peculiar young man, Mr. Thomas."

"Yes, sir. I am aware."

"What are you doing down there?"

"Recovering from a bad scare."

"What scared you?"

"A sudden recognition of my mortality."

"Have you not previously realized you are mortal?"

"Yes, sir, I've been aware of it for a while. I was just, you know, overcome by a sense of the unknown."

"What unknown, Mr. Thomas?"

"The great unknown, sir. I'm not a particularly vulnerable person. Little unknowns don't disconcert me."

"How does lying on a garage floor console you?"

"The water stains on the ceiling are lovely. They relax me."

Looking at the concrete overhead, he said, "I find them ugly."

"No, no. All the soft shadings of gray and black and rust, just a hint of green, gently blending together, all free-form shapes, not anything that looks as defined and rigid as a bone."

"Bone, did you say?"

"Yes, sir, I did. Is that a bearskin hat, sir?"

"Yes. I know it is not politically correct to wear fur, but I refuse to apologize for it to anyone."

"Good for you, sir. I'll bet you killed the bear yourself."

"Are you an animal activist, Mr. Thomas?"

"I have nothing against animals, but I'm usually too busy to march on their behalf."

"Then I will tell you that I did, indeed, kill the bear from which this hat was fashioned and from which the fur came for the collar and cuffs of this coat."

"That isn't much to have gotten from a whole bear."

"I have other fur items in my wardrobe, Mr. Thomas. I wonder how you knew that I killed the bear."

"I mean no offense by this, sir, but in addition to the fur for various garments, you received into yourself something of the spirit of the bear when you killed it."

From my extreme perspective, his many frown lines looked like terrible dark saber scars. "That sounds New Age and not Catholic."

"I'm speaking metaphorically, not literally, and with some irony, sir."

"When I was your age, I did not have the luxury of irony. Will you get up from there?"

"In a minute, sir. Eagle Creek Park, Garfield Park, White River State Park—Indianapolis has some very nice parks, but I didn't know there were bears in them."

"As I am sure you realize, I hunted the bear and shot it when I was a young man in Russia."

"I keep forgetting you're Russian. Wow, librarians are a tougher bunch in Russia than here, hunting bear and all."

"Everyone had it tough. It was the Soviet era. But I was not a librarian in Russia."

"I'm in the middle of a career change myself. What were you in Russia?"

"A mortician."

"Is that right? You embalmed people and stuff."

"I prepared people for death, Mr. Thomas."

"That's a peculiar way of putting it."

"Not at all. That's how we said it in my former country." He spoke a few words in Russian and then translated: "'I am a mortician. I prepare people for death.' Now, of course, I am a librarian at the Indiana State Library opposite the Capitol, at one-forty North Senate Avenue."

I lay in silence for a moment. Then I said, "You're quite droll, Mr. Romanovich."

"But I hope not grotesque."

"I'm still thinking about that." I pointed to the second SUV.

"You're driving that one. You'll find the keys tagged with the license number in a wall box over there."

"Has your meditation on the ceiling stains ameliorated your fear of the great unknown?"

"As much as could be expected, sir. Would you like to take a few minutes to meditate on them?"

"No thank you, Mr. Thomas. The great unknown does not trouble me." He went to get the keys.

When I rose to my feet, my legs were steadier than they had been recently.

Ozzie Boone, a four-hundred-pound best-selling mystery writer who is my friend and mentor in Pico Mundo, insists that I keep the tone light in these biographical manuscripts. He believes that pessimism is strictly for people who are over-educated and unimaginative. Ozzie counsels me that melancholy is a self-indulgent form of sorrow. By writing in an unrelievedly dark mode, he warns, the writer risks culturing darkness in his heart, becoming the very thing that he decries.

Considering the gruesome death of Brother Timothy, the awful discoveries yet to be revealed in this account, and the grievous losses forthcoming, I doubt that the tone of this narrative would be half as light as it is if Rodion Romanovich had not been part of it. I do not mean that he turned out to be a swell guy. I mean only that he had wit.

These days, all I ask of Fate is that the people she hurls into my life, whether they are evil or good, or morally bipolar, should be amusing to one degree or another. This is a big request to make of busy Fate, who has billions of lives to keep in constant turmoil. Most good people have a sense of humor. The problem is finding smile-inducing evil people, because the evil are mostly humorless, though in the movies they frequently get some of the best lines. With few exceptions, the morally bipolar are too preoccupied with justifying their contradictory behaviors to learn to laugh at themselves, and I've noticed they laugh *at* other people more than *with* them.

Burly, fur-hatted, and looking as solemn as a man should who prepares people for death, Rodion Romanovich returned with the keys to the second SUV.

"Mr. Thomas, any scientist will tell you that in nature many systems appear to be chaotic, but when you study them long enough and closely enough, strange order always underlies the appearance of chaos."

I said, "How about that."

"The winter storm into which we are going will seem chaotic—the shifting winds and the churning snow and the brightness that obscures more than it reveals—but if you could view it not at the level of a meteorological event, view it instead at the micro scale of fluid and particle and energy flux, you would see a warp and woof suggestive of a well-woven fabric."

"I left my micro-scale eyeglasses in my room."

"If you were to view it at the atomic level, the event might seem chaotic again, but proceeding into the subatomic, strange order appears once more, an even more intricate design than warp and woof. Always, beneath every apparent chaos, order waits to be revealed."

"You haven't seen my sock drawer."

"The two of us might seem to be in this place, at this time, only by coincidence, but both an honest scientist and a true man of faith will tell you there are no coincidences."

I shook my head. "They sure did make you do some pretty deep thinking at that mortician's school."

Neither a spot nor a wrinkle marred his clothes, and his rubber boots gleamed like patent leather.

Stoic, seamed, and solid, his face was a mask of perfect order.

He said, "Do not bother to ask for the name of the mortician's school, Mr. Thomas. I never attended one."

"This is the first time I've known anyone," I said, "who embalmed without a license."

His eyes revealed an order even more rigorous than that exemplified by his wardrobe and his face.

He said, "I obtained a license without the need for schooling. I had a natural-born talent for the trade."

"Some kids are born with perfect pitch, with a genius for math, and you were born knowing how to prepare people for death."

"That is exactly correct, Mr. Thomas."

"You must have come from interesting genetic stock."

"I suspect," he said, "that your family and mine were equally unconventional."

"I've never met my mother's sister, Aunt Cymry, but my father says she's a dangerous mutant they've locked away somewhere."

The Russian shrugged. "I would nevertheless wager heavily on the equivalency of our families. Should I lead the way or follow you?"

If he contained chaos on some level below wardrobe and face and eyes, it must be in his mind. I wondered what kind of strange order might underlie it.

"Sir, I've never driven in snow before. I'm not sure how I'll be able to tell, under all the drifts, exactly where the driveway runs between here and the abbey. I'd have to plow by intuition—though I usually do all right that way."

"With all due respect, Mr. Thomas, I believe that experience trumps intuition. Russia is a world of snow, and in fact I was born during a blizzard."

"During a blizzard, in a mortuary?"

"Actually, in a library."

"Was your mother a librarian?"

"No," he said. "She was an assassin."

"An assassin."

"That is correct."

"Do you mean *assassin* figuratively or literally, sir?"

"Both, Mr. Thomas. When driving behind me, please remain at a safe distance. Even with four-wheel drive and chains, there is some danger of sliding."

"I feel like I've been sliding all day. I'll be careful, sir."

"If you do start to slide, turn the wheel into the direction of the slide. Do not try to pull out of it. And use the brakes gently." He walked to the other SUV and opened the driver's door.

Before he climbed behind the wheel, I said, "Sir, lock your doors. And if you see anything unusual in the storm, don't get out of the truck to have a closer look at it. Keep driving."

"Unusual? Such as?"

"Oh, you know, anything unusual. Say like a snowman with three heads or someone who looks like she might be my Aunt Cymry."

Romanovich could peel an apple with his stare.

With a little good-luck wave, I got into my truck, and after a moment, he got into his.

After he drove around me to the foot of the ramp, I pulled in behind him.

He used his remote opener, and at the top of the incline, the big door began to roll up.

Beyond the garage lay a chaos of bleak light, shrieking wind, and a perpetual avalanche of falling snow.

CHAPTER 35

IN FRONT OF ME, RODION ROMANOVICH DROVE out of the garage into hammers of wind and shatters of snow, and I switched on my headlamps. The drowned daylight required them in this feathered rain.

Even as those beams brought sparkle to the dull white curtains of snow, Elvis materialized in the passenger seat as though I had switched him on, as well.

He was dressed in his navy-frogman scuba suit from *Easy Come, Easy Go,* possibly because he thought I needed a laugh.

The black neoprene hood fitted tightly to his head, covering his hair, his ears, and his forehead to the eyebrows. With his face thus isolated, the sensuous quality of his features was weirdly enhanced, but not to good effect. He looked not like a navy frogman but rather like a sweet little bow-lipped Kewpie doll that some pervert had dressed in a bondage costume.

"Oh, man, that movie," I said. "With that one, you gave new meaning to the word *ridiculous.*"

He laughed soundlessly, pretended to shoot me with a spear

gun, and phased from the scuba suit into the Arabian costume he
had worn in *Harum Scarum.*

"You're right," I agreed, "that one was even worse."

When making his music, he had been the essence of cool, but
in his movies he was often a self-parody embarrassing to watch.
Colonel Parker, his manager, who had picked movie scripts for
him, had served Elvis less well than the monk Rasputin had
served Czar Nicholas and Alexandra.

I drove out of the garage, stopped, and thumbed the remote to
put down the door behind me.

Using the rearview mirror, I watched until the door had closed
entirely, prepared to shift into reverse and run down any fugitive
from a nightmare that tried to enter the garage.

Apparently calculating the correct path of the driveway by a
logical analysis of the topography, Romanovich plowed without
error north-by-northwest, exposing blacktop as he ascended in a
gentle curve.

Some of the scooped-away snow spilled back onto the pavement in his wake. I lowered my plow until it barely skimmed the
blacktop, and cleaned up after him. I remained at the requested
safe distance, both out of respect for his experience and because I
didn't want him to report me to his mother, the assassin.

Wind skirled as though a dozen Scottish funerals were under
way. Concussive blasts rocked the SUV, and I was grateful that
it was an extended model with a lower point of gravity, further
anchored by the heavy plow.

The snow was so dry and the blow so relentlessly scolding that
nothing stuck to the windshield. I didn't turn on the wipers.

Scanning the slope ahead, left and right, checking the mirrors,
I expected to see one or more of the bone beasts out for a lark in

the blizzard. The white torrents foiled vision almost as effectively as a sandstorm in the Mojave, but the stark geometric lines of the creatures, by contrast, ought to draw the eye in this comparatively soft sweep of stormscape.

Except for the SUVs, nothing moved other than what the wind harried. Even a few big trees along the route, pines and firs, were so heavily weighed down by the snow already plastered on them that their boughs barely shivered in deference to the gale.

In the passenger seat, Elvis, having gone blond, had also phased into the work boots, peg-legged jeans, and plaid shirt he had worn in *Kissin' Cousins*. He played two roles in that one: a dark-haired air-force officer and a yellow-haired hillbilly.

"You don't see many blond hillbillies in real life," I said, "especially not with perfect teeth, black eyebrows, and teased hair."

He pretended to have a buck-toothed overbite and crossed his eyes to try to give the role more of a *Deliverance* edge.

I laughed. "Son, you've been going through some changes lately. You were never able to laugh this easily about your bad choices."

For a moment he seemed to consider what I had said, and then he pointed at me.

"What?"

He grinned and nodded.

"You think I'm funny?"

He nodded again, then shook his head no, as if to say he thought I was funny but that wasn't what he had meant. He pulled on a serious expression and pointed at me again, then at himself.

If he meant what I thought he did, I was flattered. "The one who taught *me* how to laugh at my foolishness was Stormy."

He looked at his blond hair in the rearview mirror, shook his head, laughed silently again.

"When you laugh at yourself, you gain perspective. Then you realize that the mistakes you made, as long as they didn't hurt anyone but yourself—well, you can forgive yourself for those."

After thinking about that for a moment, he gave me one thumb up as a sign of agreement.

"You know what? Everyone who crosses over to the Other Side, if he didn't know it before he went, suddenly understands the thousand ways he was a fool in this world. So everyone over there understands everyone over here better than we understand ourselves—and forgives us our foolishness."

He knew that I meant his beloved mother would greet him with delighted laughter, not with disappointment and certainly not with shame. Tears welled in his eyes.

"Just think about it," I said.

He bit his lower lip and nodded.

Peripherally, I glimpsed a swift presence in the storm. My heart jumped, and I turned toward the movement, but it was only Boo.

With canine exuberance, he appeared almost to skate up the hill, glorying in the winter spectacle, neither troubled by nor troubling the hostile landscape, a white dog racing through a white world.

After rounding the back of the church, we drove toward the entrance to the guesthouse, where the brothers would meet us.

Elvis had phased from carefully coiffed hillbilly to physician. He wore a white lab coat, and a stethoscope hung around his neck.

"Hey, that's right. You were in a movie with nuns. You played a doctor. *Change of Habit.* Mary Tyler Moore was a nun. Not immortal cinema, maybe not up there with the Ben Affleck-Jennifer Lopez oeuvre, but not egregiously silly."

He put his right hand over his heart and made a patting motion to suggest a rapid beat.

"You loved Mary Tyler Moore?" When he nodded, I said, "Everybody loved Mary Tyler Moore. But you were just friends with her in real life, right?"

He nodded. Just friends. He made the patting motion again. Just friends, but he loved her.

Rodion Romanovich braked to a stop in front of the guesthouse entrance.

As I pulled up slowly behind the Russian, Elvis put the ear tips of the stethoscope in his ears and pressed the diaphragm to my chest, as though listening to my heart. His stare was meaningful and colored with sorrow.

I shifted into park, tramped the emergency brake, and said, "Son, don't you worry about me. You hear? No matter what happens, I'll be all right. When my day comes, I'll be even better, but in the meantime, I'll be all right. You do what you need to do, and don't you worry about me."

He kept the stethoscope to my chest.

"You've been a blessing to me in a hard time," I told him, "and nothing would please me more than if I proved to be a blessing to you."

He put one hand on the back of my neck and squeezed, the way a brother might express himself when he has no adequate words.

I opened the door and got out of the SUV, and the wind was so cold.

CHAPTER 36

BAKED BY BITTER COLD, HALF THE FLUFF OF THE falling snow had been seared away. The flakes were almost grains now, and they stung my face as I waded through twenty inches of powder to meet Rodion Romanovich when he got out of his SUV. He had left the engine running and the lights on, as I had done.

I raised my voice above the wind: "The brothers will need help with their gear. Let them know we're here. The back row of seats in my truck are folded down. I'll come in as soon as I've put them up."

In the school garage, this son of an assassin had looked a bit theatrical in his bearskin hat and fur-trimmed leather coat, but in the storm he appeared imperial and in his element, as if he were the king of winter and could halt the falling snow with a gesture if he chose to do so.

He did not hunch forward and tuck his head to escape the bite of the wind, but stood tall and straight, and strode into the guesthouse with all the swagger you would expect of a man who had once prepared people for death.

The moment he had gone inside, I opened the driver's door of his SUV, killed the headlights, switched off the engine, and pocketed the keys.

I hurried back to the second vehicle to shut off its lights and engine as well. I pocketed those keys, too, assuring that Romanovich could not drive either SUV back to the school.

When I followed my favorite Hoosier into the guesthouse, I found sixteen brothers ready to rumble.

Practicality had required them to trade their usual habits for storm suits. These were not, however, the flashy kind of storm suits you would see on the slopes of Aspen and Vail. They did not hug the contours of the body to enhance aerodynamics and après-ski seduction, or feature vivid colors in bold designs.

The habits and ceremonial garments worn by the monks were cut and sewn by four brothers who had learned tailoring. These four had also created the storm suits.

Every suit was a dull blue-gray, without ornamentation. They were finely crafted, with foldaway hoods, ballistic-nylon scuff guards, and insulated snowcuffs with rubberized strippers: perfect gear for shoveling sidewalks and other foul-weather tasks.

Upon Romanovich's arrival, the brothers had begun to put on Thermoloft-insulated vests over their storm suits. The vests had elasticized gussets and reinforced shoulders, and like the storm suits, they offered a number of zippered pockets.

In this uniform, with their kind faces framed in snugly fitted hoods, they looked like sixteen spacemen who had just arrived from a planet so benign that its anthem must be "Teddy Bears on Parade."

Brother Victor, the former marine, moved among his troops, making sure that all the needed tools had been brought to this staging area.

Two steps inside the door, I spotted Brother Knuckles, and he nodded conspiratorially, and we rendezvoused immediately at the end of the reception lounge that was farthest from the marshaled forces of righteousness.

As I handed him the keys to the SUV that Romanovich had driven, Knuckles said, "Fortify and defend against who, son? When you gotta go to the mattresses, it's kinda traditional to know who's the mugs you're at war with."

"These are some epic bad mugs, sir. I don't have time to explain here. I'll lay it out when we get to the school. My biggest problem is how to explain it to the brothers, because it is mondo weird."

"I'll vouch for you, kid. When Knuckles says a guy's word is gold, there ain't no doubters."

"There's going to be some doubters this time."

"Better not be." His block-and-slab features fell into a hard expression suitable for a stone-temple god who didn't lightly suffer disbelievers. "There better be no doubters of you. Besides, maybe they don't know God's got a hand on your head, but they like you and they got a hunch somethin's special about you."

"And they're crazy about my pancakes."

"That don't hurt."

"I found Brother Timothy," I said.

The stone face broke a little. "Found poor Tim just the way I said he'd be, didn't you?"

"Not just the way, sir. But, yeah, he's with God now."

Making the sign of the cross, he murmured a prayer for Brother Timothy, and then said, "We got proof now—Tim, he didn't slip around to Reno for some R and R. The sheriff's gonna have to get real, give the kids the protection you want."

"Wish he would, but he won't. We still don't have a body."

"Maybe all those times I got my ears boxed is catchin' up with me, 'cause what I thought you said was you found his body."

"Yes, sir, I did, I found his body, but all that's left now is maybe the first couple centimeters of his face rolled up like on a sardine-can key."

Intensely eye to eye, he considered my words. Then: "That don't make no sense of no kind, son."

"No, sir, no sense. I'll tell you the whole thing when we get to the school, and when you hear it all, it'll make even less sense."

"And you think this Russian guy, he's in it somehow?"

"He's no librarian, and if he was ever a mortician, he didn't wait for business, he went out and made it."

"I can't puzzle the full sense of that one, neither. How's your shoulder from last night?"

"Still a little sore, but not bad. My head's okay, sir, I'm not concussed, I assure you."

Half the storm-suited monks had taken their gear outside to the SUVs and others were filing out of the door when Brother Saul, who was not going to the school, came to inform us that the abbey phones had gone dead.

"Do you usually lose the phones in a big storm?" I asked.

Brother Knuckles shook his head. "Maybe once in all the years I remember."

"There's still cell phones," I said.

"Somethin' tells me no, son."

Even in good weather, cell service wasn't reliable in this area. I fished my phone from a jacket pocket, switched it on, and we waited for the screen to give us bad news, which it did.

Whenever the crisis arrived, we wouldn't have easy communication between the abbey and the school.

"Back when I worked for the Eggbeater, we had a thing we said when there was too many funny coincidences."

"'There are no coincidences,'" I quoted.

"No, that ain't it. We said, 'Somebody amongst us musta let the FBI put a bug up his rectum.'"

"That's colorful, sir, but I'd be happy if this were the FBI."

"Well, I was on the dark side back then. You better tell the Russian he don't have a round-trip ticket."

"You've got his keys."

Carrying a toolbox in one hand and a baseball bat in the other, the last of the storm-suited brothers shouldered through the front door. The Russian wasn't in the room.

As Brother Knuckles and I stepped out into the snow, Rodion Romanovich drove away in the first SUV, which was fully loaded with monks.

"I'll be damned."

"Whoa. Careful with that, son."

"He took both sets of keys off the peg," I said.

Romanovich drove halfway back along the side of the church and then stopped, as though waiting for me to follow.

"This is bad," I said.

"Maybe this is God at work, son, and you just can't see the good in it yet."

"Is that confident faith talking, or is it the warm-and-fuzzy optimism of the mouse who saved the princess?"

"They're sort of one and the same, son. You want to drive?"

I handed him the keys to the second SUV. "No. I just want to sit quietly and stew in my stupidity."

CHAPTER 37

THE LINT-WHITE SKY SEEMED TO BRIGHTEN THE day less than did the blanketed land, as if the sun were dying and the earth were evolving into a new sun, though a cold one, that would illuminate little and warm nothing.

Brother Knuckles drove, following the devious faux librarian at a safe distance, and I rode shotgun without a shotgun. Eight brothers and their gear occupied the second, third, and fourth rows of seats in the extended SUV.

You might expect that a truckful of monks would be quiet, all the passengers in silent prayer or meditating on the state of their souls, or scheming each in his own way to conceal from humankind that the Church is an organization of extraterrestrials determined to rule the world through mind control, a dark truth known to Mr. Leonardo da Vinci, which we can prove by citing his most famous self-portrait, in which he depicted himself wearing a pyramid-shaped tinfoil hat.

Here in the early afternoon, the Lesser Silence should have been observed to the extent that work allowed, but the monks were voluble. They worried about their missing brother, Timothy, and were alarmed by the possibility that persons unknown intended to harm the children at the school. They sounded fearful, humbled, yet exhilarated that they might be called upon to be brave defenders of the innocent.

Brother Alfonse asked, "Odd, are all of us going to die?"

"I hope none of us is going to die," I replied.

"If all of us died, the sheriff would be disgraced."

"I fail to understand," said Brother Rupert, "the moral calculus that all of us dying would be balanced by the sheriff's disgrace."

"I assure you, Brother," Alfonse said, "I didn't mean to imply that mass death would be an acceptable price for the sheriff's defeat in the next election."

Brother Quentin, who had been a police officer at one time, first a beat patrolman and then a robbery-and-homicide detective, said, "Odd, who are these kid-killer wannabes?"

"We don't know for sure," I said, turning in my seat to look back at him. "But we know something's coming."

"What's the evidence? Obviously something that's not concrete enough to impress the sheriff. Threatening phone calls, like that?"

"The phones have gone down," I said evasively, "so there won't be any threatening calls now."

"Are you being evasive?" Brother Quentin asked.

"Yes, sir, I am."

"You're terrible at being evasive."

"Well, I do my best, sir."

"We need to know the name of our enemy," said Brother Quentin.

Brother Alfonse said, "We know the name. His name is legion."

"I don't mean our *ultimate* enemy," said Quentin. "Odd, we aren't going up against Satan with baseball bats, are we?"

"If it's Satan, I haven't noticed a sulfurous smell."

"You're being evasive again."

"Yes, sir."

From the third row, Brother Augustine said, "Why would you have to be evasive about whether or not it's Satan? We all know it's not Satan himself, it's got to be some anti-faith zealots or something, doesn't it?"

"Militant atheists," said someone at the back of the vehicle.

Another fourth-row passenger chimed in: "Islamofascists. The president of Iran said, 'The world will be cleaner when there's no one whose day of worship is Saturday. When they're all dead, we'll kill the Sunday crowd.'"

Brother Knuckles, behind the wheel, said, "No reason to work yourselves up about it. We get to the school—Abbot Bernard, he's gonna give you the straight poop, as far as we know it."

Surprised, indicating the SUV ahead of us, I said, "Is the abbot with them?"

Knuckles shrugged. "He insisted, son. Maybe he don't weigh more than a wet cat, but he's a plus to the team. There's not a thing in this world could scare the abbot."

I said, "There might be a thing."

From the second row, Brother Quentin put a hand on my shoulder, returning to his main issue with the persistence of a cop skilled at interrogation. "All I'm saying, Odd, is we need to know the name of our enemy. We don't exactly have a crew of trained warriors here. When push comes to shove, if they don't know who they're supposed to be defending against, they'll get so jittery, they'll start swinging baseball bats at one another."

Brother Augustine gently admonished, "Do not underestimate us, Brother Quentin."

"Maybe the abbot will bless the baseball bats," said Brother Kevin from the third row.

Brother Rupert said, "I doubt the abbot would think it proper to bless a baseball bat to ensure a game-winning home run, let alone to make it a more effective weapon for braining someone."

"I certainly hope," said Brother Kevin, "we don't have to brain anyone. The thought sickens me."

"Swing low," Brother Knuckles advised, "and take 'em out at the knees. Some guy with his knees all busted ain't an immediate threat, but the damage ain't permanent, neither. He's gonna heal back to normal. Mostly."

"We have a profound moral dilemma here," Brother Kevin said. "We must, of course, protect the children, but busting knees is not by any stretch of theology a Christian response."

"Christ," Brother Augustine reminded him, "physically threw the money changers out of the temple."

"Indeed, but I've seen nowhere in Scripture where our Lord busted their knees in the process."

Brother Alfonse said, "Perhaps we really are all going to die."

His hand still on my shoulder, Brother Quentin said, "Something more than a threatening call has you alarmed. Maybe . . . did you find Brother Timothy? Did you, Odd? Dead or alive?"

At this point, I wasn't going to say that I had found him dead *and* alive, and that he had suddenly transformed from Tim to something not Tim. Instead, I replied, "No, sir, not dead or alive."

Quentin's eyes narrowed. "You're being evasive again."

"How could you possibly know, sir?"

"You've got a tell."

"A what?"

"Every time you're being evasive, your left eye twitches ever so slightly. You have an eye-twitch tell that betrays your intention to be evasive."

As I turned front to deny Brother Quentin a view of my twitchy eye, I saw Boo bounding gleefully downhill through the snow.

Behind the grinning dog came Elvis, capering as if he were a child, leaving no prints behind himself, arms raised above his head, waving both hands high as some inspired evangelicals do when they shout *Hallelujah*.

Boo turned away from the plowed pavement and sprinted friskily across the meadow. Laughing and jubilant, Elvis ran after him. The rocker and the rollicking dog receded from view, neither troubled by the stormscape nor troubling it.

Most days, I wish that my special powers of vision and intuition had never been bestowed on me, that the grief they have brought to me could be lifted from my heart, that everything I have seen of the supernatural could be expunged from memory, and that I could be what, but for this gift, I otherwise am—no one special, just one soul in a sea of souls, swimming through the days toward a hope of that final sanctuary beyond all fear and pain.

Once in a while, however, there are moments for which the burden seems worth carrying: moments of transcendent joy, of inexpressible beauty, of wonder that overwhelms the mind with awe, or in this case a moment of such piercing charm that the world seems more right than it really is and offers a glimpse of what Eden might have been before we pulled it down.

Although Boo would remain at my side for days to come, Elvis would not be with me much longer. But I know that the image of them racing through the storm in rapturous delight will be with me vividly through all my days in this world, and forever after.

"Son?" Knuckles said, curious.

I realized that, although a smile was not appropriate to the moment, I was smiling.

"Sir, I think the King is about ready to move out of that place down at the end of Lonely Street."

"Heartbreak Hotel," said Knuckles.

"Yeah. It was never the five-star kind of joint where he should be booked to play."

Knuckles brightened. "Hey, that's swell, ain't it."

"It's swell," I agreed.

"Must feel good that you opened the big door for him."

"I didn't open the door," I said. "I just showed him where the knob was and which way it turned."

Behind me, Brother Quentin said, "What're you two talking about? I don't follow."

Without turning in my seat, I said, "In time, sir. You'll follow him in time. We'll all follow him in time."

"Him who?"

"Elvis Presley, sir."

"I'll bet your left eye is twitching like crazy," said Brother Quentin.

"I don't think so," I said.

Knuckles shook his head. "No twitch."

We had covered two-thirds of the distance between the new abbey and the school when out of the storm came a scissoring, scuttling, serpentine bewilderment of bones.

CHAPTER 38

ALTHOUGH BROTHER TIMOTHY HAD BEEN KILLED—
and worse than killed—by one of these creatures, a part of
me, the Pollyanna part I can't entirely wring out of myself, had
wanted to believe that the ever-moving mosaic of bones at the
school window and my pursuers in the cooling-tower service
tunnel had been apparitions, fearsome but, in the end, less real
than such threats as a man with a gun, a woman with a knife, or
a U.S. senator with an idea.

Pollyanna Odd half expected, as with the lingering dead and
the bodachs, that these entities would prove to be invisible to
anyone but me, and that what happened to Timothy was somehow a singularity, because supernatural presences, after all, do
not have the power to harm the living.

That hopeful possibility was flushed down the wishful-
thinking drain with the appearance of the keening banshee of
bones and the immediate reactions of Knuckles and his brothers.

As tall and long as two horses running nose to tail, ceaselessly kaleidoscopic even when traversing the meadow, the thing came out of the white wind and crossed the pavement in front of the first SUV.

In Dante's *Inferno,* in the ice and snowy mist of the frozen lowest level of Hell, the imprisoned Satan had appeared to the poet out of the winds made by his three sets of great leathery wings. The fallen angel, once beautiful but now hideous, had reeked of despair and misery and evil.

Likewise, here was misery and despair embodied in the calcium and phosphate of bone, and evil in the marrow. Its intentions were evident in its design, in its swift motion, and its every intention was pernicious.

Not one brother reacted to this manifestation with wonder or even with mere fear of the unknown, and none with disbelief. Without exception they regarded it at once as an abomination, and viewed it with as much disgust as terror, with loathing and with a righteous kind of hatred, as though upon seeing it for the first time they recognized it as an ancient and enduring beast.

If any was stunned to silence, he found his voice quickly, and the SUV was filled with exclamations. There were appeals to Christ and to the Holy Mother, and I heard no hesitation or embarrassment about labeling the thing before us with the names of demons or with the name of the father of all demons, though I'm reasonably sure the first words from Brother Knuckles were *Mamma mia.*

Rodion Romanovich brought his SUV to a full stop as the white demon passed in front of him.

When Knuckles braked, the chain-wrapped tires stuttered on the icy pavement but didn't slide, and we, too, shuddered to a halt.

The pistoning bony legs cast up plumes of snow from the meadow as the thing crossed the road and kept going, as though it was not aware of us. The trail it left in the fresh powder and the way the falling snow whirled in the currents of its wake dispelled any doubt about its reality.

Certain that the beast's disinterest in us was pretense and that it would return, I said to Knuckles, "Let's go. Don't just sit here. Go, go, get us inside."

"I can't go till he does," Knuckles said, indicating the SUV that blocked the road in front of us.

To the right, south, rose a steep bank, which the uberskeleton had descended in a centipedal scurry. We might not bog down in the deep drift, but the angle of incline would surely roll us.

In the northern meadow, the dismal light of the sunless day and shrouds of snow folded around the fantastic architecture of restless bones, but we had not seen the last of it.

Rodion Romanovich still stood on his brake pedal, and in the red taillights, snow came down in bloody showers.

To the left, the meadow dropped two feet from the driveway. We could probably have driven around Romanovich; but that was a needless risk.

"He's waiting for another look at it," I said. "Is he nuts? Give him the horn."

Knuckles pumped the horn, and the brake lights on Romanovich's SUV fluttered, and Knuckles used the horn again, and the Russian began to coast forward, but then braked once more.

Out of the north came the monster, harrowing the field of snow, moving less quickly than before, a sense of ominous intention in its more measured approach.

Amazement, fear, curiosity, disbelief: Whatever had immobilized Romanovich, he broke free of its hold. The SUV rolled forward.

Before Romanovich could build any speed, the creature arrived, reared up, extruded intricately pincered arms, seized its prey, and tipped the vehicle on its side.

CHAPTER 39

THE SUV LAY ON ITS STARBOARD SIDE. THE
slowly turning tires on the port side uselessly sought trac-
tion in the snow-shot air.

The Russian and the eight monks could exit only by the back
hatch or by the doors turned to the sky, but not with ease and not
with haste.

I assumed the beast would either pry open the doors and reach
inside for the nine men or pluck them as they tried to escape.
How it would do to them what it had done to Brother Timothy, I
didn't know, but I was certain that it would methodically gather
them to itself, one by one.

When they were harvested, it would carry them away to
crucify them on a wall as it had done with Timothy, transforming
their mortal forms into nine chrysalises. Or it would then come
after us, here in the second truck, and later in the day, the cooling
tower would be crowded with eighteen chrysalises.

Instead of proceeding with its usual mechanical insistence, the
thing retreated from the overturned SUV and waited, retaining

its basic form but continuously folding in upon itself and blooming out new vaned and petaled patterns.

With the nerveless aplomb of an experienced getaway driver,
Brother Knuckles engaged his safety harness, raised the steel plow
off the pavement, shifted gears, and reversed up the driveway.

"We can't leave them trapped," I said, and the brothers behind
me were in vociferous agreement.

"We ain't leavin' nobody," Knuckles assured me. "I just hope
they're scared enough to stay put."

Like a macabre motorized sculpture crafted by graverobbers,
the bone heap stood sentinel by the side of the road, perhaps
waiting for the doors on the overturned SUV to open.

When we had reversed fifty yards, the tipped truck became a
blur on the road below, and the sheeting snow almost entirely
camouflaged the bony specter.

I strapped myself into the shoulder harness—and heard the
brothers buckling up behind me. Even when God is your co-pilot,
it pays to pack a parachute.

Brother Knuckles slowed to a stop. With one foot on the brake,
he shifted into drive.

Except for the sound of their breathing, the monks had fallen
silent.

Then Brother Alfonse said, *"Libera nos a malo."*

Deliver us from evil.

Knuckles traded the brake pedal for the accelerator. The engine growled, the tire chains rang rhythms from the pavement,
and we raced downhill, aiming to sweep past the overturned
SUV and take out the fiend.

Our target seemed oblivious of us until the penultimate moment, or perhaps it had no fear.

Plow-first we slammed into the thing and instantly lost most of our forward momentum.

A furious hail crashed down. The windshield crazed, dissolved, fell in upon us, and with it came both loose bones and articulated structures.

An elaborately jointed array of bones landed in my lap, spasming like a broken crab. My cry was every bit as manly as that of a young schoolgirl surprised by a hairy spider. I knocked the thing off me, onto the floor.

It felt cold and slick, yet not greasy or wet, had seemed to harbor no warmth of life.

The castoff scrabbled at my feet, not with intent to harm but as the decapitated body of a snake lashes mindlessly. Nevertheless, I quickly pulled my feet onto the seat and would have gathered my petticoats tightly around me if I had been wearing any.

After coming to a stop ten yards past the overturned vehicle, we reversed until we were beside it once more, things snapping and crunching loudly under the tires.

When I got out of the truck, I found the pavement littered with twitching constructs of bones, splintered remnants of the beast's fragmented anatomy. Some were as large as vacuum cleaners, many the size of kitchen appliances—flexing, irising, folding, unfolding as if striving to obey the conjuring call of a sorcerer.

Thousands of single bones of all shapes and sizes were also scattered on the roadway. These rattled in place as if the ground were shaking under them, but I could not feel any earth tremors through the soles of my ski boots.

Kicking the debris aside, I cleared a path to the overturned

SUV and climbed onto the flank of it. Inside, tumbled brothers looked up at me, wide-eyed and blinking, through the side windows.

I pulled open a door, and Brother Rupert clambered up to assist. Soon we had pulled the Russian and the monks from the vehicle.

Some were bruised and all were shaken; but none of them had sustained a serious injury.

Every tire on the second SUV had been punctured by broken shafts of bone. The vehicle sat on flat rubber. We would have to walk the remaining hundred yards to the school.

No one needed to express the opinion that if one impossible ambulatory kaleidoscope of bones could exist, others might follow. In fact, whether because of shock or fear, few words were exchanged, and those were spoken in the softest voices.

Everyone worked urgently to unload all the tools and the other gear that had been brought to defend and fortify the school.

The rattling skeletal debris slowly grew quieter, and some bones began to break down into cubes in a variety of sizes, as though they had not been bones, after all, but structures formed from smaller interlocking pieces.

As we were setting out for the school, Rodion Romanovich took off his hat, stooped, and with one gloved hand scooped some of the cubes into that bearskin sack.

He looked up and saw me watching him. Clutching the hat in one hand as if it were a purse filled with treasure, he picked up what appeared to be a large attaché case, rather than a toolbox, and turned toward the school.

Around us, the wind seemed to be full of words, all angry and growing rapidly angrier, in a brutal language ideal for imprecation, malediction, blasphemy, and threat.

The veiled sky folded down to meet the hidden land, and the vanishment of the horizon was swiftly followed by the disappearance of every structure of man and nature. A perfect consistency of light throughout the bleak day, allowing no shadow, did not illuminate but blinded. In that white obscurity, all contours of the land faded from sight, except those directly underfoot, and we were plunged into a total whiteout.

With psychic magnetism, I am never lost. But at least a couple of the brothers might have wandered off forever, within mere yards of the school, if they had not stayed close to one another and had not received some guidance from the rapidly vanishing patches of blacktop exposed earlier by the plows.

More walking boneyards might be near, and I suspected that they would not be blinded by the whiteout, as we were. Whatever senses they possessed were not analogous—but perhaps superior—to ours.

Two steps before blundering into the segmented roll-up garage door, I saw it and halted. When the others had gathered around me, I did a count to be sure that all sixteen monks were present. They numbered seventeen. The Russian was there, but I had not mistakenly included him in the count.

I led them past the large door to a smaller, man-size entrance. With my universal key, I let us into the garage.

When everyone had passed safely inside, I closed and dead-bolted the door.

The brothers dropped their burdens on the floor, brushed snow from themselves, and pulled back their hoods.

The seventeenth monk proved to be Brother Leopold, the

novice who often came and went with the stealth of a ghost. His freckled face looked less wholesome than it had always been before, and his usual sunny smile was not in evidence.

Leopold stood next to the Russian, and there was an ineffable quality to their attitudes and postures that suggested they were in some way allied.

CHAPTER 40

ROMANOVICH WENT TO ONE KNEE ON THE garage floor, and from his bearskin hat, he spilled a collection of the white cubes onto the concrete.

The larger specimens were about an inch and a half square, the smaller perhaps half an inch. They were so polished and smooth that they might have been dice without spots, and looked not like natural objects but like manufactured items.

They twitched and rattled against one another, as though life yet existed in them. Perhaps they were agitated by the memory of the bone they had been, were programmed to reconstitute that structure but lacked the power.

I was reminded of jumping beans, those seeds of Mexican spurge that are animated by the movements of the moth larvae living in them.

Although I didn't believe that the agitation of these cubes was caused by the equivalent of moth larvae, I wasn't going to try to bite one open to confirm my opinion.

As the brothers gathered around to observe the blank dice, one of the larger specimens shook more violently—and rattled into four smaller, identical cubes.

Perhaps triggered by that action, a smaller cube turned end over end and rendered itself into four diminished replicas.

Glancing up from the self-dividing geometrics, Romanovich locked eyes with Brother Leopold.

"Quantumizing," the novice said.

The Russian nodded in agreement.

I said, "What's going on here?"

Instead of answering me, Romanovich returned his attention to the dice and said, almost to himself, "Incredible. But where's the heat?"

As if this question alarmed him, Leopold took two steps back.

"You would want to be twenty miles from here," Romanovich told the novice. "A bit late for that."

"You knew each other before coming here," I said.

With increasing rapidity, the cubes were breaking down into ever-smaller units.

Turning my attention to the brothers, expecting them to support my demand for answers from the Russian, I discovered their attention fixed not on Romanovich or Leopold, but instead half on me and half on the strange—and ever-tinier—objects on the floor.

Brother Alfonse said, "Odd, in the SUV, when we saw that thing come out of the snow, you didn't seem stunned by the sight of it like the rest of us were."

"I was . . . just speechless," I said.

"There's that eye-twitch tell," said Brother Quentin, pointing at me, frowning as he must have frowned at numerous suspects in the homicide-division interrogation room.

As the cubes continued dividing, growing dramatically in number, the collective mass of them should have remained the same. Cube an apple, and the pieces will weigh as much as the whole fruit. But mass was disappearing here.

This suggested that, after all, the beast had been supernatural, manifesting in a material with more apparent substance—but no more real physical existence—than ectoplasm.

The problems with that theory were many. For one thing, Brother Timothy was dead, and no mere spirit had killed him. The SUV had not been overturned by the anger of a poltergeist.

Judging by the ghastly expression that had drained all the sunny Iowan charm from his boyish face, Brother Leopold was clearly focused on an explanation different from—and far more terrifying than—any supernatural manifestation.

On the floor, the cubes had become so numerous and tiny that they appeared to be only a spill of salt. And then . . . the concrete was bare again, as though the Russian had never emptied anything out of his hat.

Color began to seep back into Brother Leopold's face, and he shuddered with relief.

Masterfully deflecting curiosity that might have been directed at him, Romanovich rose to his feet and, to reinforce the brothers' intuitive belief that I knew more about this situation than they did, he said, "Mr. Thomas, what *was* that thing out there?"

All the brothers were staring at me, and I realized that I—with my universal key and sometimes enigmatic behavior—had always been a more mysterious figure to them than was either the Russian or Brother Leopold.

"I don't know what it was," I said. "I wish I did."

Brother Quentin said, "No eye-twitch tell. Have you learned to suppress it or are you really not being evasive?"

Before I could respond, Abbot Bernard said, "Odd, I would like you to tell these brothers about your exceptional abilities."

Surveying the faces of the monks, each shining with curiosity, I said, "In all the world, sir, there aren't half this many people who know my secret. It feels like . . . going public."

"I am instructing them herewith," the abbot said, "to regard your revelations as a confession. As your confessors, your secrets are to them a sacred trust."

"Not to all of them," I said, not bothering to accuse Brother Leopold of being insincere in his postulancy and in the profession of his vows as a novice, but addressing myself solely to Romanovich.

"I am not leaving," the Russian said, returning the bearskin hat to his head as if to punctuate his declaration.

I had known that he would insist on hearing what I had to tell the others, but I said, "Don't you have a couple of poisoned cakes to decorate?"

"No, Mr. Thomas, I have finished all ten."

After once more surveying the earnest faces of the monks, I said, "I see the lingering dead."

"This guy," said Brother Knuckles, "maybe he evades a question when he's gotta, but he don't know how to lie any better than a two-year-old."

I said, "Thanks. I think."

"In my other life, before God called me," Knuckles continued, "I lived in a filthy sea of liars and lies, and I swam as good as any of those mugs. Odd—he ain't like them, ain't like I once was. Fact is, he ain't like nobody I ever known before."

After that sweet and heartfelt endorsement, I told my story as succinctly as possible, including that I had for years worked with the chief of police in Pico Mundo, who had vouched for me with Abbot Bernard.

The brothers listened, rapt, and expressed no doubts. Although ghosts and bodachs were not included in the doctrines of their faith, they were men who had given their lives to an absolute conviction that the universe was God-created and that it had a vertical sacred order. Having found a way to understand the existence of the monster in the storm—by defining it as a demon—they would not now be cast into spiritual or intellectual turmoil merely by being asked to believe that a nobody smart-ass fry cook was visited by the restless dead and tried to bring them justice as best he could.

They were emotional at the news that Brother Constantine had not committed suicide. But the faceless figure of Death in the bell tower intrigued more than frightened them, and they were in agreement that if a traditional exorcism would be effective with either of these two recent apparitions, it would be more likely to work on the tower phantom than on an uberskeleton that could overturn an SUV.

I couldn't tell whether Brother Leopold and Rodion Romanovich believed me, but I didn't owe those two any evidence beyond the sincerity of my story.

To Leopold, I said, "I don't believe that an exorcism will work in either case—do you?"

The novice lowered his gaze to the place on the floor where the cubes had been. He nervously licked his lips.

The Russian spared his comrade the need to answer: "Mr. Thomas, I am fully prepared to believe that you live on a ledge between this world and the next, that you see what we cannot. And now you have seen apparitions previously unknown to you."

"Are they previously unknown to *you*?" I asked.

"I am merely a librarian, Mr. Thomas, with no sixth sense. But I am a man of faith, whether you believe that or not, and now that I have heard your story, I am worried about the children as much as you are. How much time do we have? Whatever will happen, *when* will it happen?"

I shook my head. "I only saw seven bodachs this morning. There would be more if the violence was imminent."

"That was this morning. Do you think we should have a look now—past one-thirty in the afternoon?"

"Bring all your tools and the . . . weapons," Abbot Bernard advised his brothers.

The snow had melted off my boots. I wiped them on the mat at the door between the garage and the basement of the school, while the other men, who were all veterans of winter and all more considerate than I, shucked off their zippered rubber boots and left them behind.

With lunch finished, most of the kids were in the rehabilitation and recreation rooms, each of which I visited with the abbot, a few brothers, and Romanovich.

Sooty shadows, cast by nothing in this world, slid through these rooms and along the hallway, quivering with anticipation, wolfish and eager, seeming to thrill to the sight of so many innocent children who they somehow knew would in time be screaming in terror and agony. I counted seventy-two bodachs and knew that others would be prowling the corridors on the second floor.

"Soon," I told the abbot. "It's coming soon."

CHAPTER 41

WHILE THE SIXTEEN WARRIOR MONKS AND the one duplicitous novice determined how to fortify the two stairwells that served the second floor of the school, Sister Angela was present to ensure that her nuns were prepared to offer any assistance that might be wanted.

As I headed toward the northwest nurses' station, she fell in beside me. "Oddie, I hear something happened on the trip back from the abbey."

"Yes, ma'am. Sure did. I don't have time to go into it now, but your insurance carrier is going to have a lot of questions."

"Do we have bodachs here?"

I looked left and right into the rooms we passed. "The place is crawling with them, Sister."

Rodion Romanovich followed us with the authoritarian air of one of those librarians who rules the stacks with an intimidating scowl, whispers *quiet* sharply enough to lacerate the tender inner tissues of the ear, and will pursue an overdue-book fine with the ferocity of a rabid ferret.

"How is Mr. Romanovich assisting here?" Sister Angela asked.

"He isn't assisting, ma'am."

"Then what's he doing?"

"Scheming, most likely."

"Shall I throw him out?" she asked.

Through my mind flickered a short film of the mother superior wrenching the Russian's arm up hard behind his back in some clever tae kwon do move, muscling him downstairs to the kitchen, and making him sit in a corner on a stool for the duration.

"Actually, ma'am, I'd rather have him hovering over me than have to wonder where he is and what he's up to."

At the nurses' station, Sister Miriam, with *Thanks be to God* forever on her lips, or at least forever on the lower one, was still behind the counter.

She said, "Dear, the dark clouds of mystery surrounding you are getting so thick I soon won't be able to see you. This sooty whirl of smog will go past, and people will say, 'There's Odd Thomas. Wonder what he looks like these days.'"

"Ma'am, I need your help. You know Justine in Room Thirty-two?"

"Dear, I not only know every child here, but I love them like they were my own."

"When she was four, her father drowned her in the bathtub but didn't finish the job the way he did with her mother. Is that correct, do I have it right?"

Her eyes narrowed. "I don't want to think in what sort of place his soul is festering now." She glanced at her mother superior and said, with an edge of guilt in her voice, "Actually, I not only sometimes think about it, I *enjoy* thinking about it."

"What I need to know, Sister, is maybe he *did* finish the job, and Justine was dead for a couple minutes before the police or the paramedics revived her. Could that have happened?"

Sister Angela said, "Yes, Oddie. We can check her file, but I believe that was the case. She suffered brain damage from prolonged lack of oxygen, and in fact had no vital signs when the police broke into the house and found her."

This was why the girl could serve as a bridge between our world and the next: She had once been over there, if only briefly, and had been pulled back by men who had all the best intentions. Stormy had been able to reach out to me through Justine because Justine belonged on the Other Side more than she did here.

I asked, "Are there other children here who suffered brain damage from oxygen deprivation?"

"A few," Sister Miriam confirmed.

"Are they—are any of them—more alert than Justine? No, that's not the issue. Are they capable of speech? That's what I need to know."

Having moved to the counter beside the mother superior, Rodion Romanovich scowled intently at me, like a mortician who, in need of work, believed that I would soon be a candidate for embalming.

"Yes," said Sister Angela. "There are at least two."

"Three," Sister Miriam amended.

"Ma'am, were any of the three clinically dead and then revived by police or paramedics, the way Justine was?"

Frowning, Sister Miriam looked at her mother superior. "Do you know?"

Sister Angela shook her head. "I suppose it would be in the patient records."

"How long will it take you to review the records, ma'am?"

"Half an hour, forty minutes? Maybe we'll find something like that in the first file."

"Would you please do it, Sister, fast as you can? I need a child who was dead once but can still talk."

Of the three of them, only Sister Miriam knew nothing about my sixth sense. "Dear, you are starting to get downright spooky."

"I've always been, ma'am."

CHAPTER 42

IN ROOM 14, JACOB HAD FINISHED THE LATEST portrait of his mother and had sprayed it with fixative. He carefully sharpened each of his many pencils on the sandpaper block, in anticipation of the blank page of the drawing tablet on the slantboard.

Also on the table was a lunch tray laden with empty dishes and dirty flatware.

No bodachs were currently present, although the darksome spirit who called himself Rodion Romanovich stood in the open doorway, his coat draped over one arm but his fur hat still on his head. I had forbidden him to enter the room because his glowering presence might intimidate the shy young artist.

If the Russian entered against my wishes, I would snatch his hat from his head, park my butt on it, and threaten to scent it with essence of Odd if he didn't back off. I can be ruthless.

I sat across the table from Jacob and said, "It's me again. The Odd Thomas."

Toward the end of my previous visit, he had met my every

comment and question with such silence that I'd become convinced he had gone into an internal redoubt where he didn't any longer hear me or even recognize that I was present.

"The new portrait of your mother came out very well. It's one of your best."

I had hoped that he would be in a more garrulous mood than when I had last seen him. This proved to be a false hope.

"She must have been very proud of your talent."

Jacob finished sharpening the last of the pencils, kept it in his hand, and shifted his attention to the drawing tablet, studying the blank page.

"Since I was last here," I told him, "I had a wonderful roast-beef sandwich and a crisp dill pickle that probably wasn't poisoned."

His thick tongue appeared, and he bit gently on it, perhaps deciding what his first pencil strokes should be.

"Then this nasty guy almost hanged me from the bell tower, and I got chased through a tunnel by a big bad scary thing, and I went on a snow adventure with Elvis Presley."

He began lightly and fluidly to sketch the outline of something that I could not recognize at once from my upside-down point of view.

At the doorway, Romanovich sighed impatiently.

Without looking at him, I said, "Sorry. I know my interrogation techniques aren't as direct as those of a librarian."

To Jacob, I said, "Sister Miriam says you lost your mother when you were thirteen, more than twelve years ago."

He was sketching a boat from a high perspective.

"I've never lost a mother because I never really had one. But I lost a girl I loved. She meant everything to me."

With a few lines he suggested that the sea, when fully drawn, would be gently rolling.

"She was beautiful, this girl, and beautiful in her heart. She was kind and tough, sweet and determined. Smart, she was smarter than me. And so funny."

Jacob paused to study what he had thus far put on the paper.

"Life had been hard on this girl, Jacob, but she had enough courage for an army."

His tongue retreated, and he bit instead on his lower lip.

"We never made love. Because of a bad thing that happened to her when she was a little girl, she wanted to wait. Wait until we could afford to be married."

With two styles of cross-hatching, he began to give substance to the hull of the boat.

"Sometimes I thought I couldn't wait, but then I always could. Because she gave me so much else, and everything she gave me was more than a thousand other girls could ever give. All she wanted was love with respect, respect was so important to her, and I could give her that. I don't know what she saw in me, you know? But I could give her that much."

The pencil whispered over the paper.

"She took four bullets in the chest and abdomen. My sweet girl, who never hurt a soul."

The moving pencil gave Jacob comfort. I could see how he took comfort from creation.

"I killed the man who killed her, Jacob. If I had gotten there two minutes sooner, I might have killed him before he killed her."

The pencil hesitated, but then moved on.

"We were destined to be together forever, my girl and I. We had a fortune-teller's card that said so. And we will be . . . forever.

This here, now—this is just an intermission between act one and act two."

Perhaps Jacob trusts God to guide his hand and show him the very boat and the precise place on the ocean where the bell rang, so he will know it, after all, when his own time comes to float away.

"They didn't scatter my girl's ashes at sea. They gave them to me in an urn. A friend in my hometown keeps it safe for me."

As the pencil whispered, Jacob murmured, "She could sing."

"If her voice was as lovely as her face, it must have been sweet. What did she sing?"

"So pretty. Just for me. When the dark came."

"She sang you to sleep."

"When I woke up and the dark wasn't gone yet, and the dark seemed so big, then she sang soft and made the dark small again."

That is the best of all things we can do for one another: Make the dark small.

"Jacob, earlier you told me about someone called the Neverwas."

"He's the Neverwas, and we don't care."

"You said he came to see you when you were 'full of the black.'"

"Jacob was full of the black, and the Neverwas said, 'Let him die.'"

"So 'full of the black' means you were ill. Very ill. Was the man who said they should let you die—was he a doctor?"

"He was the Neverwas. That's all he was. And we don't care."

I watched the graceful lines emerge from the simple pencil gripped by the stubby fingers of the short broad hand.

"Jacob, do you remember the face of the Neverwas?"

"A long time ago." He shook his head. "A long time ago."

Cataracts of falling snow made a blind eye of the window.

In the doorway, Romanovich tapped one finger against the face of his watch and raised his eyebrows.

We might have precious little time remaining, but I could think of nowhere better to spend it than here, where I had been sent by the medium of the once-dead Justine.

Intuition raised a question that at once seemed important to me.

"Jacob, you know my name, my full name."

"The Odd Thomas."

"Yes. My last name is Thomas. Do you know your last name?"

"Her name."

"That's right. It would be your mother's last name, too."

"Jennifer."

"That's a first name, like Jacob."

The pencil stopped moving, as if the memory of his mother came so vividly to him that no part of his mind or heart remained free to guide his drawing.

"Jenny," he said. "Jenny Calvino."

"So you are Jacob Calvino."

"Jacob Calvino," he confirmed.

Intuition had told me that the name would be revealing, but it meant nothing to me.

Again the pencil moved, and the boat took further form, the vessel from which Jenny Calvino's ashes had been dispersed.

As during my previous visit, a second large drawing tablet lay closed on the table. The longer I tried and dismally failed to think of questions that might extract vital information from Jacob, the more my attention was compelled toward that tablet.

If I inspected the second tablet without permission, Jacob might consider my curiosity a violation of his privacy. Offended, he might withdraw again, and give me nothing further.

On the other hand, if I asked to see the tablet and he refused permission, that avenue of inquiry would be closed off.

Jacob's last name was not revelatory, as I had thought it would be, but in this case, I did not think that intuition would fail me. The tablet seemed almost to glow, almost to be floating above the table, the most vivid thing in the room, hyper-real.

I slid the tablet in front of me, and Jacob either did not notice or did not care.

When I turned back the cover, I found a drawing of this room's only window. Pressed to the glass was a kaleidoscope of bones, which he had rendered in exquisite detail.

Sensing that I had found something alarming, Romanovich took a step into the room.

I raised one hand to warn him to stop, but then held up the drawing so he could see it.

When I turned the page, I found another depiction of the beast at the same window, though in this one, the bones formed a pattern different from the first.

Either the thing had clung to the window long enough for Jacob to draw it in great detail, which I doubted, or he had a photographic memory.

The third drawing was of a robed figure wearing a necklace of human teeth and bones: Death as I had seen him in the bell tower, with pale hands and without a face.

As I was about to show this drawing to Romanovich, three bodachs slunk into the room, and I closed the tablet.

CHAPTER 43

EITHER NOT INTERESTED IN ME OR PRETENDING no interest, the three sinister shapes gathered around Jacob.

Their hands were fingerless, as devoid of detail as were their faces and forms. Yet they were more suggestive of paws—or the webbed extremities of amphibians—than of hands.

As Jacob worked, oblivious of his spirit visitors, they appeared to stroke his cheeks. Quivering with excitement, the specters traced the curve of his thick neck and kneaded his heavy shoulders.

Bodachs appear to experience this world with some if not all of the usual five senses, perhaps also with a sixth sense of their own, but they have no effect on things here. If a hundred were to rush past in a pack, they would make no sound, create no slightest draft.

They seemed to thrill to a radiance produced by Jacob that was invisible to me, perhaps his life force, knowing that soon it would be torn from him. When eventually the violence comes, the pending horror that has drawn them, they will shudder and spasm and swoon in ecstasy.

Previously, I have had reason to suspect that they might not be spirits. I sometimes wonder if they are instead time travelers who return to the past not physically but in virtual bodies.

If our current barbaric world spirals into greater corruption and brutality, our descendants may become so cruel and so morally perverse that they cross time to watch us suffer, bearing orgasmic witness to the bloodbaths from which their sick civilization grew.

In truth, that is a few small steps down from current audiences' fascination with the wall-to-wall disaster coverage, bloody murder stories, and relentless fear-mongering that comprise TV news.

These descendants of ours would surely look like us and would be able to pass for us if they journeyed here in their real bodies. Therefore, the creepy bodach form, the virtual body, might be a reflection of their twisted, diseased souls.

One of these three prowled on all fours around the room, and sprang onto the bed, where it seemed to sniff the sheets.

As if it were smoke drawn by a draft, another bodach slithered through a crack under the bathroom door. I don't know what it did in there, but for sure it didn't take a potty break.

They don't pass through walls and closed doors, as the lingering dead can do. They must have the crack, the chink, the open keyhole.

While they have no mass and should not be affected by gravity, the bodachs do not fly. They climb and descend stairs three or four at a time, in a lope, but never glide through the air as do movie ghosts. I have seen them race in frenzied packs, as swift as panthers but limited by the contours of the land.

They seem to be bound by some—but not all—rules of our world.

From the doorway, Romanovich said, "Is something wrong?"

I shook my head and subtly made a zip-your-lips gesture, which any real librarian should at once understand.

Although surreptitiously watching the bodachs, I pretended to be interested only in Jacob's drawing of a boat at sea.

In all my life, I have encountered just one other person who could see bodachs, a six-year-old English boy. Moments after he had spoken aloud of these dark presences, within their hearing, he had been crushed by a runaway truck.

According to the Pico Mundo coroner, the driver of the truck had suffered a massive stroke and had collapsed against the steering wheel.

Yeah, right. And the sun comes up every morning by sheer chance, and mere coincidence explains why darkness follows sunset.

After the bodachs departed Room 14, I said to Romanovich, "For a minute there, we weren't alone."

I opened the tablet to the third drawing and stared at faceless Death festooned with human teeth. The following pages were blank.

When I turned the tablet to face Jacob and put it on the table near him, he did not glance at it, but remained fixated on his work.

"Jacob, where did you see this thing?"

He did not reply, and I hoped that he had not gone away from me again.

"Jake, I've seen this thing, too. Just today. At the top of the bell tower."

Trading his pencil for another, Jacob said, "He comes here."

"To this room, Jake? When did he come?"

"Many times he comes."

"What does he do here?"

"Watches Jacob."

"He just watches you?"

The sea began to flow from the pencil. The initial tones and textures committed to the paper suggested that the water would be undulant, ominous, and dark.

"Why does he watch you?" I asked.

"You know."

"I do? I guess I forgot."

"Wants me dead."

"You said earlier that the Neverwas wants you dead."

"He's the Neverwas, and we don't care."

"This drawing, this hooded figure—is he the Neverwas?"

"Not scared of him."

"Is this who came to see you when you were sick that time, when you were full of the black?"

"The Neverwas said, 'Let him die,' but she wouldn't let Jacob die."

Either Jacob saw spirits, as I did, or this death figure was no more a spirit than had been the walking boneyard.

Seeking to establish the reality of it, I said, "Your mother saw the Neverwas?"

"She said come, and he came just the once."

"Where were you when he came?"

"Where they all wore white and squeaked in their shoes and used the needles for medicine."

"So you were in the hospital, and the Neverwas came. But did he come in a black robe with a hood, with a necklace of human teeth?"

"No. Not like that, not back in the long ago, only now."

"And he had a face then, didn't he?"

In graded tones, the sea formed, full of its own darkness, but brightened elsewhere by reflections of the sky.

"Jacob, did he have a face in the long ago?"

"A face and hands, and she said, 'What's wrong with you,' and the Neverwas said, 'What's wrong is with him,' and she said, 'My God, my God, are you afraid to touch him,' and he said, 'Don't be a bitch about it.'"

He lifted his pencil from the paper because his hand had begun to tremble.

The emotion in his voice had been intense. Toward the end of that soliloquy, his mild speech impediment had thickened.

Concerned that I might drive him into withdrawal by pressing too hard, I gave him time to settle.

When his hand stopped trembling, he returned to the creation of the sea.

I said, "You are being such a help to me, Jake. You are being a friend to me, and I know this isn't easy for you, but I love you for being such a friend to me."

He glanced almost furtively at me, then returned his gaze at once to the drawing paper.

"Jake, will you draw something especially for me? Will you draw the face of the Neverwas, the way he looked in the long ago?"

"Can't," he said.

"I'm pretty sure you have a photographic memory. That means you remember everything you see, in great detail, even from long before the ocean and the bell and the floating away." I glanced at the wall with the many portraits of his mother. "Like your mother's face. Am I right, Jake? Do you remember everything from long ago as clear as if you just saw it an hour ago?"

He said, "It hurts."

"What hurts, Jake?"

"All of it, so clear."

"I'll bet it does. I know it does. My girl has been gone sixteen months, and I see her clearer every day."

He drew, and I waited.

Then I said, "Do you know how old you were that time in the hospital?"

"Seven. I was seven."

"So will you draw me the face of the Neverwas, from that time in the hospital when you were seven?"

"Can't. My eyes was funny then. Like a window with the rain and nothing looks right through it."

"Your vision was blurred that day?"

"Blurred."

"From the sickness, you mean." My hope deflated. "I guess it might have been blurred."

I turned back one tablet page to the second drawing of the bone kaleidoscope at the window.

"How often have you seen this thing, Jake?"

"More than one thing. Different ones."

"How often have they been at the window?"

"Three times."

"Just three? When?"

"Two times yesterday. Then when I woke from the sleep."

"When you woke up this morning?"

"Yeah."

"I've seen them, too," I told him. "I can't figure out what they are. What do you think they are, Jake?"

"The dogs of the Neverwas," he said without hesitation. "I'm not scared of them."

"Dogs, huh? I don't see dogs."

"Not dogs but like dogs," he explained. "Like really bad dogs, he teaches to kill, and he sends them, and they kill."

"Attack dogs," I said.

"I'm not scared, and I won't be."

"You're a very brave young man, Jacob Calvino."

"She said . . . she said don't be scared, we wasn't born to be all the time scared, we was born happy, babies laugh at everything, we was born happy and to make a better world."

"I wish I'd known your mother."

"She said everyone . . . everyone, if he's rich or he's poor, if he's somebody big or nobody at all—everyone has a grace." A look of peace came over his embattled face when he said the word *grace*. "You know what a grace is?"

"Yes."

"A grace is a thing you get from God, you use it to make a better world, or not use it, you have to choose."

"Like your art," I said. "Like your beautiful drawings."

He said, "Like your pancakes."

"Ah, you know I made those pancakes, huh?"

"Those pancakes, that's a grace."

"Thank you, Jake. That's very kind of you." I closed the second tablet and got up from my chair. "I have to go now, but I'd like to come back, if that's all right."

"All right."

"Are you going to be okay?"

"All right, okay," he assured me.

I went to his side of the table, put a hand on his shoulder, and studied the drawing from his perspective.

He was a superb renderer, but he wasn't just that. He understood the qualities of light, the fact of light even in shadow, the beauty of light and the need for it.

At the window, though the winter twilight lay a few hours away, most of the light had been choked out of the blizzard-throttled sky. Already the day had come to dusk.

Earlier, Jacob had warned me that the dark would come with the dark. Maybe we couldn't expect that death would wait for full night. Maybe the gloom of this false dusk was dark enough.

CHAPTER 44

OUTSIDE ROOM 14, AFTER I LEFT JACOB WITH the promise to return, Rodion Romanovich said, "Mr. Thomas, your questioning of that young man—it was not done as I would have done it."

"Yes, sir, but the nuns have an absolute rule against ripping out fingernails with pliers."

"Well, even nuns are not right about everything. What I was about to say, however, is that you drew him out as well as anyone could have done. I am impressed."

"I don't know, sir. I'm circling close to it, but I'm not there yet. He has the key. I was sent to him earlier in the day because he has the key."

"Sent to him by whom?"

"By someone dead who tried to help me through Justine."

"Through the drowned girl you mentioned earlier, the one who was dead and then revived."

"Yes, sir."

"I was right about you," Romanovich said. "Complex, complicated, even intricate."

"But innocuous," I assured him.

Unaware that she walked through a cluster of bodachs, scatter-
ing them, Sister Angela came to us.

She started to speak, and I zipped my lips again. Her periwinkle blues narrowed, for although she understood about bodachs,
she wasn't used to being told to shut up.

When the malign spirits had vanished into various rooms, I
said, "Ma'am, I'm hoping you can help me. Jacob here—what do
you know about his father?"

"His father? Nothing."

"I thought you had backgrounds on all the kids."

"We do. But Jacob's mother was never married."

"Jenny Calvino. So that's a maiden—not a married—name."

"Yes. Before she died of cancer, she arranged for Jacob to be
admitted to another church home."

"Twelve years ago."

"Yes. She had no family to take him, and on the forms, where
the father's name was requested, I'm sad to say, she wrote
unknown."

I said, "I never met the lady, but from even what little I know
about her, I can't believe she was so promiscuous that she
wouldn't know."

"It's a world of sorrow, Oddie, because we make it so."

"I've learned some things from Jacob. He was very ill when he
was seven, wasn't he?"

She nodded. "It's in his medical records. I'm not sure exactly,
but I think . . . some kind of blood infection. He almost died."

"From things Jacob has said, I believe Jenny called his father to the hospital. It wasn't a warm and fuzzy family reunion. But this name—it may be the key to everything."

"Jacob doesn't know the name?"

"I don't think his mother ever told him. However, I believe Mr. Romanovich knows it."

Surprised, Sister Angela said, "Do you know it, Mr. Romano-vich?"

"If he knows it," I said, "he won't tell you."

She frowned. "Why won't you tell me, Mr. Romanovich?"

"Because," I explained, "he's not in the business of giving out information. Just the opposite."

"But, Mr. Romanovich," said Sister Angela, "surely dispensing information is a fundamental part of a librarian's job."

"He is not," I said, "a librarian. He will claim to be, but if you press the point, all you'll get out of him is a lot more about Indianapolis than you need to know."

"There is no harm," Romanovich said, "in acquiring exhaus-tive knowledge about my beloved Indianapolis. And the truth is, you also know the name."

Again surprised, Sister Angela turned to me. "Do you know the name of Jacob's father, Oddie?"

"He suspects it," said Romanovich, "but is reluctant to believe what he suspects."

"Is that true, Oddie? Why are you reluctant to believe?"

"Because Mr. Thomas admires the man he suspects. And because if his suspicions are correct, he may be up against a power with which he cannot reckon."

Sister Angela said, "Oddie, is there any power with which you cannot reckon?"

"Oh, it's a long list, ma'am. The thing is—I need to be sure I'm right about the name. And I have to understand his motivation, which I don't yet, not fully. It might be dangerous to approach him without full understanding."

Turning to the Russian, Sister Angela said, "Surely, sir, if you can share with Oddie the name and motivation of this man, you will do so to protect the children."

"I wouldn't necessarily believe anything he told me," I said. "Our fur-hatted friend has his own agenda. And I suspect he'll be ruthless about fulfilling it."

Her voice heavy with disapproval, the mother superior said, "Mr. Romanovich, sir, you presented yourself to this community as a simple librarian seeking to enrich his faith."

"Sister," he disagreed, "I never said that I was simple. But it is true that I am a man of faith. And whose faith is so secure that it never needs to be further enriched?"

She stared at him for a moment, and then turned to me again. "He is a real piece of work."

"Yes, ma'am."

"I'd turn him out in the snow if it wasn't such an unchristian thing to do—and if I believed for a minute we could manhandle him through the door."

"I don't believe we could, Sister."

"Neither do I."

"If you can find me a child who was once dead but can speak," I reminded her, "I might learn what I need to know by other means than Mr. Romanovich."

Her wimpled face brightened. "That's what I came to tell you before we got into all this talk about Jacob's father. There's a girl named Flossie Bodenblatt—"

"Surely not," said Romanovich.

"Flossie," Sister Angela continued, "has been through very much, too much, so much—but she is a girl with spirit, and she has worked hard in speech therapy. Her voice is so clear now. She was down in rehab, but we've brought her to her room. Come with me."

CHAPTER 45

NINE-YEAR-OLD FLOSSIE HAD BEEN AT ST. Bartholomew's for one year. According to Sister Angela, the girl was one of the minority who would be able to leave someday and live on her own.

The names on the door plaques were FLOSSIE and PAULETTE. Flossie waited alone.

Frills, flounce, and dolls characterized Paulette's half of the room. Pink pillows and a small green-and-pink vanity table.

Flossie's area was by contrast simple, clean, all white and blue, decorated only with posters of dogs.

The name *Bodenblatt* suggested to me a German or Scandinavian background, but Flossie had a Mediterranean complexion, black hair, and large dark eyes.

I had not encountered the girl before, or had seen her only at a distance. My chest grew tight, and I knew at once that this might be more difficult than I had expected.

When we arrived, Flossie was sitting on a rug on the floor, paging through a book of dog photographs.

"Dear," said Sister Angela, "this is Mr. Thomas, the man who would like to talk to you."

Her smile was not the smile that I remembered from another place and time, but it was close enough, a wounded smile and lovely.

"Hello, Mr. Thomas."

Sitting cross-legged on the floor in front of her, I said, "I'm so pleased to meet you, Flossie."

Sister Angela perched on the edge of Flossie's bed, and Rodion Romanovich stood among Paulette's dolls and frills, like a bear that had turned the tables on Goldilocks.

The girl wore red pants and a white sweater with an appliquéd image of Santa Claus. Her features were fine, nose upturned, chin delicate. She could have passed for an elf.

The left corner of her mouth pulled down, and the left eyelid drooped slightly.

Her left hand was cramped into a claw, and she braced the book on her lap with that arm, as if she had little other use for it than bracing things. She had been turning pages with her right hand.

Now her attention focused on me. Her stare was direct and unwavering, full of confidence earned from painful experience— a quality I had also seen before, in eyes this very shade.

"So you like dogs, Flossie?"

"Yes, but I don't like my name." If she had once had a speech impediment caused by brain damage, she had overcome it.

"You don't like Flossie? It's a pretty name."

"It's a cow's name," she declared.

"Well, yes, I have heard of cows named Flossie."

"And it sounds like what you do with your teeth."

"Maybe it does, now that you mention it. What would you prefer to be called?"

"Christmas," she said.

"You want to change your name to Christmas?"

"Sure. Everyone loves Christmas."

"That's true."

"Nothing bad ever happens on Christmas. So then nothing bad could happen to someone named Christmas, could it?"

"So, let me begin again," I said. "I'm so pleased to meet you, Christmas Bodenblatt."

"I'm gonna change the last p-p-part, too."

"And what would you prefer to *Bodenblatt*?"

"Almost anything. I haven't made up my mind yet. It's gotta be a good name for working with dogs."

"You want to be a veterinarian when you grow up?"

She nodded. "Can't be, though." She pointed to her head and said with awful directness, "I lost some smarts in the car that day."

Lamely, I said, "You seem plenty smart to me."

"Nope. Not dumb but not smart enough for a vet. If I work hard on my arm, though, and my leg, and they get b-b-better, I can work with a vet, you know, like help him with dogs. Give b-baths to dogs. Trim them and stuff. I could do a lot with dogs."

"You like dogs, I guess."

"Oh, I love dogs."

A radiance arose in her as she talked about dogs, and joy made her eyes appear less wounded than they had been.

"I had a dog," she said. "He was a good dog."

Intuition warned me that questions I might ask about her dog would take us places I could not bear to go.

"Did you come to talk about dogs, Mr. Thomas?"

"No, Christmas. I came to ask a favor."

"What favor?"

"You know, the funny thing is, I don't remember. Can you wait here for me, Christmas?"

"Sure. I got a dog book."

I rose to my feet and said, "Sister, can we talk?"

The mother superior and I moved to the farther end of the room, and confident that we could not manhandle him, the Russian joined us.

In a voice almost a whisper, I said, "Ma'am . . . what happened to this girl . . . what did she have to endure?"

She said, "We don't discuss the children's histories with just anyone," and fried the Russian with a meaningful look.

"I am many things," said Romanovich, "but not a gossip."

"Or a librarian," said Sister Angela.

"Ma'am, there's a chance maybe this girl can help me learn what is coming—and save all of us. But I'm . . . afraid."

"Of what, Oddie?"

"Of what this girl might have endured."

Sister Angela brooded for a moment, and then said, "She lived with her parents and grandparents, all in one house. Her cousin came around one night. Nineteen. A problem boy, and high on something."

I knew she was not a naïf, but I didn't want to see her saying what surely she would say. I closed my eyes.

"Her cousin shot them all. Grandparents and parents. Then he spent some time . . . sodomizing the girl. She was seven."

They are something, these nuns. All in white, they go down into the dirt of the world, and they pull out of it what is precious, and they shine it up again as best they can. Clear-eyed, over and over again, they go down into the dirt of the world, and they have hope always, and if ever they are afraid, they do not show it.

"When the drugs wore off," she said, "he knew he'd be caught, so he took the coward's way. In the garage, he fixed a hose to the exhaust pipe, opened a window just wide enough to slip the hose into the car. And he took the girl into the car with him. He would not leave her only as damaged as she was. He had to take her with him."

There is no end to the wailing of senseless rebellion, to the elevation of self above all, the narcissism that sees the face of any authority only in the mirror.

"Then he chickened out," Sister Angela continued. "He left her alone in the car and went in the house to call nine-one-one. He told them he had attempted suicide and his lungs burned. He was short of breath and wanted help. Then he sat down to wait for the paramedics."

I opened my eyes to take strength from hers. "Ma'am, once last night and once today, someone on the Other Side, someone I know, tried to reach me through Justine. I think to warn me what's coming."

"I see. I think I see. No, all right. God help me, I accept it. Go on."

"There's this thing I can do with a coin or a locket on a chain, or with most anything bright. I learned it from a magician friend. I can induce a mild hypnosis."

"To what purpose?"

"A child who's been dead and revived is maybe like a bridge between this world and the next. Relaxed, in a light hypnosis, she might be a voice for that person on the Other Side who wasn't able to speak to me through Justine."

Sister Angela's face clouded. "But the Church discourages an interest in the occult. And how traumatic would this be for the child?"

I took a deep breath and let it out. "I'm not going to do it, Sister. I just want you to understand that maybe, doing this, I could learn what's coming, and so maybe I should do it. But I'm too weak. I'm scared, and I'm weak."

"You're not weak, Oddie. I know you better than that."

"No, ma'am. I'm failing you here. I can't handle this . . . with Christmas over there and her heart so full of dogs. It's too much."

"There's something I don't understand about this," she said. "What don't I know?"

I shook my head. I couldn't think how to explain the situation.

After retrieving his fur-trimmed coat from Paulette's bed, Romanovich said in a rough whisper, "Sister, you know that Mr. Thomas lost one who was most dear to him."

"Yes, Mr. Romanovich, I am aware of that," she said.

"Mr. Thomas saved many people that day but was not able to save her. She was a girl with black hair and dark eyes, and skin like this girl here."

He was making connections that could only be made if he knew much more about my loss than was in the press.

Previously unreadable, his eyes were still storyless; his book remained closed.

"Her name," Romanovich said, "was Bronwen Llewellyn, but she disliked her name. She felt that Bronwen sounded like an elf. She called herself Stormy."

He no longer merely puzzled me. He mystified me. "Who are you?"

"She called herself Stormy, as Flossie calls herself Christmas," he continued. "Stormy was abused as a girl, by her adoptive father."

"No one knows that," I protested.

"Not many do, Mr. Thomas. But a few social workers know. Stormy did not suffer severe physical damage, mental retardation. But you can see, Sister Angela, the parallels here make this most difficult for Mr. Thomas."

Most difficult, yes. Most difficult. And as a mark of how very difficult, no twist of wit came to mind in that moment, not even a pucker of sour humor, no thin astringent joke.

"To speak to the one he lost," Romanovich said, "through the medium of one who reminds him of her . . . too much. It would be too much for anyone. He knows that using this girl to channel a spirit would be traumatic for her, but he tells himself her trauma is acceptable if lives can be saved. Yet because of who she is, of *how* she is, he cannot proceed. She is an innocent, as Stormy was, and he will not use an innocent."

Watching Christmas with her book of dogs, I said, "Sister, if I use her as a bridge between the living and the dead . . . what if that brings back to her the memory of death that she's forgotten? What if when I'm done with her, she has one foot in each world, and can never be whole in this one or know any peace here? She was already used as though she were just a thing, used and thrown away. She can't be used again, no matter what the justifications are. Not again."

From an inner pocket of the coat draped over his arm, Romanovich produced a long vertical-fold wallet, and from the wallet a laminated card, which he did not at once present to me.

"Mr. Thomas, if you were to read a twenty-page report on me

that was prepared by seasoned intelligence analysts, you would know all that is worth knowing about me, as well as much that would not have been of interest even to my mother, though my mother doted on me."

"Your mother the assassin."

"That is correct."

Sister Angela said, "Excuse me?"

"Mother was also a concert pianist."

I said, "She was probably a master chef, too."

"In fact, I learned cakes from her. After reading a twenty-page report on you, Mr. Thomas, I thought I knew everything about you, but as it turns out, I knew little of importance. By that, I do not mean only your . . . gift. I mean I did not know the kind of man you are."

Although I wouldn't have thought the Russian could be a medicine for melancholy, he suddenly proved to be an effective mood-elevator.

"What did your father do, sir?" I asked.

"He prepared people for death, Mr. Thomas."

Heretofore, I had not seen Sister Angela nonplussed.

"So it's a family trade, sir. Why do you so directly call your mother an assassin?"

"Because, you see, technically an assassin is one who proceeds only against highly placed political targets."

"Whereas a mortician is not as choosy."

"A mortician is not indiscriminate, either, Mr. Thomas."

If Sister Angela didn't regularly attend tennis matches as a spectator, she would have a sore neck in the morning.

"Sir, I'll bet your father was also a chess master."

"He won only a single national championship."

"Too busy with his career as a mortician."

"No. Unfortunately, a five-year prison sentence fell at that very point at which he was at his most competitive as a chessman."

"Bummer."

As Romanovich gave me the laminated photo-ID card with embedded holographs, which he had taken from his wallet, he said to Sister Angela, "All of that was in the old Soviet, and I have confessed it and atoned. I have long been on the side of truth and justice."

Reading from the card, I said, "National Security Agency."

"That is correct, Mr. Thomas. After watching you with Jacob and with this girl here, I have decided to take you into my confidence."

"We must be careful, Sister," I warned. "He may only mean that he is a confidence man."

She nodded but seemed no less perplexed.

"We need to talk somewhere more private," Romanovich said.

Returning his NSA credentials, I said, "I want a few words with the girl."

As once more I sat on the floor near Christmas, she looked up from her book and said, "I like cats, too, b-b-but they aren't dogs."

"They sure aren't," I agreed. "I've never seen a group of cats strong enough to pull a dogsled."

Picturing cats in the traces of a sled, she giggled.

"And you'll never get a cat to chase a tennis ball."

"Never," she agreed.

"And dogs never have mouse breath."

"Yuck. Mouse breath."

"Christmas, do you really want to work with dogs one day?"

"I really do. I know I could do a lot with dogs."

"You have to keep up rehab, get back as much strength in your arm and leg as you can."

"Gonna get it all b-back."

"That's the spirit."

"You gotta retrain the b-b-brain."

"I'm going to stay in touch with you, Christmas. And when you're grown up and ready to be on your own, I have a friend who will make sure you'll have a job doing something wonderful with dogs, if that's still what you want."

Her eyes widened. "Something wonderful—like what?"

"That'll be for you to decide. While you're getting stronger and growing up, you think about what would be the most wonderful job you could do with dogs—and that will be it."

"I had a good dog. His name was F-Farley. He tried to save me, but Jason shot him, too."

She spoke about the horror with more dispassion than I could have done, and in fact I felt that I would not maintain my composure if she said another word about it.

"One day, you'll have all the dogs you want. You can live in a sea of happy fur."

Although she couldn't go directly from Farley to a giggle, she smiled. "A sea of happy fur," she said, savoring the sound of it, and her smile sustained.

I held out my hand. "Do we have a deal?"

Solemnly, she thought about it, and then she nodded and took my hand. "Deal."

"You're a very tough negotiator, Christmas."

"I am?"

"I'm exhausted. You have worn me down. I am bleary and dopey and pooped. My feet are tired, my hands are tired, even my hair is tired. I need to go and have a long nap, and I really, really need to eat some pudding."

She giggled. "Pudding?"

"You've been such a tough negotiator, you've so exhausted me that I can't even chew. My teeth are tired. In fact my teeth are already asleep. I can only eat pudding."

Grinning, she said, "You're silly."

"It's been said of me before," I assured her.

Because we needed to talk in a place where bodachs were unlikely to enter, Sister Angela led Romanovich and me to the pharmacy, where Sister Corrine was dispensing evening medicines into small paper cups on which she had written the names of her patients. She agreed to give us privacy.

When the door closed behind Sister Corrine, the mother superior said, "All right. Who is Jacob's father, and why is he so important?"

Romanovich and I looked at each other, and we spoke as one: "John Heineman."

"Brother John?" she asked dubiously. "Our patron? Who gave up all his wealth?"

I said, "You haven't seen the uberskeleton, ma'am. Once you've seen the uberskeleton, you pretty much know it couldn't be anyone else but Brother John. He wants his son dead, and maybe all of them, all the children here."

CHAPTER 46

RODION ROMANOVICH HAD SOME CREDIBILITY with me because of his National Security Agency ID and because he was droll. Maybe it was the effect of rogue molecules of tranquilizers in the medicinally scented air of the pharmacy, but minute by minute, I grew more willing to trust him.

According to the Hoosier, twenty-five years before we had come under siege in this blizzard, John Heineman's fiancée, Jennifer Calvino, had given birth to their child, Jacob. No one knows if she had availed herself of a sonogram or other testing, but in any case, she had carried the child to term.

Twenty-six, already a physicist of significant accomplishments, Heineman had not reacted well to her pregnancy, had felt trapped by it. Upon his first sight of Jacob, he denied fatherhood, withdrew his proposal of marriage, cut Jennifer Calvino out of his life, and gave her no more thought than he would have given a basal-cell carcinoma once it had been surgically removed from his skin.

Although even at that time, Heineman had been a man of

some means, Jennifer asked him for nothing. His hostility to his deformed son had been so intense that Jennifer decided Jacob would be both happier and safer if he had no contact with his father.

Mother and son did not have an easy life, but she was devoted to him, and in her care, he thrived. When Jacob was thirteen, his mother died, after arranging for his lifelong institutional care through a church charity.

Over the years, Heineman became famous and wealthy. When his research, as widely reported, drove him to the conclusion that the subatomic structure of the universe suggested indisputable design, he had reexamined his life and, in something like penitence, had given away his fortune and retreated to a monastery.

"A changed man," said Sister Angela. "In contrition for how he treated Jennifer and Jacob, he gave up everything. Surely he couldn't want his son dead. He funded this facility for the care of children like Jacob. And for Jacob himself."

Leaving the mother superior's argument unaddressed, Romanovich said, "Twenty-seven months ago, Heineman came out of seclusion and began to discuss his current research with former colleagues, by phone and in E-mails. He had always been fascinated by the strange order that underlies every apparent chaos in nature, and during his years of seclusion, using computer models of his design, processed on twenty linked Cray supercomputers, he had made breakthroughs that would enable him, as he put it, 'to prove the existence of God.'"

Sister Angela didn't need to mull that over to find the flaw in it. "We can approach belief from an intellectual path, but in the end, God must be taken on faith. Proofs are for things of this world, things in time and of time, not beyond time."

Romanovich continued: "Because some of the scientists with whom Heineman spoke were on the national-security payroll, and because they recognized risks related to his research and certain defense applications as well, they reported him to us. Since then, we have had one of ours in the abbey guesthouse. I am only the latest."

"For some reason," I said, "you were alarmed enough to introduce another agent as a postulant, now a novice, Brother Leopold."

Sister Angela's wimple seemed to stiffen with her disapproval. "You had a man falsely profess vows to God?"

"We did not intend for him to go beyond simple postulancy, Sister. We wanted him to spend a few weeks deeper in the community than a guest might ever get. As it turned out, he was a man searching for a new life, and he found it. We lost him to you—though we feel he still owes us some assistance, as his vows allow."

Her scowl was more imposing than any of his had been. "More than ever, Mr. Romanovich, I think you are a dubious piece of work."

"You are undoubtedly correct. Anyway, we became alarmed when Brother Constantine committed suicide—because thereafter, Heineman at once stopped calling and E-mailing his old colleagues, and has not since communicated with anyone outside St. Bartholomew's."

"Perhaps," said Sister Angela, "the suicide moved him to trade his research for prayer and reflection."

"We think not," Romanovich said drily.

"And Brother Timothy has been murdered, ma'am. There is no doubt of it now. I found the body."

Although she had already accepted the fact of his murder, this hard confirmation left her stricken.

"If it helps you come to terms with the situation," Romanovich said to her, "we believe that Heineman may not be fully aware of the violence he has unleashed."

"But, Mr. Romanovich, if two are dead and others threatened, how could he not be aware?"

"As I recall, poor Dr. Jekyll did not at first realize that his quest to rid himself of all evil impulses had in the process created Mr. Hyde, whose nature was pure evil unleavened by the goodness of the doctor."

Seeing in my mind's eye the uberskeleton assaulting the SUV, I said, "That thing in the snow wasn't merely the dark side of a human personality. There was nothing human about it."

"Not his dark side," Romanovich agreed. "But perhaps *created by* his dark side."

"What does that mean, sir?"

"We aren't sure, Mr. Thomas. But I think now it is incumbent upon us to find out—quickly. You have been given a universal key."

"Yes."

"Why, Mr. Thomas?"

"Brother Constantine is one of the lingering dead. I was given a key so I could let myself into anyplace on the property where he went poltergeist. I've been trying to . . . counsel him to move on."

"You lead an interesting life, Mr. Thomas."

"You're no slouch yourself, sir."

"You are even allowed access to John's Mew."

"We connected, sir. He makes good cookies."

"You have a culinary bond."

"Seems like we all do, sir."

Sister Angela shook her head. "I can't cook water."

Romanovich threw the switch that beetled his hydraulic brow over his eyes. "Does he know of your gift?"

"No, sir."

"I think you are his Mary Reilly."

"I hope you aren't becoming enigmatic again, sir."

"Mary Reilly was Dr. Jekyll's housekeeper. For all that he concealed from her, he subconsciously hoped that she would find him out and stop him."

"Did this Mary Reilly end up killed, sir?"

"I do not recall. But if you have not actually done any dusting for Heineman, you may be safe."

"What now?" asked Sister Angela.

"Mr. Thomas and I must make it alive into John's Mew."

"And out again alive," I said.

Romanovich nodded. "We can certainly try."

CHAPTER 47

THE STORM-SUITED MONKS NUMBERED TEN more than seven. Only two or three whistled while they worked. None was unusually short. As they secured the southeast and the northwest stairwells, however, I half expected Snow White to stop by with bottled water and words of encouragement.

In the interest of safety, the stairwell doors could not be locked. At each floor, the landing was a generous space, so the door opened into the stairwell instead of outward.

At the basement level, ground floor, and third floor, the monks drilled four holes in each door frame—two on the left, two right—and fitted them with steel sleeves. Into each sleeve, they inserted a half-inch-diameter bolt.

The bolts protruded an inch from the sleeves, preventing the door from opening. This scheme engaged not merely the strength of the frame but also of the entire wall in support of the door.

Because the sleeves were not threaded and were wider than the shafts inserted into them, the bolts could be plucked out in seconds to facilitate a hasty exit from the stairwell.

At the second floor, the children's dormitory, the trick was to devise a way to prevent the doors from being pulled open in the unlikely event that something broke into the stairwell, through a bolt-reinforced door, at another level. Already the brothers were debating the merits of three security options.

From the southeast stairs, Romanovich and I enlisted Brother Knuckles, and from the northwest stairs, Brother Maxwell, for the defense of Jacob Calvino. Each of them brought two baseball bats in case the first was cracked in battle.

If the Mr. Hyde part of Brother John Heineman's personality had an animus against *all* mentally and physically disabled people, then no child in the school was safe. Every one of them might be slated for destruction.

Common sense suggested, nonetheless, that Jacob—*Let him die*—remained the primary target. He would most likely either be the only victim or the first of many.

When we returned to Jacob's room, he was for once not drawing. He sat in a straight-backed chair, and a pillow on his lap served as a hand rest when he needed it. Head bowed, intently focused, he was embroidering flowers with peach-colored thread on white fabric, perhaps a handkerchief.

At first, embroidery seemed to be an unlikely pursuit for him, but his workmanship proved to be exquisite. As I watched him finesse intricate patterns from needle and thread, I realized that this was no more remarkable—and no less—than his ability to summon detailed drawings from pencil lead with these same short broad hands and stubby fingers.

Leaving Jacob to his embroidery, I gathered with Romanovich, Knuckles, and Brother Maxwell at the only window.

Brother Maxwell had graduated from the University of Missouri

School of Journalism. For seven years, he worked as a crime reporter in Los Angeles.

The number of serious crimes was greater than the number of reporters available to cover them. Every week, scores of industrious thugs and motivated maniacs committed outrageous acts of mayhem, and discovered, to their disgruntlement, that they had been denied even so much as two inches of column space in the press.

One morning, Maxwell found himself having to choose between covering a kinky-sex murder, an extremely violent murder committed with an ax and a pick and a shovel, a murder involving cannibalism, and the assault upon and ritual disfigurement of four elderly Jewish women in a group home.

To his surprise as well as to the surprise of his colleagues, he barricaded himself in the coffee room and would not come out. He had vending machines stocked with candy bars and peanut-butter-filled cheese crackers, and he figured he could go at least a month before he might develop scurvy due to severe vitamin C deficiency.

When his editor arrived to negotiate through the barricaded door, Maxwell demanded either to have fresh orange juice delivered weekly by ladder through the third-story coffee-room window—or to be fired. After considering those options for exactly the length of time that the newspaper's vice president of employee relations deemed necessary to avoid a wrongful-termination lawsuit, the editor fired Maxwell.

Triumphant, Maxwell vacated the coffee room, and only later, at home, with a sudden gale of laughter, realized that he simply could have quit. Journalism had come to seem not like a career but like an incarceration.

By the time he finished laughing, he decided that his petit madness had been a divine gift, a call to leave Los Angeles and to go where he could find a greater sense of community and less gang graffiti. He had become a postulant fifteen years ago, then a novice, and for a decade he had been a monk under full vows.

Now he examined the window in Jacob's room and said, "When this building was converted from the old abbey, some of the windows on the ground floor were enlarged and replaced. They have wood muntins. But on this level, the old windows remain. They're smaller, and they're solid bronze—rails, muntins, everything bronze."

"Nothin's gonna chop or chew through those too easy," Brother Knuckles declared.

"And the panes," said Romanovich, "are ten-inch squares. That brute we encountered in the storm would not fit through one. Indeed, if it managed to tear out the entire window, it would still be too large to get into the room."

I said, "The one in the cooling tower was smaller than the one that smacked down the SUV. It couldn't get through a ten-inch pane, but it'll fit through an open window this size."

"Casement window, opens outward," Brother Maxwell noted, tapping the crank handle. "Even if it smashed a pane and reached through, it would be blocking the window it was trying to open."

"While clinging to the side of the building," said Romanovich.

"In high wind," Brother Maxwell said.

"Which it might be able to do," I said, "while also keeping seven plates spinning atop seven bamboo poles."

"Nah," Brother Knuckles said. "Maybe three plates but not seven. We're good here. This is good."

Squatting beside Jacob, I said, "That's beautiful embroidery."

"Keeping busy," he said, his head remaining bowed, his eyes on his work.

"Busy is good," I said.

He said, "Busy is happy," and I suspected that his mother had counseled him about the satisfaction and the peace that come from giving to the world whatever you are capable of contributing.

Besides, his work gave him a reason to avoid eye contact. In his twenty-five years, he had probably seen shock, disgust, contempt, and sick curiosity in too many eyes. Better not to meet any eyes except those of the nuns, and those you drew with a pencil and into which you could shade the love, the tenderness, for which you yearned.

"You're going to be all right," I said.

"He wants me dead."

"What he wants and what he gets are not the same thing. Your mom called him the Neverwas because he was never there for the two of you when you needed him."

"He's the Neverwas, and we don't care."

"That's right. He's the Neverwas, but he's also the Neverwill. He never will hurt you, never will get at you, not as long as I'm here, not as long as one sister or one brother is here. And they're *all* here, Jacob, because you're special, you're precious to them, and to me."

Raising his misshapen head, he met my eyes. He did not at once look shyly away, as always he had done previously.

"You all right?" he asked.

"I'm all right. Are you all right?"

"Yeah. I'm all right. You . . . you're in danger?"

Because he would know a lie, I said, "Maybe a little."

His eyes, one higher in his tragic face than the other, were pellucid, full of timidities and courage, beautiful even in their different elevations.

His gaze sharpened as I had never seen it, as his soft voice grew softer still: "Did you accuse yourself?"

"Yes."

"Absolution?"

"I received it."

"When?"

"Yesterday."

"So you're ready."

"I hope I am, Jacob."

He not only continued to meet my eyes but also seemed to search them. "I'm sorry."

"Sorry about what, Jacob?"

"Sorry about your girl."

"Thank you, Jake."

"I know what you don't know," he said.

"What is that?"

"I know what she saw in you," he said, and he leaned his head on my shoulder.

He had done what few other people have ever achieved, though many may have tried: He had rendered me speechless.

I put an arm around him, and we stayed like that for a minute, neither of us needing to say anything more, because we were both all right, we were ready.

CHAPTER 48

I N THE ONLY ROOM CURRENTLY WITHOUT CHIL-
dren in residence, Rodion Romanovich put a large attaché
case on one of the beds.

The case belonged to him. Brother Leopold had earlier fetched
it from the Russian's room in the guesthouse and had brought it
back in the SUV.

He opened the case, which contained two pistols nestled in the
custom-molded foam interior.

Picking up one of the weapons, he said, "This is a Desert Eagle
in fifty Magnum. In a forty-four Magnum or three-fifty-seven, it
is a formidable beast, but the fifty Magnum makes an incredible
noise. You will enjoy the noise."

"Sir, with that in a cactus grove, you could do some heavy-duty
meditation."

"It does the job, but it has kick, Mr. Thomas, so I recommend
that you take the other pistol."

"Thank you, sir, but no thank you."

"The other is a SIG Pro three-fifty-seven, quite manageable."

"I don't like guns, sir."

"You took down those shooters in the mall, Mr. Thomas."

"Yes, sir, but that was the first time I ever pulled a trigger, and anyway it was someone else's gun."

"This is someone else's gun. It is my gun. Go ahead, take it."

"What I usually do is just improvise."

"Improvise what?"

"Self-defense. If there's not a real snake or a rubber snake around, there's always a bucket or something."

"I know you better now, Mr. Thomas, than I did yesterday, but in my judgment you remain in some ways a peculiar young man."

"Thank you, sir."

The attaché case contained two loaded magazines for each pistol. Romanovich jammed a magazine in each weapon, put the spare magazines in his pants pockets.

The case also contained a shoulder holster, but he didn't want it. Holding the pistols, he put his hands in his coat pockets. They were deep pockets.

When he took his hands out of his pockets, the guns were no longer in them. The coat had been so well made that it hardly sagged with its burdens.

He looked at the window, checked his watch, and said, "You would not think it was just twenty past three."

Behind the white gravecloth of churning snow, the dead-gray face of the day awaited imminent burial.

After closing the attaché case and tucking it under the bed, he said, "I sincerely hope that he is merely misguided."

"Who, sir?"

"John Heineman. I hope he is not mad. Mad scientists are not only dangerous, they are tedious, and I have no patience for tedious people."

To avoid interfering with the work of the brothers in the two stairwells, we rode down to the basement in the elevator. There was no elevator music. That was nice.

When all the children were in their rooms and the stairwells were secured, the monks would call the two elevators to the second floor. They would use the mother superior's key to shut them down at that position.

If anything nefarious got into a shaft from the top or the bottom, the elevator cab itself would blockade access to the second floor.

The ceiling of each cab featured an escape panel. The brothers had already secured those panels from the inside, so nothing on the roof of the cab could enter by that route.

They seemed to have thought of everything, but they were human, and therefore they had definitely not thought of everything. If we were capable of thinking of everything, we would still be living in Eden, rent-free with all-you-can-eat buffets and infinitely better daytime TV programming.

In the basement, we went to the boiler room. The gas fire-rings were hissing, and the pumps were rumbling, and there was a general happy atmosphere of Western mechanical genius about the place.

To reach John's Mew, we could venture out into the blizzard and strive through deep drifts to the new abbey, risking encounter with an uberskeleton sans the armor of an SUV. For adventure, that route had many things to recommend it: challenging weather, terror, air so cold it would clear your head if it didn't freeze the mucus in your sinus passages, and an opportunity to make snow angels.

The service tunnels offered an avenue without weather and with no wind shriek to cover the rattling approach of the plug-uglies. If perhaps those boneyards, however many there might be, had all gone topside, to prowl around the school in anticipation of nightfall, we would have an easy sprint to the basement of the new abbey.

I took the special wrench from the hook beside the crawl-through entrance to the service passageway, and we knelt at the steel access panel. We listened.

After half a minute, I asked, "You hear anything?"

When another half minute had passed, he said, "Nothing."

As I put the wrench to the first of the four bolts and started to turn it, I thought I heard a soft scraping noise against the farther side of the panel.

I paused, listened, and after a while said, "Did you hear something?"

"Nothing, Mr. Thomas," said Romanovich.

Following another half-minute of attentive listening, I rapped one knuckle against the access panel.

From beyond exploded a frenzied clitterclatter full of rage and need and cold desire, and the eerie keening that accompanied all the frantic tap-dancing seemed to arise from three or four voices.

After tightening the bolt that I had begun to loosen, I returned the special wrench to the hook.

As we rode the elevator up to the ground floor, Romanovich said, "I regret that Mrs. Romanovich is not here."

"For some reason, sir, I wouldn't have thought there was a Mrs. Romanovich."

"Oh, yes, Mr. Thomas. We have been married for twenty blissful years. We share many interests. If she were here, she would *so* enjoy this."

CHAPTER 49

I F ANY EXITS FROM THE SCHOOL WERE BEING monitored by skeletal sentinels, the front door, the garage doors, and the mud-room door adjacent the kitchen would be the most likely places for them to concentrate their attention.

Romanovich and I agreed to depart the building by a window in Sister Angela's office, which was the point farthest removed from the three doors that most invited the enemy's attention. Although the mother superior was not present, her desk lamp glowed.

Indicating the posters of George Washington, Flannery O'Connor, and Harper Lee, I said, "The sister has a riddle, sir. What shared quality does she most admire in those three people?"

He didn't have to ask who the women were. "Fortitude," he said. "Washington obviously had it. Ms. O'Connor suffered from lupus but refused to let it defeat her. And Ms. Lee needed fortitude to live in that place at that time, publish that book, and deal with the bigots who were angered by her portrait of them."

"Two of them being writers, you had a librarian's advantage."

When I switched off the lamp and opened the drapes, Romanovich said, "It is still a total whiteout. We will be disoriented and lost ten steps from the school."

"Not with my psychic magnetism, sir."

"Do they still include prizes in boxes of Cracker Jack?"

With a twinge of guilt, I opened a couple of Sister Angela's desk drawers, found a pair of scissors, and cut off six feet of drapery cord. I wrapped one end around my gloved right hand.

"When we're outside, I'll give you the other end, sir. Then we won't be separated even if we're snow-blind."

"I do not understand, Mr. Thomas. Are you saying that the cord will act as some kind of dowsing rod leading us to the abbey?"

"No, sir. The cord just keeps us together. If I concentrate on a person that I need to find, and drive or walk around awhile, I'll almost always be drawn to him by my psychic magnetism. I'm going to be thinking about Brother John Heineman, who is in the Mew."

"How interesting. The most interesting part, to me, is the adverb *almost*."

"Well, I'm the first to admit that I don't live rent-free in Eden."

"And what does that mean when you admit it, Mr. Thomas?"

"I'm not perfect, sir."

After making sure that my hood was firmly fastened under my chin, I raised the bottom half of the double-hung window, went out into the roar and rush of the storm, and scanned the day for signs of cemetery escapees. If I'd seen any shambling bones, I would have been in big trouble, because visibility was down to an arm's length.

Romanovich followed me and closed the window behind us. We were not able to lock it, but our warrior monks and nuns could not guard the entire building, anyway; they were even now retreating to the second floor, to defend that more limited position.

I watched the Russian tie the loose end of the cord to his wrist. The tether between us was about four and a half feet long.

Only six steps from the school, I became disoriented. I had no clue which direction would bring us to the abbey.

I summoned into mind an image of Brother John sitting in one of the armchairs in his mysterious receiving room, down in the Mew, and I slogged forward, reminding myself to be alert for a loss of tension on the cord.

The snow lay everywhere at least knee-deep, and in places the drifts came nearly to my hips. Wading uphill through an avalanche couldn't have been a whole lot more annoying than this.

Being a Mojave boy, I again found the bitter cold only slightly more appealing than machine-gun fire. But the cacophony of the storm, combined with the whiteout, was the worst of it. Step by frigid step, a weird kind of open-air claustrophobia got a grip on me.

I also resented that the deafening hoot-and-boom of the wind prevented Romanovich and me from saying a word. During the weeks that he had been in the guesthouse, he'd seemed to be a taciturn old bear; but as this day had unfolded, he had become positively loquacious. I was enjoying our conversations as much now that we were allied in a cause as when I had thought that we were enemies.

Once they have exhausted the subject of Indianapolis and its many wonders, a lot of people have nothing more of interest to say.

I knew we had reached the stone stairs down to John's Mew when I stumbled into them and nearly fell. Snow had drifted against the door at the bottom of the steps.

The cast-bronze words LIBERA NOS A MALO, on the plaque above the door, had mostly been obscured by encrusting snow, so that instead of reading *Deliver us from evil*, it read simply *evil*.

After I unlocked the half-ton door, it pivoted open smoothly on ball-bearing hinges, revealing the stone corridor bathed in blue light.

We went inside, and the door closed, and we disengaged ourselves from the tether that had kept us together during the slog.

"That was most impressive, Mr. Thomas."

"Psychic magnetism isn't an earned skill, sir. Taking pride in it would be like taking pride in how well my kidneys function."

We brushed snow from our coats, and he took off his bearskin hat to shake it.

At the brushed stainless-steel door with LUMIN DE LUMINE embedded in polished letters, I knocked one foot against the other to shed as much caked snow as possible.

Romanovich removed his zippered boots and stood in dry shoes, a more considerate guest than I.

Translating the words on the door, he said, "'Light from light.'"

"'Waste and void, waste and void. Darkness on the face of the deep,'" I said. "Then God commanded light. The light of the world descends from the Everlasting Light that is God."

"That is surely one thing it means," said Romanovich. "But it may also mean that the visible can be born from the invisible, that matter can arise from energy, that thought is a form of energy and that thought itself can be concretized into the very object that is imagined."

"Well, sir, that's a mouthful to get out of three words."

"Most assuredly," he agreed.

I flattened the palm and fingers of my right hand against the plasma screen in the wide steel architrave.

The pneumatic door slid open with the engineered hiss intended to remind Brother John that in every human enterprise, no matter with what good intentions it is undertaken, a serpent lurks. Considering where his work apparently had led him, perhaps in addition to the hiss, loud bells should have rung, lights should have flashed, and an ominous recorded voice should have said *Some things men were never meant to know.*

We stepped into the seamless, wax-yellow, porcelain-like vessel where buttery light emanated from the walls. The doors hissed shut at our backs, the light faded, and darkness enveloped us.

"I have no sense of motion," I said, "but I'm pretty sure it's an elevator, and we're going down a few floors."

"Yes," Romanovich said, "and I suspect that surrounding us is an enormous lead reservoir filled with heavy water."

"Really? That thought hadn't occurred to me."

"No, it would not."

"What is heavy water, sir, besides being obviously heavier than ordinary water?"

"Heavy water is water in which the hydrogen atoms have been replaced with deuterium."

"Yes, of course. I'd forgotten. Most people buy it at the grocery store, but I prefer to get the million-gallon jug at Costco."

A door hissed open in front of us, and we stepped into the vestibule bathed in red light.

"Sir, what is the purpose of heavy water?"

"It is used chiefly as a coolant in nuclear reactors, but here I believe it has other purposes, including perhaps, secondarily, as an additional layer of shielding against cosmic radiation that might affect subatomic experiments."

In the vestibule, we ignored the plain stainless-steel doors to the left and right, and went forward to the door in which were embedded the words PER OMNIA SAECULA SAECULORUM.

"'For ever and ever,'" said Romanovich, scowling. "I do not like the sound of that."

Pollyanna Odd, surfacing again, said, "But, sir, it's merely praising God. 'For thine is the kingdom and the power and the glory, for ever and ever, amen.'"

"No doubt that was Heineman's conscious intention when he chose these words. But one suspects that unconsciously he was expressing pride in his own achievements, suggesting that his works, performed here, would endure for ever and ever, beyond the end of time, where only God's kingdom otherwise endures."

"I hadn't thought of that interpretation, sir."

"No, you would not, Mr. Thomas. These words might indicate pride beyond mere hubris, the self-glorification of one who needs no word of praise or approval from others."

"But Brother John is not an egomaniacal nutbag, sir."

"I did not say that he was a nutbag. And more likely than not, he sincerely believes that, through this work, he is devoutly and humbly seeking to know God."

Without a hiss, *For ever and ever* slid aside, and we proceeded into the thirty-foot-diameter chamber where, at the center, standing on a wine-colored Persian carpet, four wingback chairs were served by four floor lamps. Currently, three lamps shed light.

Brother John, in tunic and scapular, with his hood pushed back from his head, waited in one of those three chairs.

CHAPTER 50

IN THE COZINESS OF HONEY-COLORED LIGHT, WITH the surrounding room in shadows and the curved wall darkly lustrous, Romanovich and I settled in the two chairs to which we had clearly been directed.

On the tables beside our chairs, where usually three fresh warm cookies would have been provided on a red plate, no cookies were in evidence. Perhaps Brother John had been too busy to bake.

His hooded violet eyes were as piercing as ever, but they seemed to reveal no suspicion or hostility. His smile was warm, as was his deep voice when he said, "I have been inexplicably weary today, and at times even vaguely depressed."

"That is interesting," Romanovich remarked to me.

Brother John said, "I am glad you came, Odd Thomas. Your visits refresh me."

"Well, sir, sometimes I think I make a pest of myself."

Brother John nodded at Romanovich. "And you, our visitor from Indianapolis—I have only seen you once or twice at a distance and have never had the pleasure of speaking with you."

"That pleasure is now yours, Dr. Heineman."

Raising one large hand in genteel protest, Brother John said, "Mr. Romanovich, I am not that man anymore. I am only John or Brother John."

"Likewise, I am only Agent Romanovich of the National Security Agency," said the assassin's son, and produced his ID.

Rather than lean forward from his chair to accept and examine the laminated card, Brother John turned to me. "Is he indeed, Odd Thomas?"

"Well, sir, this feels true in a way that librarian never did."

"Mr. Romanovich, Odd Thomas's opinion carries more weight with me than any identification. To what do I owe the honor?"

Putting away his ID, Romanovich said, "You have quite a vast facility here, Brother John."

"Not really. The vastness you sense may be the scope of the work, rather than the size of the facility."

"But you must need many specialists to keep it functioning."

"Only six brothers who have had intense technical training. My systems are all but entirely solid-state."

"On occasion, tech support comes in from Silicon Valley by helicopter."

"Yes, Mr. Romanovich. I am pleased but surprised the NSA would be interested in the work of a spiritual seeker."

"I am a man of faith myself, Brother John. I was intrigued when I heard that you have developed a computer model that you believe has shown you the deepest, most fundamental structure of reality, even far below the level of quantum foam."

Brother John sat in silence, and finally said, "I must assume that some of my conversations with former colleagues, which I allowed myself a couple of years ago, were reported to you."

"That is correct, Brother John."

The monk frowned, then sighed. "Well, I should not hold them to blame. In the highly competitive secular world of science, there is no expectation of keeping a confidence of this nature."

"So you believe you have developed a computer model that has shown you the deepest structure of reality?"

"I do not believe it, Mr. Romanovich. I *know* that what the model shows me is true."

"Such certitude."

"To avoid a bias toward my views, I didn't create the model. We inputted the entirety of substantive quantum theory and the evidence supporting it, allowing the computer array to develop the model with no human bias."

"Computers are creations of human beings," said Romanovich, "so they have bias built in."

To me, Brother John said, "The melancholy I've struggled with today does not excuse my bad manners. Would you like some cookies?"

That he offered cookies only to me seemed significant. "Thank you, sir, but I'm saving room for two slices of cake after dinner."

"Back to your certitude," Romanovich said. "How can you *know* what the model shows you is true?"

A beatific look overcame Brother John. When he spoke, his voice had a tremor that might have been inspired by awe. "I have applied the lesson of the model . . . and it works."

"And what is the lesson of the model, Brother John?"

Leaning forward in his chair, seeming to refine the silence of the room to a hush by the force of his personality, he said softly, "Under the final level of apparent chaos, one finds strange order again, and the final level of order is *thought*."

"Thought?"

"All matter, when seen at its root, arises out of a base web that has all the characteristics of thought waves."

He clapped his hands once, and the previously dark, lustrous walls brightened. Across them, around us, floor to ceiling, intricate interlacing lines of numerous colors presented ever-changing patterns that suggested layers like thermal currents in an infinitely deep ocean. For all their complexity, the lines were clearly ordered, the patterns purposeful.

This display possessed such beauty and mystery that I was at the same time mesmerized by it and compelled to look away, struck both by wonder and fear, by awe but equally by a sense of inadequacy, which made me want to cover my face and confess all the baseness in myself.

Brother John said, "What you see before you is not the thought patterns of God that underlie all matter, which of course we have no way of actually seeing, but a computer representation of them, based on the model I mentioned."

He clapped his hands twice. The astonishing patterns faded, and the walls went dark again, as though the display had been controlled by one of those devices that some elderly people use to turn the room lights on and off without having to get out of bed.

"This little exhibition so profoundly affects people," Brother John said, "resonates with us on some level so deep, that witnessing more than a minute of it can result in extreme emotional distress."

Rodion Romanovich looked as shaken as I suppose I did.

"So," said the Russian, after regaining his composure, "the lesson of the model is that the universe—all its matter and forms of energy—arises out of thought."

"God imagines the world, and the world becomes."

Romanovich said, "Well, we know that matter can be transformed to energy, as burning oil produces heat and light—"

"As splitting the nucleus of an atom produces the nuclei of lighter atoms," Brother John interrupted, "and also the release of great energy."

Romanovich pressed him: "But are you saying that thought—at least Divine thought—is a form of energy that can shape itself into matter, the reverse of nuclear fission?"

"Not the reverse, no. This is not merely nuclear fusion. The usual scientific terms do not apply. It is . . . imagining matter into existence by the power of the will. And because we have been given thought, will, and imagination, albeit on a human scale, we too have this power to create."

Romanovich and I locked eyes, and I said, "Sir, have you ever seen the movie *Forbidden Planet*?"

"No, Mr. Thomas, I have not."

"When this is all over, I think we should watch it together."

"I will make the popcorn."

"With salt and just a pinch of chili powder?"

"So shall it be."

Brother John said, "Are you sure you won't have some cookies, Odd Thomas? I know you like my cookies."

I expected him to make sorcerous gestures toward the table beside my chair, conjuring chocolate-chip treats from thin air.

Romanovich said, "Brother John, you said earlier that you have applied the lesson of your computer model, the lesson being that all matter as we know it has arisen out of thought. The universe, our world, the trees and the flowers and the animals . . . all imagined into existence."

"Yes. You see, my science has led me back to faith."

"How do you mean you *applied* what you believe you've learned?"

The monk leaned forward in his wingback chair, his hands fisted on his knees as if he were struggling to contain his excitement. His face appeared to have shed forty years, returning him to boyhood and the wonder thereof.

"I have," he whispered, "created life."

CHAPTER 51

THIS WAS THE CALIFORNIA SIERRA, NOT THE Carpathian Mountains. Outside, snow flew rather than rain, without thunderclaps or bolts of lightning. In this room I found a disappointing lack of bizarre machines with gold-plated gyroscopes, crackling arcs of electricity, and demented hunchbacks with lantern eyes. In the days of Karloff and Lugosi, they really understood the demands of melodrama better than our mad scientists do these days.

On the other hand, it is true that Brother John Heineman was less mad than misguided. You will see that this is true, though you will also see that between the mad and the misguided, the line is as thin as a split hair that has been split again.

"This chamber," said Brother John with a curious mix of glee and solemnity, "isn't merely a room but is also a revolutionary machine."

To me, Rodion Romanovich said, "This is always trouble."

"If I envision an object and consciously project that image,"

Brother John continued, "the machine receives it, recognizes the projected nature of it separate from all other kinds of thought, amplifies my directed mental energy to several million times its initial power, and produces the object imagined."

"Good Lord, sir, your electrical bill must be outrageous."

"It's not inconsiderable," he acknowledged, "but it isn't as bad as you might think. For one thing, it's not volts that matter so much as amps."

"And I suppose you receive a high-user discount."

"Not only that, Odd Thomas, my laboratory has certain rate advantages because it is in fact a religious organization."

Romanovich said, "When you say you can imagine an object and the room will produce it—you mean like the cookies you have mentioned."

Brother John nodded. "Certainly, Mr. Romanovich. Would you like some cookies?"

Glowering, the Russian said, "Cookies are not alive. You said you had created life."

The monk sobered. "Yes. You're correct. Let's not make a parlor game out of it. This is about First Things, man's relationship to God and the meaning of existence. Let's go directly to the main show. I will create a floppy for you."

"A what?" Romanovich asked.

"You will see," Brother John promised, and smiled knowingly.

He sat back in his chair, closed his eyes, and furrowed his forehead as if in thought.

"Are you doing it now?" I asked.

"If I am allowed to concentrate, yes."

"I thought you would need a helmet of some kind, you know, with all kinds of wires trailing from it."

"Nothing so primitive, Odd Thomas. The room is attuned to the precise frequency of my brain waves. It's a receiver and an amplifier, but only of my projected thoughts, no one else's."

I glanced at Romanovich. He looked as bearishly disapproving as ever I had seen him.

Perhaps twenty seconds had passed before the air felt thicker, as though the humidity had abruptly increased, but this heaviness had no moist quality. Pressure pushed in upon me from all sides, as if we had been descending into oceanic depths.

On the Persian carpet, in front of Brother John's chair, arose a silvery shimmering, like a reflection of light that had bounced off a bright object elsewhere in the room, although that was not the explanation for it.

After a moment, tiny white cubes had formed apparently out of nothing, as rock sugar crystallizes on a string that is suspended in a glass of highly sweetened water. The number of tiny cubes rapidly increased, and at the same time they began to fuse with one another, as if I were watching a rewinding video of the incident in the garage.

Romanovich and I rose to our feet, no doubt motivated by the same thought: *What if a "floppy" is the pet name Brother John has given to the ambulatory boneyards?*

We need not have been alarmed. What formed before us was a creature the size of a hamster. All white, combining features of a puppy, a kitten, and a baby bunny, it opened huge eyes that were as blue as—but less predatory than—the eyes of Tom Cruise, gave me a winning smile, and made an appealing, musical burbling sound.

Brother John opened his eyes, smiled at his creation, and said, "Gentlemen, meet your first floppy."

* * *

I was not present in the school to witness this, but following is what I was told of events unfolding parallel to Brother John's revelations in the Mew:

In Room 14, as Jacob does needlepoint, Brother Knuckles places a chair in the open doorway, where he sits, a baseball bat across his knees, and observes the activity in the hallway.

Brother Maxwell, fifteen years downriver from his journalism career, is perhaps hoping that he has not come all this way and time only to encounter the same mindless violence that he could have had *without* a vow of poverty, in Los Angeles.

Maxwell sits in a chair near the only window. Because the whirl of snow half hypnotized him, he has not been focusing on the fading day beyond the glass.

A noise more crisp than the wind, a series of faint clinks and squeaks, draws his attention to the window. Pressed to the far side of the panes is a shifting kaleidoscope of bones.

Rising slowly from his chair, as if a sudden movement might agitate the visitor, Maxwell whispers, "Brother Salvatore."

In the open doorway, with his back to the room, Brother Knuckles is thinking about the latest book by his favorite author, which isn't about either a china rabbit or a mouse who saves a princess, but is nonetheless wonderful. He doesn't hear Brother Maxwell.

Backing away from the window, Brother Maxwell realizes that he has left both his baseball bats beside the chair he vacated. He again whispers for Salvatore, but perhaps no louder than before.

The patterns of bone at the window constantly change, but not in an agitated fashion, almost lazily, conveying the impression that the creature may be in a state similar to sleep.

The dreamy quality of the kaleidoscopic movement encourages Brother Maxwell to return to his chair to pick up one of the baseball bats.

As he bends down and grips that weapon, he hears a pane of glass crack above him, and as he startles upright, he shouts, "*Salvatore!*"

* * *

Although it had formed out of cubes, the floppy was as furry, cuddly, and floppy as its name. Its huge ears drooped over its face, and it brushed them back with one paw, then rose on its hind feet. The Pillsbury Doughboy might have something like this as his pet.

His face a portrait of enchantment, Brother John said, "All my life, I've been obsessed with order. With finding order within chaos. With imposing order *on* chaos. And here is this sweet little thing, born out of the chaos of thought, out of the void, out of nothing."

Still standing, no less wary than when he had expected one of the boneyards to rise up before him, Romanovich said, "Surely you have not shown this to the abbot."

"Not yet," Brother John said. "In fact, you're the first to see this . . . this proof of God."

"Does the abbot even know your research was leading to . . . this?"

Brother John shook his head. "He understands that I intended to prove that at the bottom of physical reality, under the last layer of apparent chaos is ordered thought waves, the mind of God. But I never told him that I would create *living* proof."

"You never told him," Romanovich said, his voice groaning under the weight of his astonishment.

Smiling at his creation as it tottered this way and that, Brother John said, "I wanted to surprise him."

"Surprise him?" Romanovich traded astonishment for disbelief. "*Surprise* him?"

"Yes. With proof of God."

With barely throttled contempt, more directly than I might have said it under these circumstances, Romanovich declared, "This is not proof of God. This is *blasphemy*."

Brother John flinched as if he had been slapped, but recovered at once. "I'm afraid you haven't entirely followed what I've told you, Mr. Romanovich."

The giggling, toddling, big-eyed floppy did not at first glance seem like a work of supreme blasphemy. My initial take was: *furry, cute, cuddly, adorable.*

When I sat down on the edge of my chair and leaned forward to have a closer look at it, however, I got a chill as sharp as an icicle in the eye.

The floppy's big blue peepers did not engage me, did not have the curiosity of a kitten's or puppy's eyes. They were vacant; a void lay beyond them.

The musical burbling and the giggle charmed, like the recorded voice of a toy—until I reminded myself that here was *not* a toy, that here was a living being. Then its utterances reminded me of the low muttering of dead-eyed dolls in nightmares.

I rose from the chair and took a step or two back from Brother John's dark miracle.

"Dr. Heineman," Romanovich said, "you do not know yourself. You do not know what you have done."

Brother John appeared bewildered by the Russian's hostility. "We have a different perspective, I see, but—"

"Twenty-five years ago, you rejected your deformed and disabled child, disowned and abandoned him."

Shocked that the Russian was privy to that transgression but also clearly stricken by shame, Brother John said, "I am not that man anymore."

"I will grant that you became remorseful, even contrite, and you did an amazingly generous thing by giving away your fortune, taking vows. You are reformed, you may be a better man, but *you are not a different man*. How can you convince yourself of such a thing when you are so conversant with the theology of your faith? From one end of this life to the other, you carry with you all that you have done. Absolution grants you forgiveness for it, but does not expunge the past. The man you were still lives within you, repressed by the man you have struggled to become."

I said, "Brother John, have you ever seen Fredric March in *Dr. Jekyll and Mr. Hyde*? If we get through this alive, maybe we can watch it together."

CHAPTER 52

THE ATMOSPHERE IN THE MEW WAS NOT healthy, which is like saying that you might not want to have a picnic in the cone of a dormant volcano if the ground is rumbling underfoot.

Brother John's feelings had been hurt when his miraculous work had been received with less enthusiasm than he had expected. And his disappointment had about it a quality of wounded pride, a thinly masked resentment, a disturbing child-like peevishness.

The cute, creepy, cuddly, soulless floppy sat on the floor, playing with its feet, making all the noises of a creature that was wonderfully amused with itself, showing off for us, as if confident that we would at any moment coo with admiration for it. Its giggle, however, sounded more humorless by the second.

The bone beasts, the tower phantom, and now this demonic Beanie Baby had exhibited a vanity unseen in genuine supernatural entities. They existed outside the vertical sacred order of human beings and spirits. Their vanity reflected the vanity of their troubled creator.

I thought of Tommy Cloudwalker's three-headed coyote-man and realized that another difference between the genuinely super-natural and the bizarre things we had seen in the past twelve hours was the fundamentally *organic* character of what is super-natural, which is no surprise, really, since true spirits once lived as flesh.

The bone beasts had seemed not organic but like machines. When Death had leaped from the bell tower, it had disassembled in flight, had broken apart into geometric fragments, as might a failed machine. The floppy was not the equivalent of a puppy or a kitten, but of a wind-up toy.

Standing with his hands in the pockets of his coat, as if he would at any moment withdraw the .50-caliber Desert Eagle and blow the floppy to smithereens, Rodion Romanovich said, "Dr. Heineman, what you have made is not life. Upon death, it does not decompose. It deconstructs itself in some process similar to fission but not fission, producing no heat, leaving nothing. What you have created is *anti*life."

"You simply do not grasp the achievement," said Brother John. Like the facade of a summer hotel being boarded up for the off-season, his face steadily put away its former light and animation.

"Doctor," Romanovich continued, "I am sure that you built the school as atonement for abandoning your son, and I am sure that you had Jacob brought here as an act of contrition."

Brother John stared at him, still withdrawing behind shutters and boarded windows.

"But the man you were is still within the man you are, and he had his own motivations."

This accusation aroused Brother John from his withdrawal. "What are you implying?"

Pointing to the floppy, Romanovich said, "How can you put an end to that thing?"

"I am able to think it out of existence as efficiently as I created it."

"Then for the love of God, do so."

For a moment, Brother John's jaw clenched, his eyes narrowed, and he did not appear disposed to oblige the request.

The Russian radiated not just the authority of an officer of the state but also moral authority. He removed his left hand from a coat pocket and made a hurry-up gesture.

Closing his eyes, furrowing his forehead, Brother John imagined the floppy out of existence. Mercifully, the giggling stopped. Then the thing disassembled into rattling, twitching cubes. It vanished.

When the scientist monk opened his eyes, Romanovich said, "You yourself noted that you have been obsessed with order all your life."

"Any sane man sides with order over anarchy, order over chaos," said Brother John.

"I agree, Dr. Heineman. But as a young man, you were so obsessed with order that you not only decried disorder, you *despised* it as if it were a personal affront. You abhorred it, recoiled from it. You had no patience for anyone whom you felt furthered disorder in society. Ironically, you exhibited what might be called an intellectual rather than an emotional obsessive-compulsive disorder."

"You have been talking to envious men," said Brother John.

"When your son was born, his deformities and disabilities struck you as biological disorder, the more intolerable because it came from your loins. You disowned him. You wanted him to die."

"I never wanted him to die. That is outrageous."

I felt a little like a traitor to him when I said, "Sir, Jacob remembers when you visited him in the hospital and urged his mother to let his infection run its course untreated."

Atop his tall lanky body, his round face bobbed like a balloon on the end of a string, and I could not tell whether he was nodding in agreement or shaking his head in denial. He might have been doing both. He could not speak.

In a voice no longer characterized by accusation, opting for a note of quiet entreaty, Romanovich said, "Dr. Heineman, have you any conscious awareness that you have been creating abominations that have materialized outside this room, that have killed?"

* * *

At the school, in Room 14, Brother Maxwell stands tense, his baseball bat raised, while Brother Knuckles, having dealt with more than his share of wiseguys in years past, and having recently mowed down an uberskeleton with an SUV, is wary but not wound tight.

In fact, leaning almost insouciantly on his bat as if it is a cane, Knuckles says, "Some big guys, they think struttin' the muscle will put your tail between your legs, but all they got is strut, they ain't got the guts to back up the brag."

"This thing," says Maxwell, "doesn't have either guts or muscle, it's all bones."

"Ain't that what I'm tellin' you?"

Half the cracked pane breaks out of the bronze muntins, shatters on the floor.

"No way this chump gets through the window, not with all them little squares."

The remaining portion of the broken pane cracks loose and falls to the floor.

"You don't scare me," Knuckles tells the dog of the Neverwas.

Maxwell says, "It scares *me*."

"No it don't," Knuckles assures him. "You're good, Brother, you're solid."

A clutching gnarl of flexing bones gropes through the hole in the casement window.

Another pane cracks, and a third explodes, spraying shards of glass onto the two monks' shoes.

Toward the farther end of the room, Jacob sits with the pillow on his lap, his head bowed to his embroidery, exhibiting no fear, creating beautiful order out of blank white cloth and peach thread, while the disorderly creation at the window shatters two more panes of glass and strains against the bronze muntins.

Brother Fletcher steps in from the hall. "Showtime. You need some backup?"

Brother Maxwell says yes, but Brother Knuckles says, "Seen tougher mugs than this in Jersey. You watchin' the elevator?"

"It's covered," Brother Fletcher assures him.

"Then maybe stay beside Jacob, move him out fast if this chump gets through the window."

Brother Maxwell protests: "You said it won't get through."

"It ain't gonna, Brother. Yeah, it's makin' a big show, but the true fact is—this geek, he's scared of us."

The stressed bronze muntins and rails of the casement window creaked, groaned.

* * *

"Abominations?" Brother John's round face seemed to swell and redden with the pressure of new dark possibilities that his mind could barely contain. "Create without conscious awareness? It isn't possible."

"If it is not possible," Romanovich said, "then have you created them intentionally? Because they do exist. We have seen them."

I unzipped my jacket and removed from within a folded page that I had torn out of Jacob's tablet. As I opened the sheet of paper, the drawing of the beast flexed with an illusion of movement.

"Your son has seen this at his window, sir. He says it is the dog of the Neverwas. Jennifer called you the Neverwas."

Brother John accepted the drawing, spellbound by it. The doubt and fear in his face belied the confidence in his voice when he said, "This is meaningless. The boy is retarded. This is the fantasy of a deformed mind."

"Dr. Heineman," the Russian said, "twenty-seven months ago, from things you said to your former colleagues in calls and E-mails, they inferred that you might have already . . . created something."

"I did. Yes. I showed it to you moments ago."

"That pathetic flop-eared creature?"

Pity more than scorn informed Romanovich's voice, and Brother John met it with silence. Vanity receives pity as a wasp receives a threat to its nest, and a desire to sting brought an unholy venomous shine to the monk's violet, hooded eyes.

"If you have advanced no further in these twenty-seven months," Romanovich said, "could it be because something happened about two years ago that frightened you off your research, and you have only recently begun again to power up this god-machine of yours and 'create'?"

"Brother Constantine's suicide," I said.

"Which was not a suicide," said Romanovich. "Unconsciously, you had dispatched some abomination into the night, Dr. Heineman, and when Constantine saw it, he could not be allowed to live."

Either the drawing cast a dark enchantment over the scientist monk or he did not trust himself to meet our eyes.

"You suspected what had happened, and you put your research on hold—but twisted pride made you return to it recently. Now Brother Timothy is dead . . . and even at this hour, you stalk your son through this monstrous surrogate."

With his gaze still upon the drawing, a pulse jumping in his temples, Brother John said tightly, "I long ago accused myself of my sins against my son and his mother."

"And I believe your confession was even sincere," Romanovich conceded.

"I received absolution."

"You confessed and were forgiven, but some darker self within you did not confess and did not think he needed to be forgiven."

"Sir, Brother Timothy's murder last night was . . . horrendous, inhuman. You have to help us stop this."

All this time later, I am saddened to write that when Brother John's eyes welled with tears, which he managed not to spill, I half believed they were not for Tim but for himself.

Romanovich said, "You progressed from postulant to novice, to professed monk. But you yourself have said you were spooked when your research led you to believe in a created universe, so you came to God in fear."

Straining the words through his teeth, Brother John said, "The motivation matters less than the contrition."

"Perhaps," Romanovich allowed. "But most come to Him in love. And some part of you, some Other John, has not come to Him at all."

With sudden intuition, I said, "Brother John, the Other is an angry child."

At last he looked up from the drawing and met my eyes.

"The child who, far too young, saw anarchy in the world and feared it. The child who resented being born into such a disordered world, who saw chaos and yearned to find order in it."

Behind his violet windows, the Other regarded me with the contempt and self-regard of a child not yet acquainted with empathy and compassion, a child from whom the Better John had separated himself but from whom he had not escaped.

I called his attention to the drawing once more. "Sir, the obsessed child who built a model of quantum foam out of forty-seven sets of Lego blocks is the same child who conceived of this complex mechanism of cold bones and efficient joints."

As he studied the architecture of the bone beast, reluctantly he recognized that the obsession behind the Lego model was the same that inspired this eerie construction.

"Sir, there is still time. Time for that little boy to give up his anger and have his pain lifted."

The surface tension of his pent-up tears abruptly broke, and one tracked down each cheek.

He looked up at me and, in a voice thick with sadness but also with bitterness, he said, "No. It's too late."

CHAPTER 53

FOR ALL I KNOW, DEATH HAD BEEN IN THE ROOM
when the curved walls had bloomed with colorful patterns
of imagined God thought, and had moved as our heads had
turned, to stay always just out of our line of sight. But it came at
me now as if it had just swept into the chamber in a cold fury,
seized me, lifted me, pulled me face to face with it.

Instead of the previous void in the hood, confronting me was a
brutal version of the face of Brother John, angular where his was
round, hard where his was soft, a child's idea less of the face of
Death than of the face of Power personified. The young genius
who had recognized and feared the chaos of the world but
who had been powerless to bring order to it had now empowered
himself.

His breath was that of a machine, rife with the reek of smoking
copper and scalding steel.

He threw me over the wingback chair, as if I were but a knotted mass of rags. I slammed into the cool, curved wall and jacked
myself up from the floor even as I landed.

A wingback chair flew, I ducked and scooted, the wall rang like a glass bell, as it had not done when I struck it, the chair stayed where it fell, but I kept moving. And here came Death again.

* * *

At the window, the bronze rails and muntins strain and slightly tweak but do not fail. The keening of the frustrated attacker grows louder than the clatter of its busy bones.

"This geek," Brother Maxwell decides, "isn't scared of us."

"It's gonna be before we're done," Knuckles assures him.

Out of the kaleidoscopic beast and through one of the empty spaces where a windowpane had been, an urgent thrusting tentacle of scissoring bones invades five feet into the room.

The brothers stagger back in surprise.

The extruded form breaks off or is ejected from the mother mass, and collapses to the floor. Instantly the severed limb assembles into a version of the larger creature.

Pincered, spined, barbed, and hooked, as big as an industrial vacuum cleaner, it comes roach-quick, and Knuckles swings for the bleachers.

The Louisville Slugger slams some corrective discipline into the delinquent, splintering off clusters of bones. Knuckles steps toward the thing as it shudders backward, demolishes it with a second swing.

Through the window comes another thrusting tentacle, and as it detaches, Brother Maxwell shouts to Brother Fletcher, "Get Jacob out of here!"

Brother Fletcher, having played some dangerous gigs in his salad days as a saxophonist, knows how to split a dive when customers start trading gunfire, so he is already scramming from the room with Jacob before Maxwell shouts. Entering the hall-way, he hears Brother Gregory cry out that something is in the elevator shaft and is furiously intent on getting through the roof of the blocking cab.

*   *   *

As Death rushed me again, Rodion Romanovich rushed Death, with all the fearlessness of a natural-born mortician, and opened fire with the Desert Eagle.

His promise of incredible noise was fulfilled. The crash of the pistol sounded just a few decibels softer than the thunder of mortar fire.

I didn't count how many rounds Romanovich squeezed off, but Death burst apart into geometric debris, as it had done when leaping down from the bell tower, the fragmenting robe as brittle as the form it clothed.

Instantly, the shards and scraps and splinters of this unnatural construct twitched and jumped with what looked like life but was not—and within seconds remanifested.

When it turned toward Romanovich, he emptied the pistol, ejected the depleted magazine, and frantically dug the spare out of his pants pocket.

Less shattered by the second barrage of gunfire than by the first, Death rose swiftly from ruin.

John, not a brother at this moment, but now a smug child, stood with eyes closed, thinking the Death figure into existence again, and when he opened his eyes, they were not those of a man of God.

*   *   *

Brother Maxwell slams a home run through the second intruder in Room 14, then sees that Knuckles is again hammering at the first one, which has rattled itself back together with the swiftness of a rose blooming in stop-motion photography.

A third scuttling extrusion of the mother mass assaults, and Maxwell knocks it apart with both a swing and backswing, but the one he had first demolished, now reassembled, rushes him in full bristle and drives two thick barbed spines through his chest.

When Brother Knuckles turns, he witnesses Maxwell pierced and, with horror, sees his brother transformed, as if by contamination, into a kaleidoscope of flexing-pivoting-rotating bones that shreds out of the storm suit as if stripping away a cocoon, and combines with the bone machine that pierced it.

Fleeing the room, Knuckles frantically pulls shut the door and, holding it closed, shouts for help.

Some consideration has been given to such a predicament as this, and two brothers arrive with a chain, which they loop to the levered handle of the door. They join that handle to the one at the adjacent room, ensuring that each door serves as the lock of the other.

The noise from the elevator shaft grows tremendous, rocking the walls. From behind the closed lift doors comes the sound of the cab roof buckling, as well as the thrum and twang of cables tested nearly to destruction.

Jacob is where he will be safest, between Sister Angela and Sister Miriam, whom surely even the devil himself will treat with wary circumspection.

*   *   *

Reborn again, Death shunned me and turned toward the Russian, who proved just two steps faster than the Reaper. Snapping the spare magazine into the Desert Eagle, Romanovich moved toward the man whom I had once admired and shot him twice.

The impact of .50-caliber rounds knocked John Heineman off his feet. When he went down, he stayed down. He wasn't able to imagine himself reconstructed, because no matter what that lost dark part of his soul might believe, he was not his own creation.

The Death figure reached Romanovich and laid a hand on his shoulder, but did not assault him. The phantom focused instead on Heineman, as if thunderstruck that its lowercase god had been laid low like any mortal.

This time Death deconstructed into a spill of cubes that split into more cubes, a mound of dancing dice, and they cast themselves with larval frenzy, rattling their dotless faces against one another until they were only a fizz of molecules, and then atoms, and then nothing at all but a memory of hubris.

CHAPTER 54

BY ELEVEN O'CLOCK THAT NIGHT, AS THE STORM began to wane, the initial contingent of National Security agents—twenty of them—arrived in snow-eating monster trucks. With the phones down, I had no idea how Romanovich contacted them, but by then I had conceded that the clouds of mystery gathered around him made *my* clouds of mystery look like a light mist by comparison.

By Friday afternoon, the twenty agents had grown to fifty, and the grounds of the abbey and all buildings lay under their authority. The brothers, the sisters, and one shaken guest were exhaustively debriefed, though the children, at the insistence of the nuns, were not disturbed with questions.

The NSA concocted cover stories regarding the deaths of Brother Timothy, Brother Maxwell, and John Heineman. Timothy's and Maxwell's families would be told that they had perished in an SUV accident and that their remains were too grisly to allow open-casket funerals.

Already, a funeral Mass had been said for each of them. In the spring, though there were no remains to bury, headstones would be erected in the cemetery by the edge of the forest. At least their names in stone would stand with those whom they had known and loved, and by whom they themselves had been loved.

John Heineman, for whom also a Mass had been offered, would be kept in cold storage. After a year, when his death would not seem coincidental with those of Timothy and Maxwell, an announcement would be made to the effect that he had died of a massive heart attack.

He had no family except the son he had never accepted. In spite of the terror and grief that Heineman had brought to St. Bartholomew's, the brothers and sisters were agreed that in a spirit of forgiveness, he should be buried in their cemetery, though at a discreet distance from the others who were at rest in that place.

Heineman's array of supercomputers were impounded by the NSA. They would eventually be removed from John's Mew and trucked away. All the strange rooms and the creation machine would be studied, meticulously disassembled, and removed.

The brothers and sisters—and yours truly—were required to sign oaths of silence, and we understood that the carefully spelled-out penalties for violation would be strictly enforced. I don't think the feds were worried about the monks and nuns, whose lives are *about* the fulfillment of oaths, but they spent a lot of time vividly explaining to me all the nuances of suffering embodied in the words "rot in prison."

I wrote this manuscript nonetheless, as writing is my therapy and a kind of penance. If ever, my story will be published only when I have moved on from this world to glory or damnation, where even the NSA cannot reach me.

Although Abbot Bernard had no responsibility for John Heineman's research or actions, he insisted that he would step down from his position between Christmas and the new year.

He had called John's Mew the adytum, which is the most sacred part of a place of worship, shrine of shrines. He had embraced the false idea that God can be known through science, which pained him considerably, but his greatest remorse arose from the fact that he had been unable to see that John Heineman had been motivated not by a wholesome pride in his God-given genius but by a vanity and a secret simmering anger that corrupted his every achievement.

A sadness settled over the community of St. Bartholomew's, and I doubted that it would lift for a year, if even then. Because the beasts of bone that breached the second-floor defenses of the school had collapsed into diminishing cubes at the moment of Heineman's demise, as had the figure of Death, only Brother Maxwell had perished in the battle. But Maxwell, Timothy, and again poor Constantine would be mourned anew in each season that life here went on without them.

Saturday evening, three days after the crisis, Rodion Romanovich came to my room in the guesthouse, bringing two bottles of good red wine, fresh bread, cheese, cold roast beef, and various condiments, none of which he had poisoned.

Boo spent much of the evening lying on my feet, as if he feared they might be cold.

Elvis stopped by for a while. I thought he might have moved on by now, as Constantine appeared to have done, but the King remained. He worried about me. I suspected also that he might be choosing his moment with a sense of the drama and style that had made him famous.

Near midnight, as we sat at a small table by the window at which a few days earlier I had been waiting for the snow, Rodion said, "You will be free to leave Monday if you wish. Or will you stay?"

"I may come back one day," I said, "but now this isn't the place for me."

"I believe without exception the brothers and the sisters feel this will forever be the place for you. You saved them all, son."

"No, sir. Not all."

"All of the children. Timothy was killed within the hour you saw the first bodach. There was nothing you could have done for him. And I am more at fault for Maxwell than you are. If I had understood the situation and had shot Heineman sooner, Maxwell might have lived."

"Sir, you're surprisingly kind for a man who prepares people for death."

"Well, you know, in some cases, death is a kindness not only to the person who receives it but to the people he himself might have destroyed. When will you leave?"

"Next week."

"Where will you go, son?"

"Home to Pico Mundo. You? Back to your beloved Indianapolis?"

"I am sadly certain that the Indiana State Library at one-forty North Senate Avenue has become a shambles in my absence. But I will be going, instead, to the high desert in California, to meet Mrs. Romanovich on her return from space."

We had a certain rhythm for these things that required me to take a sip of wine and savor it before asking, "From space—do you mean like the moon, sir?"

"Not so far away as the moon this time. For a month, the lovely Mrs. Romanovich has been doing work for this wonderful country aboard a certain orbiting platform about which I can say no more."

"Will she make America safe forever, sir?"

"Nothing is forever, son. But if I had to commend the fate of the nation to a single pair of hands, I could think of none I would trust more than hers."

"I wish I could meet her, sir."

"Perhaps one day you will."

Elvis lured Boo away for a belly rub, and I said, "I do worry about the data in Dr. Heineman's computers. In the wrong hands . . . "

Leaning close, he whispered, "Worry not, my boy. The data in those computers is applesauce. I made sure of that before I called in my posse."

I raised my glass in a toast. "To the sons of assassins and the husbands of space heroes."

"And to your lost girl," he said, clinking my glass with his, "who, in her new adventure, holds you in her heart as you hold her."

CHAPTER 55

THE EARLY SKY WAS CLEAR AND DEEP. THE snow-mantled meadow lay as bright and clean as the morning after death, when time will have defeated time and all will have been redeemed.

I had said my good-byes the night before and had chosen to leave while the brothers were at Mass and the sisters busy with the waking children.

The roads were clear and dry, and the customized Cadillac purred into view without a clank of chains. He pulled up at the steps to the guesthouse, where I waited.

I hurried to advise him not to get out, but he refused to remain behind the wheel.

My friend and mentor, Ozzie Boone, the famous mystery writer of whom I have written much in my first two manuscripts, is a gloriously fat man, four hundred pounds at his slimmest. He insists that he is in better condition than most sumo wrestlers, and perhaps he is, but I worry every time he gets up from a chair, as it seems this will be one demand too many on his great heart.

"Dear Odd," he said as he gave me a fierce bear hug by the open driver's door. "You have lost weight, I fear. You are a wisp."

"No, sir. I weigh the same as when you dropped me off here. It may be that I seem smaller to you because you've gotten larger."

"I have a colossal bag of fine dark chocolates in the car. With the proper commitment, you can gain five pounds by the time we get back to Pico Mundo. Let me put your luggage in the trunk."

"No, no, sir. I can manage."

"Dear Odd, you have been trembling in anticipation of my death for years, and you will be trembling in anticipation of my death ten years from now. I will be such a massive inconvenience to all who will handle my body that God, if he has any mercy for morticians, will keep me alive perhaps forever."

"Sir, let's not talk about death. Christmas is coming. 'Tis the season to be jolly."

"By all means, we shall talk about silver bells roasting on an open fire and all things Christmas."

While he watched, and no doubt schemed to snatch up one of my bags and load it, I stowed my belongings in the trunk. When I slammed the lid and looked up, I discovered that all the brothers, who should have been at Mass, had gathered silently on the guesthouse steps.

Sister Angela and a dozen of the nuns were there as well. She said, "Oddie, may I show you something?"

I went to her as she unrolled a tube that proved to be a large sheet of drawing paper. Jacob had executed a perfect portrait of me.

"This is very good. And very sweet of him."

"But it's not for you," she said. "It's for my office wall."

"That company is too rarefied for me, ma'am."

"Young man, it's not for you to say whose likeness I wish to look upon each day. The riddle?"

I had already tried on her the *fortitude* answer that Rodion Romanovich had made sound so convincing.

"Ma'am, intellectually I've run dry."

She said, "Did you know that after the Revolutionary War, the founders of our country offered to make George Washington king, and that he declined?"

"No, ma'am. I didn't know that."

"Did you know that Flannery O'Connor lived so quietly in her community that many of her fellow townspeople did not know that she was one of the greatest writers of her time?"

"A Southern eccentric, I suppose."

"Is that what you suppose?"

"I guess if there's going to be a test on this material, I will fail it. I never was much good in school."

"Harper Lee," said Sister Angela, "who was offered a thousand honorary doctorates and untold prizes for her fine book, did not accept them. And she politely turned away the adoring reporters and professors who made pilgrimages to her door."

"You shouldn't blame her for that, ma'am. So much uninvited company would be a terrible annoyance."

I don't think her periwinkle eyes had ever sparkled brighter than they did on the guesthouse steps that morning.

"*Dominus vobiscum,* Oddie."

"And also with you, Sister."

I had never been kissed by a nun before. I had never kissed one, either. Her cheek was so soft.

When I got into the Cadillac, I saw that Boo and Elvis were sitting in the backseat.

The brothers and sisters stood there on the guesthouse steps in silence, and as we drove away, I more than once looked back at them, looked back until the road descended and turned out of sight of St. Bartholomew's.

CHAPTER 56

THE CADILLAC HAD BEEN STRUCTURALLY RE-inforced to support Ozzie's weight without listing, and the driver's seat had been handcrafted to his dimensions.

He handled his Cadillac as sweet as a NASCAR driver, and we flew out of the mountains into lower lands with a grace that should not have been possible at those speeds.

After a while, I said to him, "Sir, you are a wealthy man by any standard."

"I have been both fortunate and industrious," he agreed.

"I want to ask you for a favor so big that I'm ashamed to say it."

Grinning with delight, he said, "You never allow anything to be done for you. Yet you're like a son to me. Who am I going to leave all this money to? Terrible Chester will never need all of it."

Terrible Chester was his cat, who had not been born with the name but had earned it.

"There is a little girl at the school."

"St. Bartholomew's?"

"Yes. Her name is Flossie Bodenblatt."

"Oh, my."

"She has suffered, sir, but she shines."

"What is it that you want?"

"Could you open a trust fund for her, sir, in the amount of one hundred thousand dollars, after tax?"

"Consider it done."

"For the purpose of establishing her in life when she leaves the school, for establishing her in a life where she can work with dogs."

"I shall have the attorney specify it exactly that way. And shall I be the one to personally oversee her transition from the school to the outside world, when the time comes?"

"I would be forever grateful, sir, if you would."

"Well," he said, lifting his hands from the wheel just long enough to dust them briskly together, "that was as easy as eating cream pie. Who shall we set up a trust for next?"

Justine's profound brain damage could not be restored by a trust fund. Money and beauty are defenses against the sorrows of this world, but neither can undo the past. Only time will conquer time. The way forward is the only way back to innocence and to peace.

We cruised awhile, talking of Christmas, when suddenly I was struck by intuition more powerful by far than I had ever experienced before.

"Sir, could you pull off the road?"

The tone of my voice caused his generous, jowly face to form a frown of overlapping layers. "What's wrong?"

"I don't know. Maybe not anything wrong. But something . . . very important."

He piloted the Cadillac into a lay-by, in the shade of several majestic pines, and switched off the engine.

"Oddie?"

"Give me a moment, sir."

We sat in silence as pinions of sunlight and the feathered shadows of the pines fluttered on the windshield.

The intuition became so intense that to ignore it would be to deny who and what I am.

My life is not mine. I would have given my life to save my lost girl's, but that trade had not been on Fate's agenda. Now I live a life I don't need, and know that the day will come when I will give it in the right cause.

"I have to get out here, sir."

"What—don't you feel well?"

"I feel fine, sir. Psychic magnetism. I have to walk from here."

"But you're coming home for Christmas."

"I don't think so."

"Walk from here? Walk where?"

"I don't know, sir. I'll find out in the walking."

He would not remain behind the wheel, and when I took only one bag from the trunk of the car, he said, "You can't just walk away with only that."

"It has everything I need," I assured him.

"What trouble are you going to?"

"Maybe not trouble, sir."

"What else would it be?"

"Maybe trouble," I said. "But maybe peace. I can't tell. But it sure is calling me."

He was crestfallen. "But I was so looking forward . . ."

"So was I, sir."

"You are so missed in Pico Mundo."

"And I miss everyone there. But this is the way it has to be. You know how things are with me, sir."

I closed the lid of the trunk.

He did not want to drive away and leave me there.

"I've got Elvis and Boo," I told him. "I'm not alone."

He is a hard man to hug, with so much ground to cover.

"You have been a father to me," I told him. "I love you, sir."

He could say only, "Son."

Standing in the lay-by, I watched him drive away until his car had dwindled out of sight.

Then I began to walk along the shoulder of the highway, where intuition seemed to lead me.

Boo fell in at my side. He is the only ghost dog I have ever seen. Animals always move on. For some reason he had lingered more than a year at the abbey. Perhaps waiting for me.

For a while, Elvis ambled at my side, and then he began to walk backward in front of me, grinning like he'd just played the biggest trick ever on me and I didn't know it yet.

"I thought you'd have moved on by now," I told him. "You know you're ready."

He nodded, still grinning like a fool.

"Then go. I'll be all right. They're all waiting for you. Go."

Still walking backward, he began to wave good-bye, and step by backward step, the King of Rock and Roll faded, until he was gone from this world forever.

We were well out of the mountains. In this California valley, the day was a mild presence on the land, and the trees rose up to its brightness, and the birds.

Perhaps I had gone a hundred yards since Elvis's departure before I realized that someone walked at my side.

Surprised, I looked at him and said, "Good afternoon, sir."

He walked with his suit jacket slung over one shoulder, his shirtsleeves rolled up. He smiled that winning smile.

"I'm sure this will be interesting," I said, "and I am honored if it's possible that I can do for you what I did for him."

He pulled on the brim of his hat, as if tipping it without taking it off, and winked.

With Christmas only days away, we followed the shoulder of the highway, walking toward the unknown, which is where every walk ever taken always leads: me, my dog Boo, and the spirit of Frank Sinatra.

NOTE

The books that changed Brother Knuckles's life were both written by Kate DiCamillo. They are *The Miraculous Journey of Edward Tulane* and *The Tale of Despereaux,* and they are wonderful stories. How they could have turned Knuckles from a life of crime to a life of goodness and hope *more than a decade before they were actually published,* I do not know. I can only say that life is filled with mystery, and that Ms. DiCamillo's magic may have had something to do with it.

—Odd Thomas

ABOUT THE AUTHOR

DEAN KOONTZ is the author of many #1 *New York Times* bestsellers. He lives with his wife, Gerda, and their dog, Trixie, in southern California.

Correspondence for the author should be addressed to:

Dean Koontz

P.O. Box 9529

Newport Beach, California 92658